Love Bites

(Book 1 of the Darkness & Light Duology)

By TL Clark

Love & Light

Published in the United Kingdom by:

Steamy Kettle Publishing

First published in electronic format and in print in 2017.

ISBN: 978-0-9956117-3-3

Acknowledgements

Cover image drawn by Mark Manley
www.markmanley.co.uk/

Cover design by Robin Ludwig Design Inc.
www.gobookcoverdesign.com

My deepest love and gratitude go to my husband.
Thank you for being so supportive and understanding.

I also send massive thanks to my proof readers, beta reader, bloggers, reviewers and fellow authors who have shown tremendous support.

And last but by no means least, thank you to all my readers. Without you I am silent.

Table of Contents

Chapter	Page No.

Chapter 1 – Meet Shakira

Shakira's life was changing. She had changed her location, she had changed her job, and now she felt as if she were changing herself into a new woman.

One thing wasn't changing though. Shakira rubbed her back again; she was in agony, but she was starting to get used to it. Back pain was becoming part of her everyday life. If anything, it was getting worse.

She was naturally tall, so stooping over coffee machines all day really didn't help her posture. As soon as she could creep away from the serving counter she snuck two ibuprofen out of her handbag and chucked them down her throat without even pausing to get a glass of water.

She wondered how long she'd be able to do this job for, but for now it's all she could get. Maybe she'd get used to it?

The bell jingled as another customer came in. Shakira smiled every time someone came in as she listened to the noise. It made her think of that film where they say that an angel gets their wings every time a bell rings.

This visitor looked a bit long in the tooth to be an angel though. She was one of the coffee shop's regulars apparently.

Shakira had only been here two weeks but she was getting to know her customers already. Mrs Evans was a Friday morning person.

Shakira's fingers ran nervously over her chestnut brown ponytail, checking it was in place. If she could have seen her green eyes in a mirror they would probably have shown her anxiety too.

She aimed to look presentable at all times, but felt like she failed. She was always the odd one out.

She could feel her teeth worrying her lip as she forced her 'customer service smile' into place.

"Good morning Mrs Evans. Black coffee and a doughnut for you?" she asked brightly, already knowing the answer.

"Yes please," Mrs Evans chuckled, looking forward to the sugary goodness.

Shakira found it oddly amusing that this little old lady in the heart of a Welsh village should like this treat.

When she moved here she'd expected the picture postcard views of rolling hills and little old ladies in traditional costume, black hats and all. But as soon as she arrived she'd realised how stupid she'd been.

Why should an elderly lady not enjoy a simple coffee and doughnut like anyone else? Shakira's problem was she had grown up in a very busy town in Surrey, England. She'd hated every minute of it, and was now striking out on her own to find a bit of peace.

In her hometown everybody conformed to 'normality' and they were all too busy with their own 'important' lives to concern themselves with others. Here it was very different. Here the community spirit still thrived, and everybody knew everybody. Shakira was still a newcomer, and most residents treated her with suspicion.

Mrs Evans was nice though, even if she did have those beady eyes which seemed to see everything.

"That back of yours still playing up?" she asked in her sing-song Welsh accent.

"Is it that obvious?" Shakira asked, concerned people could tell.

What if her boss noticed and fired her? She didn't want to go back home. Failure was not an option.

"Only to me," she replied, patting her own back.

"Touch of sciatica myself," she winked.

"Oh, I'm sorry," Shakira said over her shoulder as she prepared the fresh coffee.

"Why? Did you cause it?" Mrs Evans dismissed matter-of-factly.

"I'm sorry you're in pain," she reiterated, trying to be patient.

"Pah, I've had worse," was the reply, accompanied with a wave of the hand.

"And this makes me feel better," she added with a smile as she took her cup and plate.

She looked almost bird-like as she waddled away as quickly as she could with her prize, and sat down at a table near the window.

Shakira shook her head in amusement whilst wiping the equipment down.

As Shakira stood there she tried easing her back by slowly rising up on her toes and lowering back down again.

She considered the difference of her situation. The coffee chain she worked in back home had been constantly busy all day and she'd flop down on her bed exhausted at the end of each shift. Oddly her back hadn't hurt so much then though. She shrugged the thought away.

Back in Surrey people barked their orders of 'skinny mocha, no foam, soy milk, blah blah blah' without so much as a hello or smile.

This place already felt more like home, but she couldn't explain it.

Although the customers looked her up and down with wariness they still smiled and said hello. Most were curious about her, and weren't shy in asking questions. They were beginning to get to know her already, even if it was as 'that odd English girl who's just moved in'.

And the customers were few and far between, just dropping in at regular intervals. She was not overworked at all. It was nice. She had time to read in between customers.

She didn't know why or how she'd ended up here. She recalled her parting conversation with her mum…

"Where are you going, Shakira?"

"For the last time, I don't know, mum," had been her curt response.

"At least you must have some idea of direction? Why won't you tell me?"

Her mum had been very worried.

"I really don't know. I'll call you when I finally get there though."

Shakira had been getting really irritated. She'd had that argument too many times, and she just wanted to go. But part of her had realised her mum's motive of concern, so she'd added a more gentle, "Promise."

Her mum had packed a whole hamper of food, so her darling daughter wouldn't go hungry. And she had watched with tears streaming down her face as Shakira drove away in her little old Ford Puma.

Shakira just followed her heart. She didn't care where she ended up as long as it wasn't there. She just couldn't live in the large town anymore. She'd been suffocating.

It was as if the car was driving itself. She'd expected to find a midway point and stay in a motel overnight, but she'd driven all day, across the Severn Bridge and into a remote spot.

She just knew she'd arrived at her destination as soon as she pulled into the village.

She had parked in the public car park and strolled down the tiny high street and walked straight into the coffee shop which had a job vacancy sign in the window. She felt the hand of fate at work and happily complied.

Shakira smiled as she recalled how easy it had all seemed, and how she'd instantly fallen in love with this area.

The rest of the afternoon was daydreamed away, and Shakira went back to her cottage feeling content. It really was a very small property; one of the old coal miner's cottages. There were so many empty houses now all the mines had closed.

Her first few nights in the village had been spent in a lovely B&B, whose owner had helped her find the rental cottage. Her new home happened to be owned by her employer at the café as she'd discovered later.

She was still settling in, and felt amazed at how everything was falling into place. It had to be a very good sign, she decided. And she felt so grown up having a whole house (even a small one) all to herself. How many twenty year olds could say they had the same?

She'd chosen not to go to university. The very few remaining friends she'd had had all disappeared off and had lost contact with her. She felt shunned for her decision, but she really didn't see the point of studying any longer.

She had no real idea what she wanted to do in life, but she was sure her career wouldn't need a degree. So she'd started working for the aforementioned coffee chain whilst trying to find her way.

But as time had worn on she had found herself getting increasingly restless; like there was an itch that just wasn't getting satisfied.

She had fallen into the habit of being the family dog walker, not that she liked the little mutt much, but it got her into the open air. She often managed to get Jack, the aggressive little Jack Russell into the woods. She let it wander where it wanted, secretly hoping it'd run off so she didn't have to live with it anymore.

The nasty little thing was so yappy, and it often tried to bite people's feet, particularly hers (unsuccessfully) when they were here. Fortunately she was too fast to get nipped by its snapping jaws.

Sometimes she let it off the lead and took off at a full run, knowing the mutt would chase her. It'd never catch her, and it would tire it out.

The dog always seemed more aggressive out in these woods, but she liked the location. She was drawn to the trees.

Being in nature soothed her spirit, but it still wasn't enough. She needed more. She just didn't know what.

And that's what had been in her head as she started driving the day she left 'home'.

'Funny word, home,' she mused to herself. It suggested all sorts of feelings, but she never really felt like she'd had one. Not really, not in the true sense of the word.

She'd always been the odd one out, which is possibly why the wary reception of these villagers didn't bother her.

She gingerly climbed the stairs of her little house and started running a bath. Whilst the water was running she went into her bedroom, threw off her work clothes and went through some yoga stretches in just her underpants, making sure the curtains were closed.

Her lip involuntarily curled as she performed the 'downward dog'.

"Stupid name for it," she grizzled as she moved into 'child pose'.

Pulling back up onto all fours she went into 'cat stretch', arching her back and letting it sag. She sighed at the relief this offered her.

Before long she scurried into the bathroom so she could soak in her luxurious hot bath with her book in hand. Her life felt surreal at the moment, and she was hoping she could escape into a fantasy world.

Chapter 2 – A Walk in the Woods

Saturday had been a hard day for Shakira. Another shift had induced more back spasms. So it was a great relief to have a day off on Sunday. No shops were open in the village, and she was free to do as she pleased.

She'd heard about many great walks in the area, so she decided to explore her surroundings. She hopped into her trusty car, dressed in her warm jogging outfit and literally headed for the hills.

However, as she drove she discovered an immense forest. The trees called to her, so she found a parking area to pull up in. It was incredibly overgrown and looked completely unused.

"All the better for me," thought Shakira, who was in the mood for quiet solitude.

Settling her iPod into its pouch she headed along the path at a brisk walking pace, careful to warm up her muscles before doing anything strenuous.

The smell invaded her nostrils deliciously. It had been raining and the smell of pine invigorated her senses.

She breathed deeper, getting her fill of the divine scent of petrichor. The sharp pine scent wafted along with that musty fern and earth smell. Shakira practically bathed in it.

"Glorious," she marvelled out loud to the trees.

The trees were denser here and as she broke into a jog Shakira strayed off the path to explore the 'forest proper'. She hurdled over logs and tree stumps, laughing with joy. She skipped over the many tree roots, letting her lush dark brown hair flow out freely behind her.

She picked up speed as her confidence grew amidst the beautiful surroundings. She felt the wind in her hair, and the pure air in her lungs.

She had always been good at cross country running at school, her stamina surpassing her classmates. She hadn't even broken a sweat yet. She was happy; properly from root to tip, through to her soul happy.

She had no real idea of where she was, she just trusted her feet to take her to where she needed to be. And at last she came across a clearing.

There was a slight buzzing sensation which ran through her as she broke cover, and ventured into the open area. It felt sacred, like an ancient druid site, or something. She couldn't quite put her finger on why she should feel that way. It just felt peaceful.

She pressed her iPod's stop button.

All was still around her; complete silence. She was aware the birds which had been singing, accompanying her jaunt had fallen silent. It was slightly unnerving, but she forced herself to respect the reverence of the space without panicking.

Shakira reached the centre of the clearing and sat down, cross legged in lotus pose. She took long deep breaths, steadying her breathing after her run. In through the nose, out through the mouth. Her eyes closed and she felt her energy centering.

She traced the rainbow of colours through her chakras from the red base she was sitting on, all the way up to the purple of her third eye at her forehead. She felt her energy pulse as her focus hit each point. Her heart chakra was filled to bursting in this blissful spot.

As the energy reached the top of her head bright white light poured out like a Roman Candle firework, cascading down and around her whole body.

A calm like nothing she'd ever felt before surrounded her, travelling through every fibre of her being. Shakira just sat there in silence, absorbing it all.

Meanwhile, not far away, a shout of alarm travelled through a whole community.

A message went out to the Leader, *'Sir. There's a disturbance. Elan and Arwyn are on their way to investigate.'*

'Good. Keep me informed,' came the gruff response.

Rhion wasn't overly concerned, nobody ever came out here. It was probably just another damned squirrel, too distracted in its hunt for nuts to respect the barrier.

Shakira felt a shudder, and realised she probably should make a move. As lovely as it was sitting there, she probably shouldn't sit too long. Worried her muscles would start to seize up, she reluctantly stood up, and brushed off the stray bits of bark, fern and mud from her bottom.

"Definitely my new favourite spot," she declared to herself, promising this would be her frequent meditation zone.

She walked back into the woods, and slowly built herself back up to a run as she retraced her footsteps. She'd always had a good inner compass, and knew she'd find her way back to her car without any problems.

Rhion heard the retraction of the call, '*Stand down. It's gone.*'

'*Bloody squirrels*,' he griped to no one in particular.

Back at her car, Shakira paused a moment to catch her breath before fumbling for her keys.

She grabbed her water bottle from the car and took a slurp, wiping the stray drip from her mouth with the back of her hand.

She reached back into her car for her hoodie and wrapped it around herself to keep her muscles warm on the drive home.

She drove back to her little cottage and ran upstairs to take a quick shower. She let the water run over her, washing away any remnants of negativity.

She felt great, completely re-energised. But she realised she was famished. Breakfast was long forgotten. She didn't want to cook though, and had a wild hankering for beef. So she headed to the village pub for a roast lunch.

A deathly hush echoed around the room as she walked into the pub. Dozens of pairs of eyes glared straight at her in recognition of her status as 'not a local'.

"Shakira," someone shouted across the room in a heavy Welsh accent.

'Oh thank God,' thought Shakira, 'At least someone recognises me.'

She recognised Annie from the coffee shop as she bounded over. Annie was in fact the owner and therefore her employer.

"How are you? Good, I see. You've got some colour in your cheeks at last. I was worried about you," Annie prattled on.

"Mmm…yeah, I've just been out for a run," Shakira interrupted.

"Exercising in nature. That is good, isn't it? I prefer horses myself, but each to their own I say."

"There's just something restorative about being outside. I hate being cooped up in a gym."

"Quite. Come, there's some friends I want you to meet," she said dragging her employee along by the arm.

"Oh no, I wouldn't like to intrude," she tried to decline.

"Nonsense. We've not ordered yet. Join us for lunch. I won't hear of any noes."

Shakira let herself get dragged to the table where everyone shuffled up to make room for the interloper.

"This is Daniel, Sheila, Janet and Gwen. Gwen runs the hairdresser's here. Everyone, this is my newest recruit, Shakira."

"What sort of name is that?" scoffed Daniel.

"An Arabic one," she explained, bored of explaining her name all her life.

She cursed her mother for giving it to her.

"Ooh, Arabic, eh?" Daniel said disdainfully, "You don't look very foreign to me."

"I'm not. My mum just liked the singer, and thought the name sounded exotic."

"Oh, I know. The one who shakes her bottom around a lot," he almost sang with a wicked grin on his face.

This earned him a jab in his ribs from his wife, Janet.

"Sorry about him," apologised Janet.

"He gets a bit weird and grumpy when he's not eaten."

"I know the feeling," replied Shakira.

"Right, what's good here? I could eat a horse," she added as she grabbed a menu.

"Haha, you're going to fit right in here, I can see," grinned Gwen.

Twenty minutes later the steaming hot food arrived, and Shakira was practically salivating. She began to tuck into her rare roast beef ravenously.

"Tidy! A carnivore after my own heart, I see," Daniel remarked.

Shakira made no reply, she just carried on devouring her meal. She was even hungrier than she'd realised.

Annie had ordered red wine for the table, and Shakira gulped down some of the ruby liquid. She looked up, realising she'd finished before anyone else was even halfway through their meal.

Embarrassed, she apologised, "I guess I worked up an appetite."

"No drama. It's good to see a girl with a healthy appetite," Daniel consoled.

"When I first set eyes on you I was worried you were one of those salad munching city types, being as you're so thin," he continued.

Daniel had winced as he'd spoken, and Shakira correctly supposed his wife's elbow had found his ribs again.

"But here you are having been outdoors and eating like a wolf."

Daniel winced again.

"Please woman. I'm paying the girl a compliment. I'm allowed to do that, aren't I?"

"Compliments are good Daniel Owens, but not the way you tell them. Stop being twp."

"It's OK," Shakira diffused, making a mental note to look up 'twp' (which she later learned means foolish/stupid).

"I prefer straight talking to fake frills any day," Shakira admitted.

"See?" Daniel gloated at his wife.

"Are you sure you weren't born around here?" he jokingly quizzed Shakira.

"Sorry, English girl. But I'm happy to be adopted by the Welsh if you'll have me."

Her smile faded as she realised she was already distancing herself from her family, and the brevity of her words hit her.

Once they'd all finished Shakira was paraded around the pub, so she could be introduced to everyone.

She'd instantly been accepted, and was to be an outsider no longer. She was still new, and would never be quite one of them. But she was 'not a stranger'.

Finally back in her house Shakira was able to happily reflect this strange new feeling.

"Yes, I may be happy here," she sighed quietly, smiling.

Chapter 3 – Weird Person

It was with some reluctance that Shakira went to her next shift at the coffee shop. It seemed to take away the serenity she'd felt in the forest, and she knew it would make her back feel worse. Having eased its pain she didn't want to damage herself again.

As she poured hot drinks she couldn't help but wonder what she was doing here. She'd run away from all she'd ever known, without really knowing why. And now she was here, in the middle of nowhere.

Sure, she'd made some friends in the pub, but it wasn't the same. They were all middle aged and she was only twenty.

She'd still not met anyone her own age. Not that she should mind. Nobody her own age had really ever been nice to her. Any friends she'd ever had were only on a superficial level.

Shakira sighed as the thought dawned on her that she'd never *belonged* anywhere.

Her height and appearance had always made her stand out, and not in a good way. She was the 'tall sturdy girl', not generally thought of as pretty. Boys weren't really interested and girls thought her too dowdy to be bothered with.

She'd hoped that her escape would lead her to somewhere different. She wanted a home.

The people here had already been nicer than any she'd met before. But they still held her at arm's length. It was as if they were being nice so they could learn about this curiosity who'd turned up in their village. She was in danger of becoming like a stray dog; nice to pet, but not welcome in their own homes.

The tinkling of the bell on the door brought her out of her sullen reverie. She looked up and smiled at the customer walking in. She'd not seen this person before, and she was like an answer to her unspoken prayer.

At last there was someone young to talk to. And there was a comforting quietness about her which Shakira noticed as soon as she set eyes on her.

She placed this customer in her mid-twenties, just a little older than herself. She was a fair bit shorter though, not that that was difficult. They shared the same brunette colouring, but this woman's eyes were hazel and beady.

As she looked on, Shakira felt herself being drawn into those eyes. She felt a wisdom coming from them which she was being pulled into. She felt uncomfortable; like she was being looked at as much as she was looking.

Shakira shook herself as the customer approached the counter, releasing herself from the inappropriately long gaze.

Shakira caught a strong waft of incense, making her take a deep breath.

"Hello. What can I get for you?" Shakira asked with a genuine smile.

"Hmm…you are new," was the puzzling response.

Shakira noted the sing-song lilt of the woman's Welsh accent. But instead of the usual cheeriness that went along with that association, she detected a gruffness too.

"Yes, I moved in two weeks ago. I've not seen you before though."

"I've been on holiday," the odd person said absent-mindedly.

As if realising she was actually speaking to a person and not just herself the young woman shook her head.

"Sorry. Where's my manners? My name's Cerys. I run the metaphysical store up the road."

"Oh, I've seen that shop. I wanted to go in, but it's been closed since I got here," Shakira noted.

"Sorry about that. I only get the chance to take one holiday a year, so I make the most of it. Nobody else wants to step in to run it in my absence. I don't usually have enough customers to worry about it. Was there anything specific you wanted?"

"Err, not really. I just wanted a nose. Besides, I'm supposed to be asking you that question," Shakira said with a wry smile.

"What a pity, I think I'm all out of noses. But I'll have a caramel latte please," Cerys said with a muted chuckle.

"So, did you go away somewhere nice?" Shakira asked over the hiss of the coffee machine, ignoring the weird joke.

"America. Tucson actually. There's a great gem show there this time of year. So it was sort of a work trip really. But then I enjoy my work. I've got some great crystals now, so feel free to pop in soon," Cerys said as she grabbed her coffee to go.

Shakira liked this woman very much. She rabbited on in her own way, but she could have listened to her all day.

She made a mental note to visit the shop as soon as she could. But for now it was time to get back to the grindstone as the bell rang again, alerting her to Gwen's presence.

"Oooh, pour us a brew," she requested.

"That's your second already today," Shakira commented, preparing a tea. "Don't you have tea in the salon?"

"Yes, but that's for the customers, and you make it so much better."

"If I didn't know better, I'd say you were checking up on me," Shakira said with a knowing wink.

"Well maybe a little. But only to make sure you're OK."

"To make sure I'm not slacking you mean?"

"I knew I liked you. You're not backwards in coming forwards. But no, it's not that at all actually. I just wanted to be sure the others aren't giving you a tough time."

"Sorry. Thanks," she replied sheepishly.

Shakira felt ashamed of herself. She'd been grumping about being judged, yet here she was judging one of her new friends, and only seeking negatives.

Perhaps it was learned behaviour though, she reasoned with herself. She'd seldom had cause to give others the benefit of the doubt. It seemed she'd have to start learning fast, or risk losing her new friends.

Gwen left happily with her takeaway cup of tea. She really did like the way Shakira made her drinks. She'd never really contemplated it before, but having tasted tea made by this girl, it made her realise how wonderful the drink could really be.

The shop had several loose teas and coffee beans and Shakira enjoyed making special blends, specially refined to each person.

The shop went mercifully quiet again, and Shakira took a seat on her stool to start reading her book.

Just as she was settling into the flow of her book the bell rang again. Shakira hastily got up and made herself look busy. She was surprised to see Cerys again so soon, and even more so when she pushed a small jar of leaves across the counter at her.

"This is to help with the pain," Cerys said simply.

"Sorry?" Shakira asked in alarm.

She hadn't mentioned any pain to her.

"Your back *is* causing you grief, isn't it?"

"Yes, but…"

"Don't worry. I'm weird like that. I just sensed it. You're nice. I wanted to help. Before you go to sleep tonight make a tea with this. Just one cup, mind."

"Umm…thanks. How much…" she began to ask but her query was wafted away with a hand.

"No charge. Did I mention a monetary exchange?" Cerys asked.

Afraid of causing offence Shakira just took the jar and thanked her. But she was wondering if she should trust her. Receiving a free jar of unknown herbs from a stranger felt exceedingly dodgy.

"Relax. It's nothing dodgy, and if I wanted to poison you I wouldn't be so blatant," Cerys said as if reading her mind.

Shakira felt the truth in the slightly gruff words. Shakira offered a faint smile and just like that Cerys disappeared from the shop.

'Weird. Very weird,' Shakira thought.

More customers came into the coffee shop in the afternoon, and Shakira's back felt increasingly painful. Her usual ibuprofen remedy didn't seem to help. By the time she got home her back was really hurting.

Shakira found herself longing to return to her special meditation zone, but it was already dark, and she didn't want to go scampering around alone in the woods without any light. She could make her way in the dark, but it felt more dangerous. Why risk it?

Out of desperation she took the jar of herbs from her bag and brewed a tea as Cerys had told her to. She sniffed at it suspiciously, but it actually smelled really nice. It was aromatic and quite sweet.

She took a cautious sip. It was delicious.

'Well, that's it,' she thought, 'This really can't do me any good. Rule number one; if it tastes bad it's good for you. And this tastes far too nice to be medicinal. Oh well.'

She slurped down the rest of the liquid ambrosia anyway, savouring its delectable taste. She had to admit it felt very soothing.

She changed into her pyjamas and crawled into bed. She picked up her book and began to read, but soon drifted off to sleep.

She had strange dreams that night, filled with the smell of pine and spice. She was being chased by wild animals with glowing eyes. Just as they were about to catch up with her she woke up, terrified.

Shakira took deep breaths, trying to calm down.

"It's only a dream," she told herself repeatedly.

As she steadied herself she realised her back didn't hurt any longer.

"Well, that's one good thing, I suppose," she murmured.

She turned over, re-fluffed her pillow and tried to get back to sleep. But the memory of her nightmare haunted her still.

'Where did that come from?' she wondered, trying to think of the last horror film she'd watched. She drew a blank though. She'd not watched any scary films for a while. She usually just got annoyed at them. She considered them unrealistic mumbo jumbo.

She turned back over and pulled her duvet up high. Feeling safe in her snuggly cocoon, she wriggled a little and found herself soon going back to the land of nod.

Chapter 4 – Curiosity Shop

"OK, fess up. What did you give me?" Shakira asked bluntly as she walked into the metaphysical shop the next day.

"Tea," Cerys said simply.

"Yes, but what was in it?"

"Herbs from my own garden. It worked, didn't it?" Cerys checked calmly.

"Well, yes it helped my back, but..."

"Yes. There are certain side effects. I am sorry. I should have warned you about that, but if I told you it would reveal hidden secrets would you have drunk it?"

Shakira hesitated.

"No need to answer," Cerys gently interjected with her knowing smile.

"But, but, why did I have nightmares?"

"You did? Come and sit with me," she responded with concern, getting up and leading the way to her consultation room.

Shakira felt compelled to follow this odd young lady. She found herself in a strange little room, decorated in the fashion of a travelling gypsy fortune teller. It was dark with only a few quirky lamps and swathes of hanging chiffon.

"Don't mind that dear, it's what the tourists expect and I do hate to disappoint," Cerys apologised.

"Are you going to tell me my fortune?" Shakira joked.

"Oh please. I don't think you'd believe me even if I did. No, it's just more comfortable to talk in here. Please sit."

Both women sat down around the small round table, which was covered in cloths.

"What? No crystal ball?" Shakira quipped.

"No, I draw the line at those. I don't need one, and it takes up space."

"Riiight, of course," she said incredulously.

"So you didn't like what you saw?" Cerys asked, bringing her back to the important conversation.

"No. I was chased by wild animals."

"Hmm…running away, eh? Interesting…"

"But just as they were about to catch me I woke up."

"Pity. Oh well it can't be helped."

"Pity? I woke up before I got killed and you think that's a pity?" Shakira was getting cross now.

"Killed? What makes you think they were going to kill you?"

"Silly me. Big animals chase me through a dark forest just to give me a big fluffy hug all the time."

"Sarcasm won't get you anywhere."

"I just don't see how I can interpret it any other way."

"No, you don't, do you? Most peculiar."

"I'm sorry, did I miss something?"

"You're about twenty years old, yes?"

"Yes, not that I see how that has anything to do with it."

"And you didn't grow up around here."

"No. I grew up in Surrey."

"Hmm, I see. And your parents…?"

"My parents? What the hell?"

"Please don't be upset. I didn't mean anything by it."

"Don't be upset?"

"So, you're not running away from them?"

"Oh. That's what you were asking. Sorry. I'm a little on edge. Um, no. My parents are lovely. It's not them I'm running away from."

"Not rogue then," Cerys whispered.

Shakira didn't think she was supposed to hear the side comment. But she couldn't ignore it. This conversation and the last twenty-four hours were just too strange.

"I'm sorry, I can't do this. I don't understand. Thanks for trying to help and everything," Shakira said as she got up and started to leave.

Instead of trying to stop her as Shakira had expected, Cerys merely put a business card in her hand.

"I'm so sorry. I misjudged…Just call when you're ready to talk more, OK?"

It was the first time Shakira had seen her struggle for words. She nodded, and tried to make her escape.

Cerys suddenly reached out to grab Shakira's hand firmly and stared into her eyes.

"Promise me. I'm here for you. I will understand."

Shakira frowned but agreed before freeing herself.

She almost ran back to the coffee shop. She looked at the clock, and realised she'd taken a longer lunch break than she'd intended. But it didn't look like she'd missed much.

Business was slow that afternoon, giving Shakira plenty of time to rehash the odd conversation over and over in her head.

What did Cerys mean by "not rogue"? And why was she so sure those animals weren't trying to kill her? And all those questions?

The more she tried to make sense of it all the less she understood. She tied herself up in knots until her head hurt.

She decided she didn't care about the dark. Shakira felt so stressed by the time she closed the shop that evening she drove to her forest spot.

As she got out of her car she checked her mobile phone had signal. It was low but there was one bar on her display. Shakira huffed. She didn't care. She didn't need anyone. She could look after herself she thought as she stomped along the path.

She was surprised how well she could see. It was really dark now, but she could see the path in front of her. She didn't want to stray from that path. She promised herself she'd be happy just to be out in nature.

As her eyes adjusted to the darkness even more she started to break into a jog. And before she knew it she was running, her feet pounding through her frustrations.

"Stupid know-it-all freak. Interfering bloody woman. Who asked her anyway," she muttered as she ran.

"Running away from my parents? Huh! Some psychic she is. I'm not running away from them. I'm running away from me."

Shakira suddenly halted in her tracks.

"Me?" she pondered. "Why am I running away from me?"

She turned around and gently started jogging back to her car.

Along the way she had that strange buzzing feeling again, but she ignored it and didn't stop until she got back to her car. She hurriedly got in and drove home. She'd worked up an appetite.

Annoyed that she'd let herself get too hungry she grabbed a couple of hamburgers out of the freezer and shoved them under the grill to cook whilst she tossed a green leafy salad to go with them.

She was so hungry she didn't even let the burgers cook to her usual 'medium', but ate them rare. She licked her lips as she devoured her food.

She chugged down some orange juice and realised she still felt hungry.

Shakira hated it when she forgot to eat, she always got a bad case of the munchies. So she reached for a bowl of cereal too, trying to pretend it was the healthy option despite the high sugar content. It helped, but as she sat down to dig into her book she had some dried apricots ready to tuck into as well.

When she got up from her sofa Shakira realised she'd been sitting in one position too long, and had to stretch to relieve the ache. Her body was hurting from top to toe, including her sinuses.

She hoped she wasn't getting a cold. Maybe she should have wrapped up more against the cold air when she went jogging? Just to be on the safe side she drank more orange juice before heading off to bed.

But in the morning she felt worse. Her head felt like there was a sledgehammer smashing into her skull. She downed more ibuprofen before heading off to work.

Cerys stopped in for a coffee mid-morning.

"Oh dear," she exclaimed.

"Please don't start," Shakira groaned.

"You didn't drink any more tea?"

"No, I really didn't want any more nightmares."

"I'm sorry about that. I really didn't expect you to have bad dreams. But maybe you won't next time?"

"I'd rather not risk it. I feel bad enough as it is."

"Shakira, I'm not trying to hurt you."

"I know."

"Please let me help you. I hate to see anyone in so much pain."

"Have you got anything that helps colds hidden up your sleeves?"

"You're getting a cold?"

"Sure feels that way."

"Mmm…" she said shaking her head slightly.

"So have you?"

"Have I what?"

"Got anything that can help a cold? Modern medicine seems to be failing me lately. Besides, I don't like to take too much of it."

"Very sensible too. Hmph, you won't like my remedy though."

"Please. I'm really sorry about yesterday. And I'm desperate here."

"Evidently. Very well, my answer is to drink more of that tea. You do have some left, don't you?"

"Yeees…"

"Worth another go?"

"Fine," Shakira huffed.

"That's better," she smiled. "And stop by at lunchtime, I may have a couple of other bits you'll be interested in."

And then the strange woman disappeared out of the shop, coffee in hand.

Shakira smiled, deciding her original thought of 'odd' was still highly appropriate in regards to Cerys. But she was intrigued at the same time. She did seem genuinely sorry she'd upset her, and appeared to want to help. What was the worst that could happen?

Shakira found herself stepping into the metaphysical store again at lunch time. Cerys greeted her warmly and invited her to browse the store.

Shakira wandered from shelf to shelf, trying to take in all the wonderful trinkets and doodads on display. She couldn't really focus on any one thing until she went to the cabinet of crystals.

It was quite dark in the shop, which Shakira liked. The dim lighting gave the place an ethereal yet homely feel. It also helped ease her headache a little.

Her gaze suddenly focussed on a beautiful emerald necklace. The gem was fairly small, but beautifully encased in a gold setting with a fine gold chain which matched her gold bracelet. It was a present from her parents and rarely left her wrist.

"Hmm…that lights your eyes up," Cerys chuckled.

"My eyes?" Shakira blushed.

People had often commented on her eyes, yet she never got used to it. They were large, almond shaped and a vivid green colour.

She instinctively touched her hair, making sure her ponytail was still neat and in place. It was a simple self-comforting action she made whenever she felt nervous or self-conscious.

"Yes, the colour of the stone brings out the colour of your eyes. Yes, this is the one for you."

"Maybe, but it looks expensive?"

Although Shakira had some money to back her up, she was trying her best to live within her wages, which wasn't much. She was biting her lower lip, feeling pensive.

"Perhaps not as much as you fear. It's only small. That piece is £35."

"Really?" Shakira was expecting it to be much more.

"Really."

"There's earrings to match."

"No. No thank you. Just the necklace will be fine," she replied hurriedly.

Cerys took the necklace out of the cabinet and carried it over to the till.

"Do you want to wear it now?"

"Yes please."

Having taken payment, Cerys helped put the necklace around Shakira's neck then reached into the basket by the till.

"Here, have this too," she gently commanded. "Hold it when the pain gets bad."

"Err…thanks" Shakira said, whilst doubting how a little white heart-shaped stone could possibly help.

"By the way, I don't suppose you've had a chance to explore much yet, have you?"

"Not really. I've wandered the town and been out to the forest up the road, but not got any further than that. I know I'm probably missing a lot."

"I would stay away from those woods if I were you."

"What makes you say that?"

"Oh, just folks around here don't go there anymore."

"I noticed the car park was quite overgrown and unloved. But why would people stop going to such a beautiful place?"

"There was some talk of a panther."

"Like the Beast of Bodmin Moor?"

"Yes, similar sort of tale."

"I stopped believing in fables when I was a child."

"Every tale starts with some truth. They all come from somewhere."

"Don't tell me you believe that nonsense."

"Well, you hear something enough times…"

"But a panther?"

"I didn't say I believed it was a panther. I just meant that there is something I would be worried about coming across."

"Well, I'll believe it when I see it."

"I doubt that."

Shakira noticed Cerys had that sly grin again.

"What's that supposed to mean?"

"You seem to have stopped believing in a lot of things, my friend."

"Maybe I had reason to."

"Yes. Yes, maybe you did," she said sadly.

Cerys made a concerted effort to smile.

"Anyway, enough of this mindless chatter. You'll be missed if you don't get back soon," Cerys warned.

Shakira smiled politely as she said goodbye and left to return to work.

She caught the sight of her reflection in a shop window and admired her new jewellery. It really did seem to make her eyes sparkle.

She grabbed hold of the small selenite heart stone Cerys had given her, and started to feel a bit better.

"Nothing like a bit of retail therapy," she silently mused as she sauntered back to work.

Chapter 5 – A Close Encounter

Shakira drank more herbal tea that night, perhaps against her better judgement. The weird nightmares she'd experienced before had really scared her, but Cerys had reassured her this was supposed to help. And it tasted nice at least.

She wriggled under her covers, trying to get comfortable. The heart stone was under her pillow. She was sure it was all in her mind, but her pain had seemed to lessen this afternoon. And now the tea was soothing her that little bit more.

She folded down the top of her duvet as she decided she was too hot. She drew deep breaths as she forced herself to relax. She desperately tried to reassure herself that she was going to have sweet dreams.

In…and out…she breathed. A sense of calm wrapped itself around her and drew her steadily into a deep slumber.

She dreamed of being back at home with her parents, happily playing in her back garden as a little girl. As she turned back to look at her house it started to get hazy. She tried to walk towards the door, but as she did she found herself walking through her primary school's corridor.

She wanted to get to her classroom, but the corridor went on and on. It started to get dark and the walls became trees.

Shakira could smell the musty scent of trees and earth after a rain storm. She could hear voices, but couldn't understand what was being said. Her head was against something soft and warm. She felt safe. She was being carried.

She saw those glowing eyes again and heard a shout and she felt herself being jolted as the person who carried her began to run. She began to cry as she felt frightened. And then it all went quiet.

She smelled incense and relaxed. She felt safe again.

Shakira stirred into a semi-awake state, feeling troubled and confused. But she managed to drift back off, unable to wake herself up fully.

This time she saw a lot of strange faces. She didn't know who the people were, but she felt 'home'. The people had long hair and big eyes, just like hers. It was light and she could make out different faces as they smiled at her.

She jolted awake as she saw sharp teeth revealed in those smiles.

"What are they?" Shakira wondered out loud, now fully awake in her own bedroom.

She didn't recognise any of those strange people in her dream.

"I really have to stop reading so many books," she shrugged as she rolled over, trying to find a more peaceful sleep.

The rest of her night was filled with pleasant dreams of her parents. So much so that when she woke up in the morning she felt homesick. She promised herself she'd phone them that evening. She needed to hear their voices.

Her day at work felt very long. She couldn't seem to settle and felt restless.

When Cerys came in the woman was uncharacteristically quiet. She just gave Shakira a knowing smile as she collected her coffee and left.

"Definitely very odd," mused Shakira.

She daydreamed and worried her day away apart from that odd encounter. Her thoughts were haunted by strange images from her nightmare. She just couldn't shake the uneasy feeling it had left her with. It had just felt so real.

Finally evening arrived and Shakira phoned her parents.

"Hi mum."

"Shakira darling. Are you OK?"

"Yes, I'm fine."

"You're eating alright? People are being nice to you?"

"Yes mum. I'm fine. I just wanted to say hello."

"Hello," her mum laughed, teasing her.

"Mum, did we ever go camping?"

"Camping? Oh dear me, no. You know me better than that."

"Not even a caravan trip to a forest?"

"No. Why are you asking?"

"No reason really. It's silly."

"Silly in which way?"

"Oh, it was just a dream."

"You dreamed we went camping?"

"No, I dreamed of a weird forest. Not like the woods near us. I don't know where."

"Dreams are dreams, Shakira. They're not real."

"I know. It just felt…it just felt so real."

"I think you're too old to be thinking like that. Are you sure you're okay? Do you want to come home for a visit? We'd love to see you."

Shakira heard her father in the background telling her mother to stop being such a 'mother hen'.

"Leave the girl alone. She's a big girl. She'll come home when she wants to," he told his wife.

"Tell dad he's right," Shakira smiled. "Look, I'd better go. I've not had dinner yet. I just wanted to ask that one thing. I know it was daft. Sorry I troubled you."

"Don't be silly. You don't have to go yet. Please stay on the phone. I want to hear all about your new place."

"Not tonight mum. I'll call again soon, I promise."

And with that they ended the call.

It had been nice just to hear their familiar voices. And Shakira had eased her mind. She chided herself for being such a baby over a silly little dream.

Now she thought about it in the cold light of day, it did seem a little bit like the forest she'd been jogging in. And her memories of that must have mingled with some weird horror film and the odd dream had been the result.

That sounded perfectly plausible. More than plausible; it was what any sane, rational person would think. It was the only logical answer.

Shakira went to raid her fridge. She pulled out a packet of beef mince and made a lasagne. She'd promised herself just to eat half and freeze the rest, but she devoured the whole lot in one sitting.

Pouring herself a glass of red wine, Shakira settled down with her book. It was dark now, but she merely lit a candle so she had enough light to read by. Anything more than that seemed to spark off headaches.

The rest of her week seemed to go much more smoothly. Shakira began to find a hint of the peace she'd been searching for. The coffee shop was getting busier, and she had made friends.

She no longer felt the pressures of the past, and she felt more relaxed. Even her back pain seemed to be all but gone.

All she needed now was another jaunt into the forest to jog away any remaining tension and her happiness would be complete.

As soon as she got her next day off she took the opportunity to drive out to her favourite place.

As she got out of her car she realised she'd forgotten her iPod holder, and cursed out loud. Not wanting to go all the way back to her house for such a small object she decided she'd just have to hold the device in her hand as she jogged. It was a nuisance, but she shrugged it off.

Shakira began her brisk walk and built up to a run. The music was blaring in her ears, and she was heedless as to where she was going. She just needed to run, and she sprinted through the forest, leaping over logs and skipping over roots.

The forest grew denser and darker as she carried on. Out on her own she took her hair out of its usual ponytail and let her long, lush, brown locks flow freely. She felt so alive. Her blood pumped round her system rapidly. She was beaming as she ran.

She neared her meditation zone. Her iPod shuffled to another song, which she decided she wasn't in the mood for. This area required something more soothing.

She looked at the device in her hand and fiddled with the dial to skip the track.

She wasn't looking where she was going, and almost fell over as she bumped into a tree. She rebalanced herself quickly and screamed as she looked up. The tree had eyes! No, not a tree. A person. And those eyes were glaring down at her, and glowing.

As she screamed her reflexes kicked in and she sprinted away. She ran faster than she'd ever run before.

The man she'd bumped into was frozen to the spot for a moment. He was stunned. Nobody ever came out here. And even if they had he would have known of their presence. How in the world had someone bumped into him?

Too late his feet began to carry him after the girl. He tried hard to catch her up but she outpaced him. He was utterly dumbfounded.

He got to the car park just in time to see her drive away. He just stood there, mouth wide open. Who the hell was that? He was intrigued. He had to find out. But how?

He slowly skulked back to where he had been standing, and to report back in to the others. There was a noise he was unfamiliar with. He traced its origin and saw a strange object on the ground. He picked it up.

As Shakira sped away her heart was in her mouth. She was terrified.

"All only a dream my arse," she huffed out loud to herself.

She drove as fast as she could back to the village. She had no idea how or why, but she ended up at the metaphysical shop. She supposed she was seeking refuge, and her very odd friend was the closest thing to sanctuary she could think of.

She ran into the shop.

"Cerys, Cerys, help," she screeched.

The good lady ran over to the petrified girl and wrapped her in her arms.

"Good goddess, what has happened?" she asked with great concern.

"He…he…he…." Shakira was almost hyperventilating.

"Come. Sit down," she said as she directed her friend to a chair.

Cerys put the closed sign up on the door as she locked it. She poured a cup of soothing lemon balm tea for each of them.

"Here, drink this and take deep breaths."

Shakira managed a weak smile of gratitude. The cup and saucer shook as she took it.

Cerys sat patiently and quietly as she let Shakira take sips of tea. Seeing her visibly start to regain her composure she prompted her friend to speak.

"Now, what happened?"

"I was out in the forest."

"I thought I warned you about going there," she moaned, raising an accusing eyebrow.

"You said there was a panther."

"I said to stay away as there was something I'd be worried about bumping into."

"But this was a man."

"You saw a man? That doesn't sound scary."

"No, I bumped into a man."

"Bumped?"

"Yes, literally bumped into him. I was running along and then bam! I thought I'd run into a tree but then I looked up into glowing eyes."

Cerys caught her breath but hid it behind a cough. She took a sip of tea as if to soothe the cough, but was really steadying herself and buying time.

"Dear girl, please take a moment to think about what you just said."

Cerys took hold of Shakira's free hand as she continued, "You're telling me you were in the forest, completely alone. But you bumped into a man with glowing eyes. Now, does that sound likely?"

"Well, no. But I know what I saw."

"Didn't you have a nightmare similar to this?"

"Yes."

"So, could it not just be that you did in fact bump into a tree? Isn't that what you said you thought you'd done?"

"Yes, but trees don't have glowing eyes."

"Neither do men, sweet girl."

"No. But…"

"Could it just have been a trick of the light and your imagination? Or perhaps an owl in a tree?"

"I suppose."

"And it gave you a start, so your mind put two and two together and came up with three."

"Now you put it like that," Shakira admitted as she began to feel foolish.

"It's perfectly understandable. Please don't look so embarrassed. You've had a rough time of things. Take your time, and finish your tea. You'll feel right as rain in no time."

As soon as she had finished her drink Shakira made her excuses and took herself home. She still felt stupid. How could she even think she'd seen a man with glowing eyes? It was absurd.

As she walked in through her front door she saw her iPod holder.

"Damn," she exclaimed as she realised she'd dropped her iPod in the forest.

Chapter 6 – Lost and Found

It was dark by the time Cerys got home. She lived at the edge of the village, in a cottage on its own. As far as anyone in the village was concerned it had been passed down through the generations of her family.

She had a fair sized garden, where she could grow plenty of herbs and vegetables. It was protected by a barrier of conifers, and there was a forest around the rear perimeter of the property. It was secluded and quiet, just the way she liked it.

Cerys heard the wind chimes gently jangle by her back door.

"Greetings Pryderi. I wondered how long I'd have to wait before you showed yourself."

She carefully pronounced his name "pruh-DAIR-ee", so he would sense her displeasure.

Pryderi just harrumphed at her. She rounded on him.

"And just what the bloody hell did you think you were playing at, eh? You know she saw you. Why didn't you just create a billboard poster or hire a town crier?"

"I didn't…"

"Think? No, you clearly weren't bloody thinking, were you? I'd expect that sort of error in a youngling, but you're supposed to be an adult now Pryderi."

"But…"

"Don't you 'but' me. There are no excuses. I ought to report you…"

"No. Please," he begged, looking shocked and scared at her threat; physically retreating a step, holding his hands up.

"I said I ought to. But I won't. Not this time. You're just lucky she came to me. I managed to *persuade* her you were a tree."

Pryderi couldn't help but smile at that.

"Don't you look so happy with yourself. She told me herself she thought she'd bumped into a tree. The path of least resistance seemed the best way forward. She's as stubborn as you are," she gruffled, her Welsh accent becoming accentuated.

"Who is she?" Pryderi managed to ask.

It was Cerys' turn to smirk.

"And you want to know why?" she quizzed, raising an eyebrow.

"She is…"

"Yes, she's like you. But not like you. Careful how you proceed. She knows nothing."

"How can that be?"

"I'm trying to find that out myself. In the meantime you keep your distance. You hear me?"

He nodded and held up the iPod.

"What is this?" he asked.

"An intelligent boy, sorry, man like you should be able to work that out."

"It plays some sort of music."

Pryderi had been fiddling with the device all afternoon. The music it played was strange and exciting. He had wanted to hear more but it had stopped, and he decided he'd better ask Cerys for advice anyway.

"Yes. I suppose this was found in the forest? You better tell me that's where you found it. There'll be hell to pay if you've been stalking her."

"Yes she dropped it."

"Well you'd better put it back there."

"I thought you would say that," he said sadly. "Pity. It is good."

"Hmmm…don't get too used to it. It's not for the likes of you."

Her visitor pushed out his full protruding lips a little further as he sighed, "I know."

He looked so dejected Cerys took pity on him.

"When the time is right, she works in the coffee shop."

Pryderi visibly brightened at this piece of intelligence.

"The collection is soon," he beamed.

Smiling broadly, he receded back into the night from whence he came.

Cerys was left alone again, and was most certainly not feeling as happy as her visitor had been. She needed more time. But then, how much more time did Shakira have left? She couldn't help but worry about the girl.

Meanwhile the said girl was mourning the loss of her mp3 player. It was too late, too dark, and if she was honest with herself, she was too scared to go back for it now.

She was sitting in her bath in silence. Her back was hurting her again, and she felt odd. She felt sick, but she never got ill.

Growing up, she'd seen her mother fall ill with colds frequently. The sore feeling in her face was like the one her mother had complained of when her sinuses were inflamed; an ache which travelled through her cheeks and reached down through her teeth. She was hoping yet another bath and herbal tea would help soothe this as well as her back.

As she leant back against the bath she closed her eyes and let her mind wander. In her mind she saw herself back in the forest, running wild. She breathed in deeply as she imagined the smells of the forest, and she relaxed.

However, the next morning she wasn't feeling much better, so she promised herself a trip to Cerys' shop to see if she had any other cold remedies.

"Oh dear, you look peaky," Cerys commented as Shakira entered her shop the next day.

"Is it that obvious?"

"Remember who you're talking to. Not to worry. Now let me see," she said absently as her fingers hovered across glass bottles and jars.

"Ahh yes, this should do the trick."

The green glass bottle she handed over was cloudy. Shakira unstoppered it and took a sniff. The smell made her nose crinkle.

"Eww, what the hell is that?"

"One of my most potent remedies, my dear."

"Another tea?"

"No. Oh no. This is an elixir. Take one teaspoon in the morning and two before you go to sleep."

Shakira pulled a face as she imagined forcing the foul smelling liquid down her throat.

Cerys pincered Shakira's chin between her thumb and forefinger.

"Aww now, no need for faces. Hold your nose at the same time, and chase it down with a spoonful of honey and all will be well."

Cerys wished it could be that easy. She knew her potion would help for now, but there were rough times ahead and she had no idea how to prepare the girl for it. She was still waiting for news from her sisters to confirm her suspicions.

That evening Shakira was so exhausted she couldn't face cooking. She bunged a shop bought spaghetti bolognese into the popty ping, as the locals called the microwave, and poured herself a glass of red wine. It was simple comfort food to cheer herself up.

She had bought garlic bread too, but decided she didn't want to wait that long. She was famished, and the microwave meal was ready in mere minutes.

She curled up with a blanket on her sofa and tucked into her food. The hot food and wine were soporific. Having worn herself out at work whilst feeling under the weather she decided it was time for an early night.

She shoved her plate onto the side, not even bothering to wash up. She opened a jar of honey, and plunged a spoon in. Having made preparations she took another spoon and dispatched the elixir Cerys had given her, and followed it up with her honey chaser.

"Yuck. Bleurgh," she moaned, "This had better work."

The honey didn't conceal the foulness well enough. But it worked. She only just made it to bed before zonking out.

The next day was a rest day and Shakira let herself wallow in a lie in that morning. The marshmallowy goodness of her bed was simply too enticing.

She stretched her arms and legs out and recognised she felt a lot better already. She had to admit to herself that Cerys may be a wise woman after all.

She wrapped her duvet around her a little tighter, and let her head sink back into the downy pillows. She felt as snug as a bug in a rug, and she didn't want to move. She was determined to give herself some TLC.

She wondered if she'd been working too hard, and the stress of leaving home had perhaps got on top of her, causing her to feel unwell.

The sunlight was peeking into her bedroom and she could hear the birds chirruping outside.

'Ahh, this is the life,' she thought to herself.

But no sooner than she had the thought she felt the urge to go outside into the sunshine.

"I can't waste the whole day away in bed," she remonstrated with herself.

She dressed in her jogging clothes, and skipped downstairs to top up with her morning dose of elixir, just to make sure she was OK. She had a bowl of sugary cereal to hand this time to help disguise the taste, and followed that up with a banana.

Having refuelled, she was good to go. She took deep breaths as she prepared herself to retrieve her iPod. She considered yet again that she could just go and buy another one. But her parents had bought her this one as a leaving present, and her heart ached at the thought of it being lost forever.

Shakira braced her arms straight against her steering wheel as she set off on her drive out to the forest. She reflected how odd it was, that her place of sanctuary now seemed to be a place of foreboding.

She felt as if she was creeping along on tiptoe as she got out of her car. She told herself off for being childish and set out with long confident strides.

'I'm a big girl. A big girl just going to fetch her iPod,' she told herself internally.

She picked up her pace and swung her arms as she continued her mission.

'Big brave girl,' she thought.

As she reached further into the dense woodland she couldn't shake off the unnerving feeling that she was being watched.

'It's broad daylight. I'm a big brave girl. Just picking up what's mine.'

These thoughts were becoming less believable with every step she took, so she started to hurry her footsteps. She had intended to take it easy given she had felt so unwell the previous day, but now she was breaking out into a jog.

A bramble bush argued with her as she neared the spot where she thought she'd dropped her iPod. She hissed and shook her hand as she got scratched. The thorns had drawn blood, and she sucked her finger to soothe it.

The simple action made her smile and lick her lips.

She froze as she heard something that sounded like a sharp intake of breath. Her senses were all on high alert as she looked about her.

There seemed to be shadows all around, and her heart started beating faster. She forced herself onwards, but she kept looking over her shoulder and from side to side as she went.

There. Thank goodness, she found her beloved device at last. She stooped to pick it up but withdrew her hand immediately as she felt a sharp tingle.

"Bloody brambles," she grumbled, shaking her hand again.

She reasoned with herself that her hand was still complaining from the scratch she'd incurred. What else could it be?

She reached out to her iPod again and this time successfully picked it up. Something felt wrong. She detected an odd scent and there was a sort of electricity in the air.

In the shadows a twig snapped. It was enough for Shakira. She sped off as fast as her legs would carry her.

She got back to her car safely.

And a very unsettled Pryderi was left behind at what he was now considering to be 'their spot'.

Chapter 7 – Discovery

"*What are you doing, Pryderi?*" his friend asked in their mother tongue.

"*Elan, you scared the crap out of me.*"

Pryderi had been so caught up in watching the girl he'd not even been aware of his friend's approach.

Elan's question had been inquisitive and laden with accusation, but it was not menacing.

"*Guilty conscience, my friend?*"

"*How long have you been there?*"

"*Now I am intrigued. You are truly guilty of something,*" Elan said, circling his friend in slow lithe steps, staring into his eyes as they came face-to-face.

"*It is none of your concern.*"

"*When someone acts dishonourably it concerns us all, brother,*" he sneered.

Elan was whispering into his friend's ear, and it made Pryderi even more uncomfortable. He was about to sweep away any accusations, but it was too late. Elan sniffed Pryderi elaborately.

"*Ahh, you smell of...lust.*"

Elan's violet eyes lit up as he continued to mock his friend, "*Do I excite you?*"

Elan, like Pryderi, was a Watcher, and as such was one of the taller, more muscly, sleeker males of the species. He was confident and well used to both sexes making advances on him.

"*Yes. I love you dearly, Elan,*" Pryderi chided, hoping to change the subject.

"*This I already knew of course. But this is different. This is...hmmm...what should I call this? Passion? No. Deeper than that. It is more intense.*"

Pryderi pushed Elan playfully yet firmly away.

"*Please. How can I love her when I don't know..?*" He smacked his hand over his mouth and his pupils dilated.

"*Oh ho ho, my friend. It is about time. Tell me, who is she?*"

"*I cannot.*"

"*You can tell me anything.*"

"*No. I cannot.*"

Elan caught the seriousness, and the teasing was dropped.

"*In what way cannot?*"

"*Elan, you don't want to know. Please. I don't want to bring you into this.*"

"*Too late, brother.*"

" *This. This cannot be shared with the clan. They won't understand.*"

" *Not share with the clan? Pryderi, what are you saying?*"

" *She is not...*"

" *Oh no, not human. Please don't tell me she's human.*"

" *No. Of course not.*" Pryderi looked horrified at the suggestion.

" *So, what is the problem?*"

" *She is not one of us.*"

" *A different clan? This is no strange thing,*" Elan dismissed with a wave of his hand.

" *No. She has no clan.*"

" *What? How can this be?*"

" *I don't know. Cerys says she's not rogue.*"

" *No clan, but not rogue. I begin to think this girl is a delusion. But tell me, what does Cerys know of this?*"

" *About as much as I do. She is a puzzle. Until we can work it out please don't tell. She won't be safe. If she has no clan they will pronounce her rogue.*"

" *And that will lead to...*"

" *Don't say it. I know her life will be in their hands.*"

"How does she come to be here?"

"I have no answers. I only have questions."

"But you are already in love? Does she know this?"

"I've not spoken a word to her. She knows nothing of me or us."

"But she was just here?"

"She dropped something and came back to retrieve it."

"She was here before?"

A light flicked on in Elan's head, and he checked his hypothesis, "The breach?"

"Yes. Her."

"But..."

"She just arrived."

"On her own?"

"I had nothing to do with it."

"I didn't say you did."

"You thought it."

"Cerys is seeking information?"

Pryderi nodded.

"Fine. We keep our own counsel. We let her find out more before we speak. We have nothing to tell anyway. Without detail this looks bad for you both."

Pryderi thanked his friend and lightly punched him on the shoulder as they headed back home.

Meanwhile, Cerys had finally found a lead, but her sister was being very elusive, even for a witch.

"I need to see you face to face, not like this," Lily said as her image wavered in the mirror.

"You're scaring me. This is surely secure enough? What are you not saying?"

"I'll come by as soon as I can," she told her hurriedly in her Scottish lilt.

There was a pause as Lily looked over her shoulder.

"Thank you. Can you believe I can't get any Aconite around here? It was careless of me to run out like this."

This was Cerys' clue that Lily was being watched.

"Pop by as soon as you can. I have plenty here. I'll see you soon."

The mirrors turned back to plain mirrors as the communication link was disconnected.

"You go on a journey?" Dougal demanded sternly as he entered Lily's room.

"I would request it, Sir. I need more Aconite."

She felt obligated to carry on the lie, as she knew he had heard her say those words.

The question was more how much he'd heard. She was fairly sure it was just that last bit, but with Dougal one could never be too careful. He was a cunning, watchful and powerful Leader.

"It is so urgent?" he checked as he stepped closer to her.

Lily would not break away from his gaze. She held up a spare empty jar, glaring back up into the man's eyes.

"I don't know how it happened. I am sorry. But my guides tell me more protection is required. This is vital for that."

"I would not anger the guides. You may go tomorrow. Now we have need of you."

With that he pulled her from the room by her arm. She only just managed to grab her emergency bag as they passed it.

She was led down the dark maze of tunnels until she came to Loth's room. He lay on his cot, barely conscious. His blonde hair was a mangled mess around his bloodied head. His pallor was even paler than normal.

"And you call this training?" she hissed at Dougal, her fear of losing a life becoming greater than her fear of the clan Leader.

"Life is tough," was his only form of response.

"I need some knitbone," she commanded.

One of the younglings standing nearby ducked out to fetch the required plant.

Meanwhile Lily set about cleaning the deep bite wound to the young man's rippling right triceps. Her bag was full of antiseptic tinctures and salves. She was sadly used to this work.

She also put a few drops of oil into a bowl of spring water and soaked a flannel. She placed the moist flannel on Loth's brow.

He had clearly received a blow to his head. There were no other visible injuries, and it was the only way to explain his current condition.

But his condition itself was cause for great concern. Loth was one of the senior elinefae in her clan. He should not be laying strewn on her healing couch.

She spoke softly to him and did her best to keep him conscious. She clapped her hands in front of his face when he looked in danger of fading out entirely.

"OK clear the room," she barked as the boy came back with the knitbone herb.

The few who had been by Loth's side scurried away. Even Dougal knew to leave the witch alone when she was at work, and sloped off with the rest.

Lily made a poultice with the fresh leaves, and placed them on Loth's arm. She burned some lavender and sage, and threw some salt around. She had to work quickly; Loth was getting worse.

She chanted and cast her spell and hovered her hands over the young man. Her intent was pure. She'd always had a soft spot for this one. He had shown great promise, and had quickly risen to a prominent position in the clan. She was saddened to see him so ill used. It was wasteful and degrading.

Sparks of light flicked out from her fingers and around the darkened room as she worked. A single candle was the only other light source, but she needed no more.

The room fell eerily quiet and dark as she finished. The candle was extinguished with the force of her magick withdrawing.

The rest was up to Loth now. She could only do so much. She sat on the floor, holding his hand.

She willed the candle back into life so she could watch his chest as it rose and fell steadily. She heaved a sigh of relief as she saw the good sign. She decided to let him sleep.

Lily must have dozed off as she was awoken by someone nuzzling her cheek. It was Loth. His cheek was brushing against hers. She rubbed her hand through his hair roughly.

"Someone's feeling better," she softly acknowledged.

Bright eyes glowed at her in the darkness and she saw him nod.

"You're welcome," she said in response to his continued cheek rubbing. "Just be more careful."

The glow dimmed.

"I try," Loth said sadly, closing his eyes.

Knowing she was going to leave soon and that Loth wouldn't be granted any mercy despite his close call she quickly wove a protection spell around him. Just a little one, so he wouldn't get hurt any further whilst she was away. Another injury at this stage and even she may not be able to save him. Without her there? She shuddered at the thought.

Lily gathered her things and made her way back to her room. Her shoulders slumped and her head bent down as she mourned her loss. It was the loss of what once was. This had been such a good clan long long ago.

Soon she would rake up the old story and all the associated bad feelings that went along with it. But it seemed that the fates had decided now was the time. The time she had hoped would never come.

Chapter 8 – A Tale of Woe

Lily's feeling of anxiety increased with each stage of her journey. She had to walk out of the forest, and along the hidden paths until she came out to the human world.

She had dressed in her socially acceptable clothing but still felt like she stuck out like a sore thumb as she boarded the train. Her blonde hair was pulled back into its usual bun at the back of her head, but her coat, sweater and jeans helped her blend in. Her blue eyes were hidden behind spectacles which she didn't need but liked hiding behind.

It was warm on the train, so Lily took off her long woollen coat as she took her seat. As she was short, the coat usually scraped along the ground when she sat. Normal coats just weren't made for her stature.

Fortunately the train journey wasn't a very long one and she disembarked as inconspicuously as she could. She regretted having to take this step, but unlike Cerys, she had no car.

She wandered along the pavement and, checking she was alone, found the hidden path towards Rose's home. She had not dared to make contact from her home, so she just hoped Rose was in.

Rose had a cottage like Cerys. Lily had moved out of hers, and she missed it dearly.

She smiled as she gazed upon the bountiful roses growing around the sweet cottage. It was an indication as to which witch lived in each dwelling. As she approached the door it opened, and Rose's smiling face appeared, welcoming her.

Rose lived up to her name. Her skin was pale, but her cheeks and lips were rosy. Her auburn hair was tied in a loose ponytail. Her warm smile reached her brown eyes. Lily's tension eased upon seeing her, and she almost ran into the sister's open arms.

"Oh, I've missed you," Lily cried as she entered the welcoming embrace.

"I've missed you too sister. Enter in this place and rest before you continue."

"You know my purpose?"

"Indeed. Cerys thought you may come this way so she contacted me."

"Your crystal ball not working?" she winked, taking a step into the house.

"It's being fixed," she joked back.

All witches have psychic abilities, but they can't foresee everything. Mind you, she would always have known Lily was approaching as she drew near.

Rose picked up the old fashioned kettle from her open fire and poured two cups of herbal tea, whilst Lily installed herself into a comfy armchair and instantly found Twigs in her lap. The black cat was Rose's familiar, and he was always happy to see visitors.

Rose passed a small china plate to her friend. Lily sniffed at the delicious slice of cake which was on it.

"Mmmm...lemon balm?"

"You felt like you needed it," Rose confirmed in her milder Scottish tone.

"Unusual in a cake though."

"Oh, it's in the tea too. Besides, there's rosewater in that sponge cake too."

Lily smiled. Sometimes this witch took her name far too seriously. Even the china plate was decorated with roses. But why not when it was such a useful and pretty flower?

With their cake eaten and tea drunk the two ladies took the rare opportunity to have a catch up.

Lily couldn't help but envy the peace that Rose enjoyed. Her clan were happy and productive. Rose had few demands on her, so she was able to dedicate more time to her craft.

Rose took hold of Lily's hand.

"May I?"

Lily nodded, so Rose sent some healing through her sister's body. She felt so sorry for her. She looked haggard. She was clearly stressed and overdoing things.

Feeling a bit more prepared and a lot more relaxed, Lily unveiled herself, so she appeared in her usual clothes. She'd been so het up she hadn't realised she'd not changed back when she arrived here.

The two women set out through Rose's garden and along the path to the portal. It needed a witch at either end to operate it, otherwise the energy could de-stabilise and who knew where you may end up?

The blue light expanded and glowed. Steadying her nerves, Lily stepped through the light. It always made her feel anxious, but today was even worse.

She felt the cold tingles all over her as she carried on walking, her eyes held shut. Then she felt loving arms around her.

"You can open your eyes now," Cerys told her.

Lily turned around and shouted a thank you through the portal just before it closed.

"Oh look at you, come inside," Cerys sympathised as she led her friend towards her cottage.

Cerys had ivy growing around her home, and it only lent it a more mystical appearance.

Inside was plush and cosy. A fire was roaring in the hearth. Cerys offered Lily a cup of tea, but she declined, having only just had one with Rose.

"It was good of you to come so quickly. I thought when you said you'd see me in a few days you may take the long way round."

"No, I knew Dougal could hear me at that point, and I just needed a few days away."

"Are things really that bad?"

"Yes. I just wish I knew why. They have always been proud and fierce, but things are escalating. Their training is getting out of hand. Just yesterday I had to rescue an almost unconscious trainer. It's as if Dougal is preparing for war. And he's suspicious of everybody. I'm surprised he agreed to me leaving at all. But I suppose the offer of extra protection was the succeeding point."

"And not your powers of persuasion?"

"Well, I may have used a tinsy bit of that too," Lily blushed.

Lily was a lot softer by nature than her gruff Welsh sister. Timidity was her main attribute. She was caring, and the most empathic witch Cerys knew. She felt every pain her clan was going through.

"Well, it was wisely used. I'm very pleased to have you here."

"Oh, but I wish it was not under these circumstances. I fear you will think badly of me."

"Lily, you are the sweetest person I have ever known. You are far too nice to be living amongst those ruffians in remote Scotland."

"But I have committed a crime. Indeed I have. However unintended. Oh Cerys, I'm so sorry."

Lily was getting emotional, so Cerys stood up and walked over to her cabinet and pulled out two glasses and a bottle of elderflower wine. She poured a large measure of the sweet liquid for each of them.

"Here, I think we're going to need this," Cerys uttered as she handed Lily a glass.

"Thanks," she said, gratefully taking a sip.

"How's about you start at the beginning?"

"Very well. Well, Sinead came to our clan to marry Cailean." (pronounced kay-lin)

"I remember hearing something about that. It was a big move for her, all the way from Ireland to Scotland. They were well matched though, and it was to bring peace to a long held feud."

"And did it? Do you remember hearing of that long hoped for peace?"

"Now you come to mention it, no."

"They were well matched, but it was not a soul match. Cailean was not horrible to her. He went out of his way to make her feel welcomed, in fact. Their wedding was a big event, and all seemed happy.

But it wasn't to last. Oh, when I think of it my soul shrivels. She was properly wed, and the two went into concealment. But shortly afterwards she fell into season. She was out in the hills when it happened."

Lily began crying at this and had to take another sip of wine before she could continue.

"There was a hiker lost in the countryside," she sobbed.

Cerys audibly gasped as she guessed where this story was heading.

"Yes, a human hiker. But Sinead was desperate, and couldn't control herself. She walked up to him under the pretence of putting him on the right path. Her allure was so strong I don't think she even needed to use any of her charms."

"Oh no," Cerys breathed.

"Yes. She took him then and there. Poor Sinead. Her need was so great she had sex with the first male she saw. And of course, being a human male she couldn't let him escape."

"Oh no," Cerys repeated.

"When she had been satisfied enough she took his life."

"Oh, by the goddess."

"She'd been out too long, and Cailean had gone in search for her. He saw her kill the man and knew what she'd done. He was so ashamed of her. Her crimes would reflect badly on him. Her heat was rising again and he had no choice but to satisfy her. He hoped his scent would mask the human smell that lingered."

"Poor Sinead. Poor Cailean."

"He kept her away for the next few days, filling her needs as often as she needed. But when they returned the clan still sensed something was amiss. The mated pair tried to say it was due to her hormones, but they didn't buy it.

"When the clan learned she was pregnant the situation became worse. They knew something was wrong, but they couldn't tell what. They made me consult with them. As soon as I got near her I knew. I couldn't hide the shock from my face."

Tears were pouring down Lily's cheeks. Cerys pulled her chair closer and rubbed her arm in comfort. They both sipped their wine. Cerys had not expected anything this bad.

"I tried to brush it off as surprise she was pregnant so soon, but they didn't believe me. I'm a hopeless liar. I said I needed to consult with them before I could be certain of anything. We went out alone, and they confessed all that I already suspected.

"We returned to the clan, and I managed to convince them that the baby was sick. Sadly, although this gave a reason to the sense of wrongness, it didn't make the clan any easier. Sickness is weakness, and they didn't want a weak family.

"They told me to abort the child, but I refused. She was too far into her pregnancy to do so safely, and I could never take a life. I persuaded them that if the baby survived it was a sign of its strength.

"That worked fine until the night she gave birth. The humanity in the child couldn't have been any more obvious. The clan realised what had happened and decreed an execution order. Sinead, hours after giving birth picked up her baby and fled with her husband."

"That was quick healing," Cerys interjected.

"It was a difficult birth. I gave her aid."

"I wasn't criticising."

"May I continue?"

"Please do."

"They ran into the woods, through the wind and rain which pelted them. I heard the alarm go out that they'd escaped. Nobody thought her capable of moving, and they were to be executed at sunrise. So they weren't under guard, making it easy to slip away.

"But she was still weak, and couldn't run fast enough. She handed the baby over to Cailean, but he hesitated. The hunters caught up with them and slaughtered them. The baby fell to the ground and was silent, presumed dead.

"They were unclean and dishonoured. They were far enough away from home and not near enough to the borders to cause concern, the weather was too bad to warrant staying out any longer than necessary. Their task was done. The bodies were left for the animals to dispose of."

"Barbarians," Cerys muttered.

"But the baby was not dead. I had left camp under the pretence of going home, having been interrogated first. Fortunately I was able to persuade them I had sensed a sickness, but had never suspected human blood."

"Your powers are great indeed. And you're clearly better at lying than you give yourself credit for."

"Anyway, as I passed by I heard a faint whimper. Everybody had abandoned the cursed spot. I bent down and picked up the infant and carried it back to my cottage. I lit incense, and cleansed the babe. But I knew I couldn't keep it. I wrapped her up so she was warm and carried her away. She was so human I thought she'd be safe if I hid her amongst her own kind. I used a portal to travel as far as I could."

"On your own?" Cerys asked, shocked.

"I didn't care where I ended up. Anywhere but where we were. I reached out until I sensed a couple in need of a child. I'm afraid I left her on their doorstep with a note, but I lingered in the shadows to make sure they took her in. As soon as they saw her I knew she was safe."

"And I don't suppose the note said anything about an illegal, mixed race child who could jeopardise the peace of an entire species?"

"Well of course I did," Lily said sarcastically. "I went to all that trouble just to have them hunt her down and kill her."

"Sorry," Cerys apologised sheepishly.

"As far as the couple were aware she was the daughter of a single mum whose parents disapproved and had thrown her out."

"But you named her."

"You should have seen her. She was so innocent, so beautiful. And she deserved a chance of discovering her heritage if she needed to one day. I never thought she would though."

"Sinead and Cailean gave life to little baby Shakira."

"Yes."

"Hardly subtle, Lily."

"The clan are miles away from her. They'd never even think to look for her. They believe her to be dead."

"And when another clan discovers her?"

"Oh no," Lily was aghast.

"She wandered over here. Her feet led her straight to their site."

"No no no."

"They don't know about her yet. Well, most of them don't."

"Then we can smuggle her out?"

"She's not quite as human as you thought, you dopey witch. She's coming of age."

"Oh cripes."

"And she's met the one."

"Holy poo."

"A whole steaming pile of crap in my back yard, thank you very much."

"Oh Cerys, what are we going to do?"

"Honestly, I have no idea. But one question. The hiker; how human do you think he really was?"

Chapter 9 – A Closer Encounter

Shakira had reached her house speedily and safely, iPod in hand. She placed it on the docking station to charge and pressed play as soon as she could. She paid no attention to which song was being selected, she just needed music to soothe her frazzled nerves. Sure enough, some soothing meditation music drifted out of the speakers.

'Odd,' she thought. 'I don't remember downloading anything like that.'

But she shrugged her shoulders and unzipped her top. She started stripping off on her way to her bedroom.

She dived into her pyjamas, shmushy dressing gown and unicorn slippers. She padded downstairs to grab some Scotch Broth soup and a fresh crusty roll.

Her aches and pains were starting to rage again, so once she'd finished the warming supper she made some of the herbal tea she'd been gifted. It was soporific, making her curl up on the sofa and fall asleep.

Her muscles twitched and spasmed as she dreamed of a pale face with strange glowing, orange eyes. Her predator had caught her scent and gave chase. She fled. Her feet barely touched the earth as she tried to evade capture.

Her foot caught on a tree root and she tumbled to the ground. Within a moment he was upon her. She could feel his hard body against hers as he laid on top of her, sniffing her. He licked his lips.

Shakira was unable to move. Her body refused to budge. Her eyes had locked onto his.

The light disappeared as her captor closed his eyes and took a deep breath and hissed out. But the fire was even fiercer as his eyes opened again.

Shakira's body was finally able to move, but only so her hips could move closer to his. He met her action with a deep grind of his own. They both mewled at the contact.

She wanted him like she'd wanted no other in her life. She panted with lust. Her whole body was aflame as it sought more of this strange man. But more she must have.

Shakira woke up with a start.

She was sweating yet shivering. The desire was still there in her waking moments.

In her half wakeful state her hand found its way down her pyjamas to relieve her suffering. As her fingers glided to her nub she realised just how slick she was. Her fingers were instantly coated as they slid up and down.

It didn't take her long to find her release, her mind still set on the mysterious stranger.

"Well, at least the pain's gone," she muttered to herself as she went to take a shower.

But even as the hot water revived her, Shakira couldn't help but think about the delectable stranger.

In her head, she'd just made love to a delicious morsel who she'd never met. But she really wanted to see him.

She towelled herself off and sighed. Trust her to dream up someone that yummy. Now she'd never meet anyone who matched up to her dream man. She was destined to live alone. Forever.

Pryderi simultaneously had felt a stirring in his loins. Inexplicably he felt tremendously turned on. He rapidly sought out a female.

He never had to search for long in the clan. They were all highly sexed. He headed to the 'den of sin'.

Without dallying, Pryderi had hoisted up the chosen girl's leather skirt and bent her over. She had her hands against one of the den's dirt walls. She made no objection to being taken roughly from behind. In fact, she was enjoying his rough treatment.

He howled as he came inside her. She however just harrumphed at his selfishness and went to find someone who could actually satisfy her.

But Pryderi was grinning to himself as he sought his den. It really hadn't mattered who he'd been with physically. In his mind's eye he'd been with her; his stunning mystery woman.

They both slept soundly that night. It was the most restful night's sleep either had had for a long long time.

Feeling more settled Shakira verily skipped to work the next day. She had a smile for every customer, and the day sped by. Her mood wasn't even dampened by Annie's phone call.

"I'm so sorry to do this to you, but please would you stay on tonight?" Annie asked, sounding groggy.

"Of course, but until when? I didn't even know we opened late."

"We don't normally, but once in a blue moon the mountain herders come to collect their delivery."

"Collect a delivery?" Shakira asked, thinking this seemed very odd.

"It's only coffee."

"Coffee that they can't collect during the day?"

"It's when suits them. They go where the deer are. But they like to keep a good supply of coffee to help keep them going on their cold, weary travels, I guess. They pay good money for it. I don't ask too many questions."

"It still sounds odd. Sorry, but don't you think it's weird?"

"Not really. Genuinely, it is only coffee. Actually, they order so much it's why we changed from a tea house into a coffee shop. And the locals appreciated the change too. Everybody's happy."

"Fine, I'll do it."

"Thanks. My head just really hurts, I can barely move."

"Can I get you anything? Are you OK?"

"Thanks but I'll be fine. I have all I need, and will just carry on resting. I'll be fine by the time I'm due in next."

"OK, if you're sure."

"Thanks Shakira. Just stay until they collect. They shouldn't be too late. Oh, and don't worry."

"Worry?"

"They're an odd lot. I've sort of got used to their manners. They're harmless though. Just quiet and a bit sullen."

"Moody odd people collecting a large order of coffee after hours. Got it," Shakira smirked.

As she hung up Shakira still thought it sounded very odd, but she had heard of the people who kept deer numbers down. It made sense as she thought about it more.

The sun was already low in the sky as she shut up shop for the night. Shakira supposed she should feel scared in the eerie quiet of the coffee house, but she actually found it quite comforting.

The window blinds were shut, and the doors were locked. Nobody knew she was there apart from Annie. So she settled down to read.

The sky was a midnight blue, with only the full moon providing light by the time the knock came at the back door.

She peeked out and saw only a tall shadowy figure, wearing a full length Barbour coat and bushman hat.

She opened the door with trembling fingers.

"You here to collect?" she asked, and got a brief nod in return.

She turned on the light so she could find the correct boxes in the store room. She heard a hiss behind her as her visitor turned the light back off.

"Ummm...you don't want to...?" she started.

The hat shook a 'no'. The herder strode past her, with the briefest pause, and located the boxes in the dark.

Shakira tried to steady her nerves, recalling Annie's words of warning about their manners. She was alone in a small dark room with this person. But she could see where he was despite the darkness. She realised she didn't feel as threatened as she should.

The boxes got pushed to the back door, and she locked up the store room.

The coat was already wafting along as the stranger went to load the small van. The vehicle seemed slightly incongruous with what she'd heard about these people but she shrugged and hefted a box, eager to help, eager to get this over with.

The man was in the back of the van making his way out, and jumped at her presence.

She silently passed him the box she'd been carrying, their fingers brushing against each other as she did so. They both inhaled sharply at the brief contact.

The hat's peak raised, revealing dark eyes and a dazzling smile. Shakira couldn't release her breath, it was caught in her throat. She tingled all over. She was captivated.

The herder was the first to break the spell as he coughed and loaded the box into the back of the van.

"Right, coffee," she murmured as she turned around to fetch another box.

She sensed the shadow man's presence. He was behind her in the doorway, tantalisingly close. She longed to lean back to feel his body behind her. It wouldn't take much.

Instead, using every ounce of her willpower, she bent to pick up the box at her feet. She heard a groan behind her as she did so, and she knew he felt it too; this need.

She straightened with a box in hand, but as she turned there was a body in her way. He took the box from her and put it back down.

Before she knew what was happening, his hand was gently at her waist, drawing her near.

She let herself be pulled until she could feel his body next to hers. Her eyes closed as she concentrated on the intense feeling.

A hand was on her cheek, and his face was drawing close to hers.

She could offer no resistance. She didn't want to. Her whole being was begging for this to happen.

In a flash his lips were on hers, devouring her.

Her hands reached under his coat and gripped around his back, anchoring them together. She could feel his firm, rippling muscles.

They stood alone in the silent night. Silvery moonlight illuminated them from behind, their tongues caressing each other in the most passionate kiss she'd ever experienced.

Suddenly he broke apart from her.

"Errr…my apologies," he mumbled.

Shakira's body was crying out in pain at the loss. She was trembling all over. Her eyes opened. She was looking at him in the moonlight.

"It was nice," she said, her voice shaking.

"I'm not allowed," he began to provide an explanation but had to stop.

He strode off across to the far end of the car park. She saw him in silhouette as he raised his hat, and his hand brushed through his long hair. She saw this despite the fact he was half hidden by a tree.

The hat was replaced, and he returned. He silently picked up the box and restarted the process of loading up.

Shakira felt bereft. She stepped to one side and let him complete his task alone, unable to bear being so close to him without repeating their kiss.

As he shut the van doors she crossed over to him, and managed to find her voice.

"Did I do something wrong?"

"No." The hat shook from side to side again.

"Would you at least look at me?" she asked as she gripped the hat and pulled.

His reflexes were lightning quick, and he halted her progress.

"No," he softly commanded.

"Why?"

But all she got was another hat shake.

"Why?" she repeated, raising her voice.

"Rule," was the one word response.

"Oh bollocks to this," she said in frustration as she stepped in closer.

Her reactions were faster than his this time, or maybe he couldn't fight anymore.

Her mouth found his, with even more fervour than before.

He was completely lost in her as her hands reached up to paw through his hair, knocking his hat to the ground.

His hand gripped her buttocks as she raised a leg to get a better purchase against him.

He was going to lose all self-control, he wanted to have this woman here and now. He was done fighting. To hell with the consequences.

But her screams ripped through the night, making the birds who'd been softly cooing in the trees take flight in a flap. The beating of their wings added to the din.

Shakira fell towards the ground, his hands caught her before she completely collapsed.

Tears were already streaming down her cheeks, her cries ripping his heart.

What had happened? He tried comforting her, to no avail.

He couldn't get any sense out of her. She was clearly in immense pain, and he was confused and more than a little panicked.

He loaded her into the back of the van amongst the boxes and drove as fast as he could to the only place he hoped he'd find assistance.

Chapter 10 – Everything Changes

Cerys heard the tyres screech up her driveway.

"There's no need to destroy my van, Pryderi," she grumbled as she strode towards him.

He couldn't speak. He took her hand and led her to the back of the van. Only then did Cerys hear the cries.

"Good Goddess," she breathed as she opened the doors.

Lily had come out to see what the commotion was, and bore witness to a curled up ball of pain, sweat and tears.

"OK, you're going to be fine," Cerys smoothed as she released a burst of energy from her hands towards Shakira.

The girl's shrieks were reduced to crying.

"Help me get her inside," she instructed Pryderi.

Together they carried the insensible Shakira into the cottage and laid her on the bed in the spare room.

"Lily, stay here and keep up the energy flow," she said firmly as she ran out of the room, and to her medicine cabinet.

She reached in and grabbed an elixir. She proceeded to pull out jar after jar in her haste, clattering and chinking until she found the other one she was looking for; wolfsbane.

Lily's eyes widened as she saw her friend carrying it into the sick room.

"Surely not?" she asked, aghast.

"I know what I'm doing."

"What? What is it?" Pryderi questioned, agitated.

"Panther strangler," Lily replied, giving it its alternative name.

"*Like hell it is*," he yelled, taking a step towards Cerys.

He was halted in his tracks by her magickal barrier.

"What do you two take me for? Of course I'm not going to kill her."

"But it's..."

"Yes, I am well aware of the plant thank you, Lily. Honestly, I thought I would've earned a bit more trust from you both by now," she huffed.

Putting on a rubber glove she dabbed a tiny amount of wolfsbane on her finger and wiped it across the girl's mouth.

"Lily, don't stop that flow now," she urged as she noticed her sister's attention waning.

Shakira's body started convulsing.

"She's going into shock," Lily screeched.

"No, she's going into a coma," Cerys corrected, as she measured out her elixir.

Cerys wiped Shakira's lips, discarded that cloth carefully and poured the elixir into Shakira's mouth, whispering a chant as she did so.

She knew she had to get the timing precisely right. This combination should just put the girl into a deep sleep so she wouldn't experience the agony of the change.

This had all happened much sooner than she'd expected, and far more violently. She had been hoping she was wrong, and this wouldn't happen at all. But it was, and she was having to deal with it.

This was such a drastic course of action, and was her last resort. Shakira was going through her change, and so much more painfully than expected. She'd not even been able to warn the girl.

She was going to be one confused kitten when she awoke, but time for that later. Cerys had to not actually kill her first.

She tried to put the thought to the back of her mind. Without her assistance Shakira could die anyway.

They all stayed by Shakira as her body twitched and flinched. She was unconscious all the while.

When her body finally seemed ready Cerys administered more elixir. Shakira's deep breath in was loud and raspy, and rippled fear through each of the three spectators. Her body went rigid. The three onlookers held their breath.

They didn't breathe out until she exhaled on a wail.

"Just like a new-born, crying is a good sign," Cerys confirmed, before commanding, "Lily, flow like there's tomorrow, my friend."

Lily complied, sending a constant wave of healing energy into Shakira who was screaming again. The sounds of bones crunching and cracking were audible. Shakira wouldn't fully feel the pain, but she was waking up.

Cerys couldn't wait any longer. She disappeared only to emerge a few minutes later carrying a bowl of hot water, cloths and herbs.

She plunged three quarters of the herbs into the water, and dipped one of the cloths in. She wrung it out and started mopping Shakira's brow.

"Shhh," she soothed, "the worst is over now."

She stripped the girl of her clothes and wiped her down with the herb water. She heard Pryderi's groan.

"Sorry. I forgot about you," she apologised, releasing the 'stop motion' spell.

He fell forwards a little, but quickly regained his balance. He stared at the now naked body in front of him.

"Maybe you'd better leave the room," Cerys muttered.

Pryderi stood there nodding yet not moving.

"Pryderi," she warned.

"Uh, right," he said as he forced his legs to move.

Cerys took up the remaining herbs and lit them, smudging the area around Shakira. The girl had stopped crying, but was not yet compos mentis.

After the herbs were wafted and some spells were chanted Shakira finally fell still. Lily gasped in shock as she felt another energy flow, and she looked up at Cerys.

"It's not me," she replied to the unasked question in Lily's eyes.

"Then who?"

Both witches concentrated on the new energy flow, tracing the flow back to…

"Shakira," they both whispered together.

Shakira had started channelling her own healing energy.

"How human was that hiker?" Cerys repeated her earlier question, her eyebrows rising with her voice.

Lily sealed off her flow and they monitored Shakira as she took control.

A noise from the next room brought them back to the present moment. Cerys went through.

"Pryderi, you're still here," she observed.

"I couldn't leave."

The male had been pacing in the lounge, and had bumped into a table, knocking over a lamp. It was fortunately not broken.

"You'd better get that coffee back home before you're missed."

"Is she..?"

"Yes, she's alive and she'll be fine. She's over the worst. I'll keep an eye on the rest of her transition. Now get going."

Satisfied the girl would be OK he turned to leave, but turned back.

"Did I? My fault?" he asked stiltedly.

"What did you do?"

"Kiss," he hissed with a look of abject sorrow and guilt.

In her mind, Cerys received images of the events leading up to Shakira's collapse.

"You fool youngling. Did I tell you to keep away? Rules are there for a reason. Argh, yes you probably acted as a catalyst. But no, it's not your fault. This was always going to happen."

This information didn't make him feel any better. He sloped off to take the boxes to his clan.

"What took you so long?" Elan asked huffily as Pryderi pulled up into the car park.

"I had to be careful."

"Trouble?"

"Nothing I could not handle."

No more was said. The pair offloaded the boxes, and more people turned up to carry them to the clan.

Just as soon as they were finished, Pryderi drove the borrowed van back to Cerys' cottage. He was surprised to see her pacing around outside.

"OK?" he asked.

"I just needed some cooling fresh air."

"Her?"

"Yes. Sleeping. You want to check?" Cerys offered, knowing he'd be happier going back to where he belonged after a little reassurance.

She led him into the room. He sensed the energy in there, and it made him twitch slightly.

"It's hers. It's OK," Cerys comforted.

He walked up to the bed. Shakira looked so peaceful.

"Grown," he observed, surprised.

"Yes, she's already changed. And it's been harder for her than you lot."

"More."

"Yes, there was a lot more to change. She keeps surprising me. This one is very special. But still secret. I may need your help soon. Will you be able to get away safely?"

She got an eager nod in response.

"OK, home with you now."

Pryderi knelt down and planted a soft kiss on Shakira's cheek and nuzzled her gently.

He knew he should go, but struggled to tear himself away. All he wanted was to be there for her.

He heard a cough behind him, and he reluctantly stood up. He took one last long look and disappeared into the night on foot.

Cerys disappeared back inside to check up on her patient.

"What are you?" she whispered as she smoothed the girl's hair.

Satisfied Shakira was in a stable condition she went into her kitchen, poured herself a soothing chamomile tea and took it into her lounge. Lily was in one of the armchairs, head propped up against a support, happily dozing.

It had been a long night. Cerys' mind was going over it all as she slouched and sipped her tea.

'Oh my goddess, the cafe,' she thought, sitting bolt upright.

She realised that nobody had locked up. It was a quiet neighbourhood, and was safe. However, she was planning for tomorrow. Shakira wasn't going to be up to working, and Annie would expect her employee to have locked up.

"Goddess help me," she groaned as she forced her weary body out of her chair.

She just wanted to sleep. There were things to do and tracks to cover though. So she rifled through the pile of discarded clothes to find the shop keys.

She jumped into her own little car, the van having been safely hidden away again.

It didn't take long to get to the coffee house.

She checked around to make sure everything was in place, and she locked the back door. She didn't know the security code for the burglar alarm, so she had to resort to her own way.

"Alarm set," she willed aloud, and heard the beeps as the system set itself.

"Thank you," she muttered as she set off for home.

Chapter 11 - A History Lesson

The rest of the night passed by uneventfully. Cerys and Lily took it in turns to catnap. But the pair were mid conflab when they heard…

"Arghhhhhhhhhh!"

Cerys and Lily were instantly on their feet and bounded into Shakira's presence in no time.

"What? What?" Cerys asked hurriedly.

"My ears," wailed Shakira, running her fingers along the offending articles.

"Ah," Cerys uttered as she sat down on the bed.

She took one of Shakira's hands in both of hers.

"Darling girl, I'm afraid there's more to it than that."

"More?" a panicked Shakira squeaked.

"Lily, on my dresser you'll find a handheld mirror. Would you mind fetching it, please?"

"Is it wise?"

"I think it is necessary."

She turned back to look at Shakira.

"Firstly, I'm sorry. I thought I had more time. I wanted to break this to you gently."

"What's wrong with me?"

"Oh dear, there's nothing wrong at all. Just the opposite really. You're quite magnificent."

"But…"

"Hush dear. I'm trying to explain. Oh, where to start? You're a hybrid."

"Like a Prius?"

"No, you're not a car, dear. You see, you're not quite…human," she started cautiously, trying to gauge Shakira's reaction.

"Not human?"

"That's right."

"Oh thank goodness."

"You're relieved?"

"Yes, I thought this was all real, but I'm clearly just having a nightmare. OK me, it's time to wake up now," Shakira announced, glancing around and above her.

"Oh dear. I assure you this is all very real."

Lily came back with the mirror, and slowly handed it over. Shakira looked at her reflection. Her eyes went wide and her mouth fell open. Then the screaming restarted.

"Calm down," Cerys willed, but the girl's panic was beyond even her powers.

Shakira was in hysterics.

"Oh my God. What the fuck? What?" and many more obscenities spewed forth from Shakira's mouth.

Lily scooched Cerys out of the way to sit next to the frantically screaming wreck.

"Shakira, listen to me," she said softly, "Listen. This is not what you think."

"I'm a…a…v…v…vam…vampire!"

"No. Well, let's just say no for now. Come on. Breathe for me. Deeply. That's it."

She waited for Shakira to take a few steadying breaths before continuing. And Cerys disappeared to make an herbal brew.

Lily went to the curtains and pulled them apart a little, allowing sunlight to filter in.

"There now. You're not disintegrating into dust are you?"

She received a head shake, but Shakira still squinted against the bright light filtering in.

"Vampires, the ones you're talking about can't go out in daylight, right?"

That earned her a slow head nod.

"OK, now we're getting somewhere. Those vampires are mythical beings which only exist in books."

"And films," Shakira added, still huddled under the covers and hugging her knees up to her chest.

"And films. The point is they're not real," Lily stated patiently.

"Not real."

"Right. And you're not trying to attack me either."

"No offense, but you smell funny."

"Yes, well, as long as you're not being offensive," she said sarcastically.

"Sorry."

"It's OK really, dear. I know. You'll get used to it."

"Your smell?"

"Your heightened senses. And yes, hopefully the smell also."

"Oh."

Cerys brought the herbal tea in, and they all eagerly sipped the calming blend.

"Ahh, that's better," Lily sighed appreciatively.

Lily took a deep breath before continuing, "So, if you're sitting comfortably, I'll begin. It all started long ago. Right back to when homosapiens were human-like apes. There was a branch of the family tree which split off. Feline DNA got into their family lineage."

"Cats?"

"Well, up until this morning you thought you were descended merely from monkeys."

"But cats?"

"Let's not lose focus, dear. Look at your eyes."

Shakira held the mirror up. Her eyes had always been like large almonds, but now the iris was slightly elongated. She curled her top lip up to get a better look at her fangs this time.

Her cheekbones seemed more prominent, her chin came to a finer point. And the ears she'd felt when she pushed her hand through her hair when she woke up? They were larger, slightly curved and they felt silky.

Her ears had always been pointy, sort of like an elf's. It's why she always tied her hair back into a ponytail over them. She was terribly self-conscious. She chuckled as she realised that was nothing in comparison to her new self.

"I'm not dead?"

"Not even undead," Lily assured.

"You didn't actually die," Cerys picked up. "I did have to put you to sleep for a little while."

"Like a computer?"

"Please stop comparing yourself to machines. Yes, you were in sleep mode. I was thinking more like a medically induced coma. Normally the elinefae grow gradually into their adult size, and their abilities develop during transition."

"Elinefae?"

"Oh yes, dear. Elinefae, the cat people. You may have heard of references to felidae?"

"Nope."

"That's a pity. Never mind. There's many names for them, but they like to be known collectively as elinefae."

Shakira bit her lower lip in concentration as she processed the information, and winced as her new fangs pierced her skin.

Cerys held a cloth to the girl's lips momentarily.

"Lick your lips," she told Shakira.

She licked her lips as instructed, and the puncture wounds instantly healed.

"You'll learn to be careful with those. You'll get used to it," Cerys commented, depositing the cloth in the bin.

"Cerys?"

Now she was calmer Shakira noticed her lisp as she pronounced her 's's.

"Yes?"

"Where do I come from?"

"Remember I asked about your parents?"

"Yes."

"I suspected then that they weren't your real parents."

"I'm adopted?"

"It would seem so. I'm surprised they never told you."

"Do they know?"

"About you being elinefae? I doubt it. Humans aren't aware of their existence. It's a closely guarded secret."

"But you know."

"Well, I'm a witch, dear" Cerys said, as if that explained everything.

"Not human?"

"Oh I'm human, just a witch human. We have the same lineage, at least. We, like the elinefae have longer lives. And of course, I can do magick."

"So the ladies that I've seen online claiming to be witches..?"

"Ahh, well there's humans who learn elements of the craft. They call themselves witches. But strictly speaking, we're a slightly different variation of the race. They help draw attention away from us, so we let it be."

"Witches and elinefae. Should I expect werewolves?"

"Don't be silly now, dear. No. Although as you learn more about elinefae you may understand more about the werewolf myth's origins."

Shakira frowned.

"Not shape shifters. And again, they don't attack humans."

"Yeah, smelly humans. Got it. How did they manage to adopt me? My parents, I mean."

"In for a penny, in for a pound," Cerys muttered under her breath.

"It's like this…" and she regaled her with Lily's story.

They all felt exhausted by the time she finished her retelling.

Lily realised they'd not eaten yet.

"Anyone want breakfast?" she chimed.

"Yes please. I could eat a horse," Shakira replied enthusiastically.

Cerys winced. "Yes, you probably could. But we'll come to that later."

"Oh crumbs. What do we give her?" Lily asked.

"Have you lived in the wilds too long? She can jolly well eat what we eat for now."

"But she will need to feed soon."

"Soon but not just yet, don't you think?"

Shakira was looking from one witch to the other.

"Not humans," she offered helpfully.

Cerys rubbed her forehead.

"For the last time, not humans. Go and take a shower and I'll put some bacon on."

Lily rose from her perch on the bed to let Shakira get up. Fortunately she'd not gone far as she had to catch her charge.

"Ooops. New legs too," Lily apologised.

"What?" she whinged as she looked down at her limbs.

Shakira quickly tried to cover her nakedness with her hands, as she realised she had no clothes on.

"We're all women here, no need for timidity. Oh, your clothes aren't going to fit."

"Cerys," Lily called out, as the other witch had already disappeared to the kitchen.

"Yes," she hollered back.

"Clothes."

"Right you are then. Won't be a tick."

The two ladies heard footsteps and cupboard doors slamming.

"These will have to do for now," Cerys said, re-entering the room, holding up a gypsy style skirt and top.

"I can't go to work looking like you," Shakira commented, rather ungratefully.

"Shit. What time is it? The coffee shop," she added, suddenly worried as she climbed into the clothes.

"It's taken care of," Cerys told her.

She pointed to her throat, and when she began talking the others heard Shakira's voice come out of Cerys' mouth.

"I'm really sorry, Annie. I can't come in to work today. I feel really sick," she mimicked.

"Right, the witch magick," the actual Shakira mused.

"I telephoned her first thing before you woke up screaming the place down."

Cerys ran back to the kitchen to start preparing breakfast, well, more like brunch.

Lily helped Shakira stand.

"Your legs are longer, and your hips will be different," she explained.

"Actually your arms will be too, but not noticeably until you walk on them."

"Walk on my arms?"

"All fours really. Hmmm…maybe you should try that until you get used to your new legs?"

"I'm not going to start crawling like a sodding dog," she huffed.

"Cat," the witch corrected.

Falling as she tried again to take a step forwards, Shakira gave in and got onto all fours. She felt her shoulders slide back a little.

"Cats have floating joints," Lily kindly elucidated.

Her hips also felt like they moved differently. Her knees scrunched up, and she made a tentative reach out with one hand. Her diagonally opposing foot lifted at the same time, of its own volition.

"Huh, kinda cool but weird," Shakira noted.

She tried the other arm, and the same thing happened with the other leg.

After a couple more goes she leaped into a sprint, and almost skidded on the kitchen floor as she followed the scent of bacon. The hoped for shower was a forgotten memory as the smell distracted her.

"Oh, look who's found her paws," Cerys exclaimed proudly.

Shakira was shocked to hear a purr come out of her throat.

"Well, we are a fast learner. Make yourself comfy at the table, it's almost ready."

More purrs sounded as Shakira smiled as she managed to pull the chair out and sit down without falling. Lily applauded as she walked in and took her place at the table. Cerys served up the bacon sandwiches and English Breakfast tea.

"How are you feeling? Any pain?" Cerys enquired.

"Mm...none at all," Shakira answered around a mouthful of sandwich. "It's the first time in months I've not felt in agony. I feel great. Better than ever actually."

"None?" Cerys was surprised.

"None."

"Tell me, have you ever healed yourself before."

"Heal myself? I wouldn't even know where to start."

"But you did last night."

"Did I?"

"Yes. Have you ever been poorly?"

"No. I have a strong constitution, as my mother puts it. Well, the woman I call mother."

"One thing at a time. Coughs, colds?"

"Nope."

"Sore throat?"

"Well yes, but they never amounted to anything."

"Uh huh, I see." Cerys had that annoying knowing look again.

"But that would be just as true of the elinefae," Lily put in, seeing where Cerys' questions were leading.

"You told me you don't believe in magick," Cerys continued.

"Well, I didn't. But I suppose I have to now, don't I? I didn't believe in vampires either."

"Elinefae."

"Whatever."

"Don't call them vampires, they'll get upset."

"Why? They are, aren't they?"

"No. Vampires aren't real."

"But my fangs…"

"Yes, you have fangs. Yes, you will need blood."

"Eww."

"But not from humans. Look at it this way, elinefae are what inspired the stories."

"Inspired," Kiera tried the idea.

"Yes. Well, mixed with other folk tales. The kind of vampire you're imagining stems from Dracula, I think."

"That is the image fangs conjures up, yes."

"Well stop it. Elinefae are pale, yes. They live in darkness most of the time. They used to live happily alongside humans. Not in the same villages, you understand. But they could mingle. Then ridiculous stories spread. I'm not saying that there weren't any accidents in the past. But generally humans weren't considered food."

"Generally not food?"

"Only if elinefae became starved, you know, like wolves."

"Wolves?"

"That may be more confusing. Ignore wolves. Anyway, once demon and vampire stories were popularised the humans became panicked and scared. There were attacks on innocent elinefae, and they were gradually forced into hiding."

"So, elinefae live in the dark, drink blood, have fangs, but aren't undead and don't generally eat humans."

"Right. Don't ever call them vampires. It's a sore point. It's like a swear word."

"I'm going to meet them then?"

"Not yet. No. It's complicated. Oh, you're distracting me. Magick. You didn't believe in it. Why?"

"I grew up, I guess. I used to, just like any other little girl. I'd pretend I was talking to fairies all the time. But then I stopped."

"You didn't hear them anymore?"

"Oh honestly, fairies?"

"Yes, they exist. What did the faeries talk to you about?"

"I don't know, I can't remember. It wasn't even real. My mum told me enough times to grow up, and eventually I did. End of."

"Your mum didn't like it?"

"No. Maybe I was past the point I should've grown out of it. She told me I was too old to have imaginary friends. I remember she started to get really upset about it."

"Why would it upset her?"

"The other girls teased me. I didn't fit in. I never have. But my mum wanted me to make friends, and this was just one more thing stopping me."

"Just a caring mum then."

"Yeah, she was the best. Oh, what am I going to tell her?"

"Nothing yet. We need to figure this all out."

"You keep saying that. I'm elinefae. So what do we need to figure out?"

"Oh, how to keep the humans from discovering your true self. How to keep the elinefae from knowing you exist full stop. You know, nothing much."

"Why can't I meet the elinefae?"

"Did you not listen, child? Did you hear how you were brought into the world?"

"I suppose I zoned out a bit. It was a lot to take in," Shakira answered, blushing.

"Elinefae, thinking you were part human, an illegal baby that they tried to kill? Ring any bells? They killed your real parents. What do you think they'll do to you?"

"Oh. Is there not somewhere else I can go? Are there nice elinefae?"

"They are a network, Shakira," Cerys said, starting to lose patience. "The elinefae live in clans. But they communicate with each other. They have mass gatherings. They are one."

"So how come they don't know about me?"

"Argh, they presumed you were dead. You were hidden amongst humans. Concentrate."

"Alright, alright. I'm sorry. How do I know?"

Cerys took a few deep breaths before replying, "I'm sorry. This is a very unusual situation. I've become guardian of a secret, and believe it or not, I'm trying to protect you. I want to save your life."

"You could've killed me. Last night. Just a drop too much wolfy-wotsit, and no more problem."

"Yes, yes I could," Cerys huffed, but then her lips curled into a smile, and the smile turned into a chuckle.

"Wolfy-wotsit," she laughed.

Lily joined in the laughter. Shakira thought they were laughing at her at first and began to pout.

"Oh dear, I am sorry," Cerys said through tears of laughter, "Ah, this whole thing is a bit crazy. Smuggled baby, halfling growing up clueless, and then bang, a magickal kiss and she turns into a beautiful elinefae. I don't think even the brothers Grimm could conjure up such an epic tale."

"Yeah right. Oops, where's my glass slipper?" Shakira quipped, joining in on the joke.

"Here, eat my gingerbread wall."

"Someone find me a pumpkin," Lily added, joining in the laughter.

"Here prince, come kiss me," Shakira laughed, puckering up her lips.

"Oh crap. Pryderi," Cerys exclaimed, suddenly sobering up.

"What's a Prrrr..." she purred.

That started the laughter again, but only momentarily.

"pruh-DAIR-ee," Cerys said slowly.

"Prrrr-dairy."

"Oh dear, even his name makes her purr."

"Him? That's a name? I thought we were talking about some sort of elf."

Cerys began laughing again.

"Pryderi is an elinefae. He's *your* elinefae. Your mate."

"My mate? Oh no, you can't be talking about what I think you're talking about."

"Afraid so."

"But how? I've never even met him?"

"Haven't you?"

"I think I'd know if I'd met a cat person."

"You'd think so, wouldn't you?" Cerys had that amused glint in her eye.

"OK. Owl in a tree?" Cerys prompted.

"He was in that tree I bumped into?"

"He *was* the tree you bumped into."

"But you said..."

"What was I supposed to say? Yes, you bumped into an elinefae, and you're going to turn into one."

"A little heads up would've been nice."

"You weren't ready to hear it. And I thought I had more time. How was I to know your first kiss would fuel your change?"

"My first kiss?" she asked, her jaw falling open.

"Um...yes, about that."

"That delivery driver? The herdsman? He was a cat person? This Prrryderi?"

"Yes."

"But he didn't have fangs. Don't they all have fangs? Am I just a freak?"

"Yes, of course they all have fangs. That's where the vampire tales came from."

"So is *he* some sort of freak? Oh my God, I'm supposed to marry a freakier freak."

"Yes, he is a bit odd. But actually he has fangs."

"Does not. I should know, they would have been in my mouth."

"I give them false teeth, so they can spend short periods with humans."

"False teeth?"

"Yes. A bit like those vampire teeth humans wear at Samhain, I mean Halloween, but in reverse."

"Instead of fangs, there's teeth to fill the gap?"

"Clever girl."

"Wow. Sure had me fooled. But his eyes?"

"Were dark."

"Yes. My irises are, well…cat-like."

"So are his really. Contact lenses are a marvellous thing."

"But they were so dark."

"All the better to hide the glow with, my dear."

"Glow?"

"It was dark. Your eyes will glow in the dark too. Ever see a cat's eyes when they're lit by headlights?"

"Yes."

"Like that."

"Well, of course. Silly me. How did I not think of that?"

"There's no need for sarcasm."

"Well excuuu-uuuse me, but I think there is. Cat people but not vampires are called elinefae; a race which I belong to, but who want to kill me. A handsome guy snogs me, and he turns out to be one of them. I had some sort of seizure, almost died, only to wake up as a vampire accompanied by two witches. My parents aren't my parents. My real ones are dead. Oh, and fairies exist," her voice was getting higher pitched with each item on her list.

"No, that calls for hysteria, which you seem to be reaching quite nicely."

"Hysteria? I'll bloody show you hysteria," she shouted, standing up ready to hit the infuriating witch.

But instead of standing she crumpled to the floor.

"Bloody stupid cat legs," she huffed as she sat there feeling sorry for herself.

Cerys reached down to help her to her feet.

"Aren't you worried I'll hit you?"

"No dear. Firstly, look at what just happened. You're not physically capable. Secondly, I'm protected. We witches mingle with elinefae a lot. They can be...temperamental, so it's best to always be on your guard."

Shakira dusted herself off.

"Yeah, what's with that? Why do you hang around with them?"

"Oh right, we've not got to that bit. Well, we're healers and protectors. My lot actually don't need me so much these days, bit Lily lives with some rough ones. They fight, well, train hard, and get hurt. Also, we protect them from the outside world. We put up barriers, to help with that."

"Phew, I don't know about you two, but I'm exhausted. My head hurts," Lily moaned.

"Sorry dear, there's a lot to tell you, and I fear we don't have much time to get you up to speed," Cerys apologised to Shakira.

"Cerys. Why do you keep calling me dear? It's rather condescending, especially as you're my age."

"Sorry. Force of habit. And I'm not exactly the same age."

Chapter 12 – A Steep Learning Curve

Having finished their meal, Cerys realised it was time for a lesson in deportment. She helped Shakira to her feet.

"There we are. You have extra cartilage to contend with now. Your wrists and ankles will have adapted so you can run on all fours just as easily as walking on your hind legs. You'll be even better than you were when you came into the kitchen. Your hips are now slinky. Sink into them as you walk. It will give you a sexy wiggle," she winked and chuckled.

"I don't think I've ever been called sexy in my life," Shakira lamented.

"Well, I think that will soon be remedied. Now first one foot," she promptly guided.

"Hhhhh…" Shakira hissed as her leg buckled.

Cerys caught her.

"Up up up. Your knees are now more…flexible. Remember what they felt like when you were on all fours?"

"They're bendier."

"Flexible. When you walk on your hind legs you need to remember this. Concentrate on stiffening them. Stretch your legs out a little more than you used to."

Shakira took a tentative step forward.

"There we go. Now sink that hip and raise the other as you lift that foot."

It was shaky progress, but at least she didn't fall flat on her arse.

"Use your arms for balance, swing them gently as you go. Right foot left arm."

Shakira tried, but her arms were stiff as she tensed in anticipation of falling.

"Here like this," Cerys said as she demonstrated.

This time Shakira's arms glided, her shoulder blades gently rolling in time with her opposing hip.

"Now, back straight, head up. That's it."

Shakira's steps became less faltering as she paraded around the house like a catwalk model.

"By jove, I think she's getting it," Cerys beamed, proud of her protégée.

"There's a full length mirror in my room. Go and see how stunning you are."

Shakira slinked off, leaving Cerys and Lily on their own.

"Well?" Lily asked.

"I just don't know," Cerys said, raking her hands over her face.

"I liked your thinking about not getting ill, but really that's just as much an elinefae trait."

"If only she'd shown some other signs. Now her elinefae side has taken over it's even harder to tell."

"There was the fae contact."

"But they stopped talking to her."

"Or she stopped listening."

"Curious how they never shared their information," Cerys pondered.

"Hmmm, she grew up in Surrey."

"And you still have a day left before you need to be back with your slave master."

"I am not a slave," Lily contradicted, more firmly than she intended.

"No, but he does a good job of playing a dictator. I don't like it. What's he up to?"

"I wanted to get ideas from you, but we seem to have been preoccupied."

"As the goddess wills it," Cerys said, hands outstretched in resignation to the fates.

They heard footsteps approaching and swiftly halted their conversation.

Both ladies took a deep breath in as they saw Shakira walk back in. Not Shakira the elinefae, but Shakira the human.

"What did you do?" Cerys gasped.

"Nothing really. I was looking in the mirror, trying to get used to my new look, which is growing on me, by the way. But then I started comparing it to what I used to look like, and I was just thinking about it, and my reflection shimmered and changed."

"By the goddess, and all the pantheons!"

Cerys tried to conceal her wonderment, but it was difficult. This girl, who supposedly never performed magick before just glamoured herself. This was no mean feat.

The most that even the best witches could do was change outfits, at least without performing the right ritual and casting a spell. It wasn't something which was done by accident.

"I think I'd best be hitting the road," Lily flustered.

"No rush. Could you two perhaps put on some more tea for us? I just need to pop to the bathroom."

The ladies nodded, and Cerys did indeed go to her bathroom. But not to use the toilet. She waved and chanted before the mirror in there.

"Merry meet, Heather."

"Cerys. A joyous surprise. Merry meet. Blessed be."

"Heather, I'm in a bit of a hurry. Are you in to callers?"

"Oh how lovely. Yes, always happy to receive a sister."

"I can't say more, but this is top secret. Please. Nobody must know. I hate asking this of you."

"Oh, I like a good mystery. Of course, I swear to secrecy," Heather waved her arms in vow formation as she said this.

"Thank you sister. I'm sending Lily to see you soon. Only for a day. We don't have long at all."

"I'll be ready."

"Thank you. Blessed be."

And with a wave of her hand the mirror turned back into a normal mirror.

Cerys flushed the loo, for the benefit of Shakira's new hearing. She'd soundproofed the room, but lifted it now, so as to give her story credibility. Well, there was no use exciting the girl more than necessary. She knew nothing for certain at this stage.

She hurried back to the kitchen.

"Do you take shhhggghh," Shakira struggled.

"Oh my. Oh dear. Um, no sugar thank you dear. Oh this will never do," she chuckled.

"I don't ssseee what's ssso funny," Shakira lisped.

"Hmmm, your teeth are settling in nicely, whatsyourname."

"You know my name is Shhhhkkkk," she hissed and spluttered.

"Oh yes, what a great name to give an elinefae," Cerys smirked.

"In my defence, it was in keeping and I didn't know she'd even turn. She seemed so human."

"Yes, well that seems more of an indictment on your judgement."

"Hindsight is 50/50," Lily defended, but was smiling.

"Besides, how can anyone ask after her whereabouts?" she added cockily.

Cerys narrowed her eyes at her sister, recognising her shrewdness.

"Well, deportment is going well. Perhaps elocution should be on the agenda this afternoon? And a name change?" Lily was still smiling as she spoke.

Having drunk their tea, the witches left Shakira inside practicing walking whilst they went into the garden.

Cerys opened her portal, and waited until the connection was confirmed.

"Merry meet," Heather chimed through the opening.

Lily had turned pale and was fidgeting.

"Oh, you can't fain fear now, Lily. I know what you did," Cerys chided.

"And that's what scared me. I have more power than I realised."

"Well, put it to good use, sister. Come on, time to put on your big girl pants."

That made Lily smile. With a steadying breath she stepped through and found herself wrapped in Heather's arms.

They closed the portal, and Cerys returned to her fledgling elinefae as Lily was welcomed to Surrey.

"I can't linger long, Heather. And it's best if I don't tell you why I'm here. Time is of the essence."

"Are you in trouble?"

"Not yet. But I don't want to put you in jeopardy. I must go out straight away. Have you a vehicle I can borrow, please?"

Heather's lifestyle was much like Cerys'. A thoroughly modern witch. She lived amongst the humans.

"Yes, but it's only a little Micra."

"That's fine. I just need to get somewhere. I'll return it in a few hours, I promise. Please tell me it's an automatic."

"Well yes, actually."

"That's a relief. I don't have to use cars often myself. Oh, and have you any birch wine lurking?"

"Birch wine? Yes, but…?"

"Ask me no questions and I shall tell you no lies, sister. But if you have a drop of honey I can pinch too?"

This told Heather more than enough for her to guess Lily's mission. She just didn't know the why of it. But she trusted Lily when she said it was better for her not to know. So she went to her store cupboard and retrieved the requested items.

With a brief hug the ladies parted company. Lily sped off in the little car.

She was feeling more than a little nervous. Fae were infamously tricksy beings to deal with. But this was for Shakira.

The car's satnav took her to the edge of the woods where she thought the fae were most likely to be, presuming they'd not fled the location entirely. Lily parked up and started trudging through the woodland, clutching her offerings.

She was on high alert, as she tried to sense any fae nearby. It didn't take too long for her to get the tell-tale tingling sensation. It was like a homing beacon, getting stronger with each step.

She picked up a stray acorn cup, found a fallen tree and sat down on it. She poured the wine into the lid and placed it on the log next to her. She dished up some honey in the acorn cup and put that next to the wine.

Closing her eyes, she began to chant,

"Little folk within this woodland dwell,

I call upon you with this spell.

My sole intent is pure and true,

Unto me yourselves reveal. Please do."

There was a buzzing and fluttering, then Lily saw a glowing flicker coming towards her.

The sound of tiny wings grew stronger and nearer. And as it did, Lily could make out a golden brown figure with wild blonde hair flowing around her elfin face. It landed on the log by the treats.

The faery stood there regarding the witch, twisting her mouth and scrunching her nose.

"Why are you calling, demanding our presence?"

"Ummm…hello. I do apologise but this is urgent, otherwise I wouldn't dare intrude. And I said please."

"Ever thought of just saying hello? Typical sodding witches. Why be civil when you can summon folk with a spell, and force them to show up whether they wish to or not?"

"I honestly didn't know I could do that. I thought I had to cast to see you. I'm really very sorry."

"At least you brought goodies," the little winged being said as she tipped the wine lid towards her.

The liquid splashed over the sides a little, but she managed to drink some of it.

"Sorry. It was the best I could do at short notice," Lily apologised again.

Wiping her mouth, the faery piped up, "Well, it tastes nice. What do you want, witch?"

"I'm Lily. I come on behalf of the halfling Shakira."

The faery froze mid slurp.

"You do know the name at least, then?" Lily's remark was really more of a statement than a question.

"Don't try to trick me, witch."

"Look, I'm just trying to get to the point. Her life may, no, her life is in danger."

"Has been all her life."

"Yes, but now she's transitioned."

"Well, what do you know? She's all grown up. So which way did it go?"

"Which way?"

"What did she become?"

"Well, elinefae, of course."

"No of course about it, witch."

"Lily. My name is Lily."

"Yes yes. And I'm Frydah. Blah blah blah. What do you want?" This was said with her hands planted on her lips, and Frydah staring at Lily in the eyes as she flitted up to face level.

"Frydah, I need to know. Why were you in contact with her?"

"Who says I was?" she asked huffily as she landed back on the tree.

"She did. Well, she said she used to talk to faeries, but she dismissed it as a childhood fantasy."

"Oooh, that human mother of hers really got in the way. If I wasn't so nice, she wouldn't still be breathing."

"I'm sorry. I heard she objected. I don't know why."

"Stupid humans. It's always the same. Scared of what they don't know. There was a time when they believed." Frydah's glow dimmed as she wallowed in sadness.

"Yes," Lily sighed, "there were simpler times. But it's sort of easier this way. They can go about their business, and we can go about ours."

"I suppose," the faery shrugged as she landed next to the honey, and scooped some up with her finger.

Frydah took a long suck on her honey drenched finger before sighing, "It's sort of lonely without them though."

"Frydah, why were you in contact with Shakira?"

The faery was on full alert again. "Oh no. I'm not telling. No way."

"But why?"

"Why why why? You sound like a stupid human with your stupid whys. Why do you need to know?"

"Because…because she's different. She's not pure elinefae. She's special. And we need to know how to help her. And how on Earth do we integrate her?"

Frydah laughed, but there was no joy in it.

"Integrate? A halfling? Can you hear yourself?"

"But she can't remain with the humans, not for long. No matter how well she can glamour."

"She can glamour? Well, what do you know?" Frydah said, actually smiling.

"Will you help her?"

"Wit…Lily, you seem nice. I'd like to help you, but I just can't. I'm sorry. Truly. But it's more than my life's worth. Besides, what can I do? She's a misfit. She can't live amongst humans, as you so rightly pointed out. But nor can she dwell with elinefae. They'll never accept her. Maybe she can live with one of you?"

With a final shrug Frydah flitted away and hid behind a tree. She waited for Lily to leave. Her heart sank as she watched the dejected witch walk away.

Frydah finished off the rest of the honey and the lid of wine. Lily had taken the open bottle with her. Feeling giddy, she drunkenly found the nearest mushroom and curled up underneath it.

"Stupid humans. Stupid witches. Stupid elinefae. Stupid Threaris," she huffed as she wriggled to get comfy.

"They should all learn to co-operate," she yawned into her arms folded under her face.

Chapter 13 – The Return

Lily scurried back to Heather's home, and handed back the open bottle of wine.

"Just as well I have spare stoppers," Heather said wryly noticing the missing top.

"I do apologise, dear. Things got a bit…fraught. I need to go straight back to Cerys. May I ask for your assistance one more time?"

"Of course, but please let me know if I can be of any assistance."

"Hopefully we won't need to involve you any further. But I will bear it in mind, sister. Thank you."

"I do miss everyone. I feel so alone out here," she admitted sadly.

"We all do. Maybe we should convene again? I will seek opinion. This whole thing has made me realise how little information passes between us. And maybe we need to remedy that."

Heather led her out to the portal. Lily travelled back, but she found herself in a room of Cerys' shop.

"I had to come in. I can't keep the shop closed. It will arouse suspicion," she explained, greeting her friend back. "Now, what did you learn in Surrey?"

"Not a lot, I'm sad to say. I met with a faery named Frydah, but she was very tight lipped. It was more what she didn't say."

"Well, given our thoughts, you can't blame the faery for that. And the fact that one of the most prominent members of all the fae was involved speaks volumes."

"Yes, she's certainly the go-to fae for protection. But why? Did Shakira's father send her?"

"A father often wishes to protect his young."

"But why did he not claim her? If he knows of her existence..."

"Now, that's more the question. Did Frydah confirm the parentage?"

"What do you think?" Lily asked with a wry look.

"How did she react?"

"Like a frightened sprite. Yet I don't think she was wholly surprised by my visit."

"So, what do we know? We have a halfling."

"Where is she?"

"She's still at my house. She's called in sick again. I can't keep using that excuse though."

"Quite."

"Shakira is half elinefae, and presumably half sorcerer, given her abilities. But the precise sorcerer father is yet to be determined. That's quite scary in itself. He seems to have set protection up for her, but has not been directly involved."

"Maybe he was seeing how she would grow?"

"Oh, my dear. She's just reached adulthood. He wouldn't pay a visit now, would he?"

The look of fear in Cerys' eyes was self-evident.

"I can't deny the thought had occurred to me. Oh, I shouldn't have left her on her own. I need to figure out a plan, and soon."

"But where do we start? Do we hand her over to whoever her father is?"

"Well, we don't know who. And what if it's one of the dark ones?"

"I won't believe that of her. She's gentle and loving."

"She's half elinefae. Who knows what the other half could be?"

"No. She's all good. I know she is."

"I hope so. But we have the Pryderi factor. We won't be able to separate them. Not even her father would. But we can't have her go to the clan."

"Oh goodness, no. Can you imagine? An elinefae with that sort of power? They'd fear her and do goddess knows what in the name of that fear."

"Talking of fear, you'd best be getting home before Dougal throws his toys out of his pram."

"Don't remind me. I've felt like I can breathe again, being away from him."

"Be strong. All you can do is be there. Let's see what develops."

"You know my fears."

"We all share them."

"Oh, Heather and I briefly discussed a coven gathering."

"That sounds good. But what do we say about Shakira? Is it safe to confer with them?"

"Is it safe to handle this all on our own, with an unidentified sorcerer on the loose?"

"OK. Leave it with me. I'll call everyone soon."

They quickly hugged before Cerys opened the portal to Rose.

"Oh, don't forget this," Cerys exclaimed, handing her friend a jar of Aconite.

"Oh crumbs. Can you imagine what would've happened if I returned empty handed?"

"I have enough fear in my life right now, thank you very much."

"Blessings upon you, dear one."

"And unto you."

And with that Lily travelled to Rose's house.

Lily didn't stop. She quickly thanked Rose, and shrouded herself in her travelling clothes, muttering her incantation.

She hurried home. Time was getting on, and she feared Dougal's wrath.

But her own anger rose as she headed towards her den. Walking through the encampment she heard sounds of war. Dougal was clearly pushing his warriors harder than ever. And there was a queue at her door as evidence.

"*What the hell is going on?*" she spat out in Eline as she made her way up the queue.

"*Lily, thank the goddess you're home,*" one of the elinefae males exclaimed.

"*Why? Is your self-healing not working?*" she barked.

"*Not for this,*" the first in line said, holding out his arm.

Lily's eyebrows shot up as she looked at the broken arm which had obviously healed too quickly. His bones hadn't been reset.

"*I'm going to need help,*" she grumbled, shoving her door open.

As she stepped into her own den she saw a youngling already sitting there patiently waiting with piles of herbs next to him.

"*Well, that's one thing,*" she muttered.

It was as close to a thank you as she could manage under the circumstances.

She grabbed her trolley and loaded it with potions. The fire was already lit, and there was a kettle of water already boiling.

"*How long have you been waiting?*" she asked the youngling.

"*Since daybreak,*" he muttered sheepishly.

"*Gregor, is Loth intact?*"

The youngling nodded.

"*Good. Go fetch him. Quickly.*"

Gregor sped away as fast as he could.

Lily poured some hot water and herbs into a bowl and prepared some bandages and tools. She sighed, knowing it was going to be a long day.

Dougal burst into her den as she was setting up.

"*Where have you been?*" he demanded.

"*Where I said I'd be, and I've come back when I said I would,*" she countered, in no mood to bow down to this thug.

"*I have injured urgently requiring assistance, and you weren't here,*" he bellowed.

For the first time in her life she rounded on the elinefae Leader.

"*And whose fault is that?*" she shouted back, striding close to him.

"*You weren't here.*"

"*This is all your doing, Dougal. Not mine. I told you I had to get supplies. I told you that you were pushing them too hard.*"

"*How dare you?*" he raged, raising his hand.

"*How dare I? How dare you?*" she yelled, staring him down.

He tried to strike her, but his hand hit her barrier with full force.

"*And just what were you planning to do with an injured healer?*" she jeered.

He shook his hand, trying to shake away the pain. She refused to offer him aid.

" *You're pushing your luck, witch.* "

She bristled as she stood her ground.

" *No. I am stating fact,* " she said as calmly as she could.

" *I don't need to remind you who is clan Leader.* "

" *No. No you don't. But you clearly need to remember I am one witch. I am doing my best here with your carnage. I can only do so much.* "

Loth rushed in as the two were facing off. He took a step back, not wanting to get involved.

" *It's OK Loth,* " Lily said calmly, turning her face to him. " *Please come in.* "

Turning back to Dougal, she glared a challenge at him.

" *Now, if you don't mind, I have elinefae to fix.* "

Dougal was seething. Never had anyone dared to speak to him so disrespectfully.

" *We'll continue this later,* " he hissed before turning to storm out of the room.

Their conversation had been held in Eline, he wanted to show any witnesses he had nothing to hide and that he had the last say. He was the authority here.

Lily could hear him shouting at others as he made his way back to his area. He was obviously taking his wrath out on those who couldn't stand up to him. But that wasn't her concern right now.

Lily took a deep breath. And another. She poked her head around the door to where Gregor was cowering.

" *Well boy, I need tea. Come on, come on. I can't do everything.*"

The youngling scurried into her den and made her some energising tea whilst she began helping his brethren.

" *Come in then,*" she said to the first victim.

As he sat on a wooden stool she grabbed a stick and placed it in his mouth. She motioned with her head towards Loth to stand by the patient's side.

She dipped a cloth into the hot herby water and wiped his arm, muttering a chant as she did so. She then anointed the area with a numbing oil.

"I'll hold his shoulders, you pull his hand," she subtly commanded Loth in English.

He nodded and pulled with all his might until they could hear the bones crack. The patient groaned, and snapped the stick in his teeth. He was sweating.

"Hold it," she told Loth.

She quickly dipped a bandage in the water and began wrapping it around the patient's lower arm. More chanting could be heard as she wiped an unguent over the bandage, which set as she worked.

Lily measured out an elixir onto a spoon and guided it into the patient's mouth, who pulled a face as he swallowed.

"*Now now. You're a fierce warrior,*" she admonished.

"*Maybe so. But that tastes...*"

"*Yes yes. Well, you should fight better. Go on. I'm a busy person. No time to chat.*"

And with that she shooed him out and to let in the next victim of Dougal's so called training.

She paused briefly to take a sip of tea and to instruct Gregor to keep replenishing the hot water.

"What happened to you?" Loth asked her between patients.

"I grew a pair," she said slyly, winking before fetching yet another injured warrior.

She had realised she could no longer stand idly by whilst Dougal worked his warriors into the ground.

A few had died already under his regime. Well, no more. Not on her watch. She had been cowed down by his bullying. Her, a witch. She felt ashamed of herself. But she used that to fuel her new resolution.

She didn't have time to reflect on the hows and whys, or even to dwell on her feelings of inadequacy. She had a job to do, and by the goddess, she was going to do it.

Chapter 14 – Found

Cerys had not been idle. She'd contacted Rhion and asked to borrow Pryderi for some maintenance.

"Is this really needed now?" he'd grumbled.

"My trees need lopping before they cause damage to my property. And you know how I hate to do it myself. It feels like I'm cutting off my own limbs," she'd told him.

Well, it wasn't a complete lie. He'd have seen straight through that.

"Whilst he's here I'd like him to catch up with some other bits that have been neglected. It shouldn't take more than a couple of days."

"He's one of my best Watchers."

"And you feel under threat of imminent attack perhaps?"

"I feel unrest. Just between you and me, it's as if something is stirring. Tell me you don't feel it."

"I do," she had to admit.

"My clan feels a little of it. They too seem restless, particularly Pryderi. He seems distracted. It's not like him."

"What better way of distracting him by keeping him busy? And perhaps I can gleam what ails him at the same time?"

"OK, you win," he said good-naturedly. "But one day you'll have to let me win an argument."

"Pah. Argument. It was a request, and you were good enough to grant it, Sir."

"Whatever you say, Cerys."

"Oh, please can you send him over straight away? He can get started whilst I finish up at the shop."

"Argh. Demanding woman. Fine," he assented begrudgingly, yet still smiling.

He could never bring himself to say no to her. He lamented for the thousandth time that she wasn't elinefae. She'd make a great mate if not for that one point. Trying to put the unsavoury thought aside once more, he signalled Pryderi and sent him to do Cerys' bidding.

Pryderi was obviously only too glad to get back to Shakira. He tried to exit his forest home as calmly as possible, but it took every ounce of his willpower not to sprint away.

Once clear of the clan's senses he bolted. He ran faster than even he had ever run, only slowing as he approached the humans' jurisdiction.

He slowed to a brisk walk, trying to remain hidden from any human eyes. It wasn't too difficult; Cerys' house was on the edge of town. He didn't come across many people, just the odd car passing along the road. He turned up the collar of his coat and dipped his head down, his hat shading his face.

He strode on to his destination. To her. The one female who made him feel more alive than he'd ever felt. The one he'd kill for. Who he'd die for.

Pryderi went to the back door, setting off the chimes.

Shakira had been restless, doing her best to pace on her as yet unsteady feet. She'd been trying to put her thoughts into some semblance of order.

This, this was all too much to take in. It didn't matter how often she looked at herself in the mirror, she still didn't believe her reflection.

She couldn't be a vampire. They simply didn't exist. They were a creation of novelists and film makers. OK, so the witches called them elinefae. Witches! Could she even hear herself? Vampires and witches were real?

And what did this mean for her? Her life was apparently under threat. She had a family, somewhere where she may finally belong. But oh no, they wanted to kill her.

She could be accepted NOWHERE. Aside from the people she thought of as her parents, she'd never fit in anywhere. She thought she'd come close here in this town, but now she could see that for the illusion it really was. They just humoured her. She was nothing. NOTHING.

She was sobbing, alone and collapsed on the floor. Her body was shaking with the force of her cries. She screamed out, howling out her internal pain.

Pryderi was by her side in an instant. He had heard her as he approached the door. He felt her pain and rushed to her side thinking she was being attacked. His hat fell to the ground in his haste.

"You OK?" His voice broke through her pain barrier, sinking into her soul; he was here.

He was looking at her intensely with electric blue, almond shaped eyes. She was mesmerised by their brilliance. Long black lashes added to their enchantment.

She vaguely felt his arms wrap around her, his hand on her face keeping her gaze on him.

"Shhh....Sshkk...fuck. You. Are you OK?" he asked more forcibly having received no response, and struggling with her name.

She just stared, open mouthed. He tried waving his hand in front of her eyes.

"Hello," he said loudly and slowly.

She shook herself out of her stupor.

"You're here."

"Yes. Hello," he smiled. "Are you OK?"

He rubbed her shoulder as he maintained his eye contact.

"Um, no. Not really. You look different," her voice came out quietly.

She felt a million miles away as she gazed at this man. Vampire. Elinefae. Thing. His eyes were bright blue, not dark at all. They were amazing. And they sat above high cheekbones, which somehow now seemed more prominent. His cheeks were slightly hollower than she remembered.

His chin came to a point along a strong jawline. With his slightly pointy ears, she thought he looked like a very large elf. His long black hair hung loosely down his back. He was beautiful.

"Yes, but are you hurt?" he was asking her.

His worry was etched on his face. He shrugged off his coat and sat on the floor next to her, gathering her to him. She noticed his lithe yet muscled torso which was now bare. She was almost drooling.

"No. Not hurt, just, I don't know. Overwhelmed, I suppose," she said, trying to focus on the conversation.

He cocked his head to one side. He looked like he didn't understand. And he still looked worried.

"What? I'm supposed to be OK with all this? Just accept it?"

"Not hurt?"

Realisation dawned.

"No. It just sort of hurts on the inside. I don't feel I belong anywhere. I feel lost."

He gently linked his fingers in hers and guided her hand to his heart.

"You belong here," he told her softly.

His eyes were so earnest and he sounded so sincere she felt lost all over again, but totally lost in him. She felt the meaning of his words and the truth they contained.

There was the briefest pause as her breath hitched and she stared into those electric blue eyes.

"I suppose I do," she breathed.

Their faces drew slowly nearer. Everything went silent around them. There was only him and her. The world fell away. After what felt like forever their lips met.

His lips felt plump and full as they pressed against hers. Pleasure ripped through her core. Shakira's heart felt like it expanded in her chest and was ready to burst out. Her entire being felt like it was glowing, being warmly lit up from inside.

Their mouths merged and meshed as their kiss deepened.

Pryderi groaned as his deep lust fired through him.

"Shhhkkk...Kiera," he hissed on a whisper into her neck.

"Hmmm...I like that."

"What?"

"The name. Kiera," she groaned as he continued to nuzzle her neck.

He lifted her top up and over her head and gently pushed her down to the floor.

He let out a low growl as he saw her bare breasts. It was more than he could bear. He needed her. Now.

He untied his leather trousers and set his erection free.

He pushed her gypsy skirt up. Her scent accosted his nostrils, flaring up his desire further.

She widened her legs, inviting him in. Her back arched as she writhed against the cool floor. She needed him so much it almost hurt.

"Prrryderrri," she purred.

He grinned down at her, revelling in his name escaping her lips. She was magnificent and he had to be with her.

"Oh Kiera," he moaned as he found her entrance.

He pushed his way inside her, needing to claim her, to be with her, to feel her.

They howled in unison as their bodies started to move together, dancing to their own rhythm.

He glided inside her, building momentum. But nothing could quench his thirst for her.

She lifted her legs onto his lower back, needing him to go further, needing to feel him, to claim him.

They were crying out with their need.

He cupped his arms around her shoulders, gaining more of her.

She clutched onto his back, striving for release.

Their thrusts became aggressive, frantic in their search of fulfilment.

Their cries grew louder as their writhing became wilder. He bit into her shoulder, her blood seeping into his mouth like wine.

Finally the heavens burst into stars, as they climaxed. It was as if those stars were fragments of her soul. Like her entire existence had been shattered into a million pieces.

Pryderi was blasted into orgasm too.

In her mind's eye she saw the pieces of herself merge with his, and reform as one soul. It was vibrant. Lit with all the colours of the rainbow.

She held onto him with all her might, keeping him close as she climbed back down and he licked the wound he'd inflicted.

Once she calmed she held onto him all the more, needing the reassurance of his presence.

He had just become her everything. She had found home. She had found where she belonged. She had found her soulmate.

Chapter 15 – Naming

'Mine,' she heard him say.

'Mine,' she replied, but as she did she realised her lips hadn't moved.

There were no words. It was more like a feeling.

She pushed his chest just enough for her to see his face.

"Say that again," she asked, this time with words.

'Mine,' she heard, but his lips hadn't moved.

'This is how we sometimes talk,' he told her.

'Not always,' he communicated whilst showing her images of elinefae in different scenarios.

She even 'heard' an odd language.

"Not English," he said out loud.

"That explains a lot," she replied, kind of relieved.

Pryderi rolled onto his back, the floor cooling his overheated back.

"That was intense," she gasped.

"Kiera," he said, and showed her images of him with others.

"What the hell?" she screeched, getting up to her feet.

"Only you," he tried to say, reaching out towards her.

"That wasn't me. That was many many others, Pryderi," she spat.

"Not like you."

"No, I'm some odd halfling."

"No."

He tried again. This time showing her how momentous their love making was. He then showed her a dim comparison.

"Never again," he said, standing up next to her.

"What? I was just a one time thing?"

"Argh," he grunted in frustration.

He showed her him and her together, alone. He looked at her quizzically, silently asking if she understood yet.

"Just me," she mumbled.

"Yes. Only you forever."

She smiled at him. It made her eyes glow white in the now dark room. The sun had disappeared behind a cloud, casting them in shadow.

He picked up her hand and put it to his heart again.

"Love," he said simply.

"Love," she confirmed.

She noticed his eyes were now glowing orange. She wasn't scared. It was beautiful. He was beautiful. And just like in her dream, she realised happily. Her dream man.

They stood a moment just holding each other. Both needing the physical contact and the reassurance which that brought.

But eventually Kiera put her top back on, suddenly aware of her semi-nakedness.

He remained unashamedly naked. She openly ogled him, taking in every muscle, every sinew in this svelte man. It was as if Michelangelo had sculpted him.

Her fingers ran up his arm, across his well-defined bicep, and hovered over a symbol.

"My clan mark," he explained.

She looked more closely at the tattoo.

She had seen Celtic Knots before, but this was also embellished with three dragon heads which poked out of the lower connection points, the tops of the heads level with the top corners of the knot. The outline was a dark black, but there were highlights of green in the knot and dragon heads. It was beautiful. Her fingers lightly traced the lines of the symbol up, over and down.

"You like?"

"I like," she grinned.

His breath hitched, and she saw his arousal start to twitch back into life.

She shut her eyes, and forced herself to make a decision.

"I need coffee," she stated, tearing her thoughts away from dragging him into the bedroom.

"You may want to put some clothes on," she added, struggling to keep her resolve.

He looked slightly disappointed, but allowed her to take his hand and lead him to the kitchen. He scooped up his trousers en route and put them on as she busied herself in her task.

He smiled as he watched with quiet adoration as she made her way around the kitchen.

"Umm…can you please carry the cups to the lounge?" she asked, not sure she should risk scalding herself if she stumbled. Her legs felt shakier than ever in his presence.

He took the cups from the counter and let her lead the way. She was improving all the time, but he could still see how uncertain she was, how she didn't trust her feet.

He set the cups on the table and then led her outside.

"Come," he gently cajoled.

They were in Cerys' back garden, secluded by trees and plants.

He stood very close behind her. She could feel him in all sorts of places, making her heat up again.

"Nooo," he warned before encouraging, "Step."

She took a step forward but his hips behind her made her elongate her stride a little. He placed his hand on her hip and encouraged her to sink it down a bit more.

She moved her other foot. He repeated his moves. She still thought it was really hot, but she tried to concentrate on what she was supposed to be doing.

After another couple of steps he told her she was good, and jogged around just ahead of her.

She felt like a toddler learning to walk and told him as much.

"Younglings are different."

"Do all your adults go through this?"

"Mmm…a little."

"Am I just being stupid?"

"Different," was his simple, honest response.

He showed her how the transition was more gradual and less intense, by showing her images in her mind of his own transition.

"Aww, you were so cute," she told him.

He just harrumphed at her.

"I'm sorry. You're very manly now though," she added, sorry she had inadvertently insulted him.

By the time their little exchange had ended she had reached the end of the garden. He had kept taking small steps backwards. She had just continued walking, distracted by their conversation.

"You tricked me," she laughed.

He wrapped her in his arms and brushed her cheek with his.

"Helped," he corrected.

"What is that?" she asked as she took a deep breath in.

He shrugged, clueless as to what she was referring.

"That smell?"

"My scent," he smiled as he realised what she meant.

He realised she was right after all. She was more of a youngling. She knew none of this. Everything that was second nature to him. Things he didn't have to think of were all new and strange to her.

She took his hand and they walked side by side back to their cooled coffee.

They snuggled on the sofa, and sipped. They couldn't stop looking at each other. They were each committing all the little details to memory.

'Who are you?' he silently asked her, full of wonder.

'I am Kiera,' she tried to think at him.

'No. Not like that. That is your aloud name.'

He made her close her eyes. He sent her his signature.

She opened her eyes in astonishment.

"You turn into a black panther?"

"No. My name."

"Your name, Pryderi means black panther?"

"No," he laughed, "We have two names. Pryderi is like a human name, given to us by our parents. We use it when we speak. But our true name is not chosen by us. It just is. Try again. Breathe in. Smell."

She did as she was told.

"You smell like pine and…forest berries. I don't know what that is. It's sort of woody too."

"Cerys names the plant juniper and the woody scent is sandalwood. The image and smell together are me."

"I like you. You're fresh and spicy," she smiled.

"My thanks. And what is your name?" he asked, grinning.

"I don't know," she admitted with a shrug.

"Close your eyes. Try."

"Can't you tell me?"

"Yes, but you know. Try."

She closed her eyes and took a deep breath in and tried to see, but she only saw darkness.

She sighed and shook her head sadly.

"Kiera. What is your name?" he whispered.

The shivers caused by the vibrations of his voice made her retry. She closed her eyes.

"What is your name, Kiera?" he whispered again, in a low rumble close to her ear.

"Ohh," she thrilled as she shared her signature with him.

"Yes. That is my beautiful Kiera," he smiled before kissing her.

"I am so proud of you, my cloud leopard. And I'm sorry, but I must ask Cerys what you call this yellow plant. It's sweet. I see it. I just do not know how to name it."

"I don't either. It's sort of like geranium, but I know that's not exactly it."

She kissed him back, but her face fell as she pulled away.

"There's so much I don't know," she said sorrowfully.

"I will teach you," he comforted as he rubbed her cheek with his own.

He was up on his feet in the blink of an eye, and let out a roar.

Chapter 16 – The Hunt

Cerys stomped over to Pryderi and snapped him on his nose.

"Pryderi, how dare you snarl at me? In my own home too."

He had the good sense to look abashed.

"My apologies, Cerys. I did not hear you approach. I did not know it was you."

"I see," she said wryly, looking over at the girl on her couch.

"So you and Shakira have bonded, have you?" she asked, raising her eyebrow.

He nodded. His accompanying grin was so disarming she dropped the hard act in an instant.

She hugged him in congratulation, but she heard a hiss from the sofa.

"Calm down kitty," she teased.

She was still being glared at.

"Shakira, I am not after your man. He's all yours, I promise," she added coolly.

"Kiera," the young woman corrected.

"Kiera?"

"Yes. My new name. And look," she said as she showed her friend her mind signature.

Cerys went over to Kiera and kissed her cheek and gave her a hug.

"I'm so pleased for you. You're certainly a fast learner."

"I don't feel like it."

"Well you should. You've had a whole new world dumped on you. I half expected to find a shivering wreck when I got home."

"Maybe Prrryderi found one," she quietly confessed.

Cerys smiled and winked as she noted, "Still purring his name, I hear."

A loud rumbling purr was all she received in response to that.

Pryderi took a seat back next to his mate, but she moved to make Cerys a drink.

"Don't you dare," Cerys interrupted, having noticed the slight movement.

"I'm not going to be the one to separate you two. I'm quite capable of fending for myself."

The pair snuggled up as Cerys made her own drink.

She soon came and sat in an armchair near them.

"So, what are you two having for dinner?" Cerys inquired.

Pryderi looked puzzled.

"The usual?"

"Really? That will be interesting," Cerys smirked.

"What? What am I supposed to eat?" a worried Kiera asked.

Pryderi showed her images of hunting a deer.

"Oh no. No way."

"Think of it as venison. You've had that before, haven't you? Or roast beef," Cerys suggested.

"Yes, but…"

"But?" asked a curious Pryderi.

"Well, I didn't have to kill those. They didn't even look like animals."

"Didn't look like animals? This is different?" he asked, confused.

Kiera heard Cerys chuckling.

"You're enjoying this, aren't you?"

"Well, I find it mildly amusing. Elinefae hunt for food and waste nothing. Humans have others kill their food and waste much."

"But it's savage."

"It's real and it's honest."

"And supermarkets are a figment of my imagination, I suppose."

"What's a supermarket?" Pryderi chipped in.

"Are you kidding me?" Kiera let out in exasperation.

Cerys was still chuckling, but she was in danger of releasing full on laughter.

"So this is the sticking point, my dear? I tell you your vampires of stories are more or less real, you change into one of them, you use magick without thinking, you mate with an elinefae. All this is fine. But you have to eat deer and this is what you find unbelievable?"

It was too much, Cerys' laughter burst forth. She was wiping her eyes when Kiera replied.

"But it's like eating Bambi."

"Oh stop," Cerys laughed, holding her stomach, "Please stop."

A snarl had her sobering up pretty quickly.

"Sorry Pryderi. I'm not laughing at your mate. Not really. Just the situation," she apologised.

"Kiera, you can't show him your life. Not if you want to go and live with him."

"But you said I can't go there."

"Well, it's more realistic than him coming to live with you."

Cerys knelt on the floor in front of Kiera and held her gaze.

"Their way of life is protected. They don't know much of your world. He has no idea who Bambi is. He does not understand not hunting your own food. He knows practically nothing of human life."

"Enough to drink coffee."

"Well that was my fault. It was a lapse of concentration which actually turned out well. But they don't have electronics, or supermarkets, or central heating, or any of those things."

"Huh. Well I suppose that makes sense."

"I'm sorry, but what were you expecting?"

"I don't know. I thought there was just a different community. Like a village, I guess. I don't know. I feel stupid."

"You're not stupid. I just didn't explain properly," Cerys consoled, rubbing Kiera's upper arm.

"Kiera. Elinefae have an entirely different way of life. I thought you realised about the forest."

Pryderi took Shakira's hand and showed her his home.

"Ooooaaah. You actually live there in the forest?"

He nodded.

"I thought it was just like a gathering place. You know, like witches do."

Cerys cocked her eyebrow.

"Well the human ones. You know."

Cerys shook her head, bemused by Kiera's perceptions.

Kiera rubbed her hands over her face and whined, "Ooohhh, this is all too complicated."

"No it's not. It's fine. OK. Pryderi, you go chase down a bunny or two and I'll cook a quick stew for tonight."

He nodded and disappeared into the night.

"Well, it was a compromise," Cerys told Kiera with a shrug.

"Did you have to say bunny, though?"

"No, but it was funny. Sorry. But you need this. You'll see. Elinefae, blood, it all goes. They can eat cooked meat, but they don't need as much if it's raw. It's good eco sense if you look at it like that."

"Oh joy, kill fewer deer by eating them sodding well raw."

"Calm down. I'm just explaining."

"I know. I'm sorry. So, they hunt down poor defenceless deer and live like hobos."

"Firstly, deer aren't so innocent. They're hugely destructive, and their numbers need to be carefully managed."

"Oh, so they provide a service by eating Bambi?"

"Will you stop anthropomorphising them? They're majestic creatures, granted. But you eat cows and pigs and fish as a human. This is no different."

"Except the running through the forest like a wild beast bit."

"Except for the hunting of your food. Humans have totally lost contact with the reality of their food. It's so disrespectful. The hunt? The hunt you'll change your mind on. It's your nature. The beast that lies within you."

"I don't think I'll ever be able to bring myself to do that. It's just…"

"Savage. Yeah yeah. I'd say stop thinking like a human, but there's humans who hunt."

"Yes, but…"

"No buts. Just trust me."

Cerys paused for a moment before deliberating, "He's taking a long time out there. I hope he's OK."

"He could be in danger?"

"There's always the possibility of danger," Cerys muttered matter-of-factly.

Kiera was out the door like a shot. She instinctively knew where Pryderi was. She could feel him like there was a homing beacon in her heart. Her feet pounded through the grass.

There were trees on the perimeter of the property and that's where she found him.

"*Quiet*," he silently signalled to her as she approached.

She halted. Then she saw it. Night had descended but she could see a rabbit peeking around, just sitting on the ground.

The rabbit's ears pricked up and its nose twitched. It sensed Pryderi's presence and scampered off, towards Kiera.

Kiera's tongue licked her lips as instinct took control of her. She ran on all fours after the creature and bore down on it in a matter of seconds.

She found her fangs had sunk into its neck. She was tasting its blood as it trickled down her throat. The limp body hung lifelessly in her mouth. And she loved it.

She carried on sucking until there was no more red juice left in the rabbit. She opened her jaws and the carcass dropped to the ground with a thud.

As Kiera's gaze lifted she saw the orange glow of Pryderi's eyes approaching her rapidly.

He was licking the blood off her mouth before she could say hello. His rough tongue lapped her lips before delving inside her mouth, tasting the heady combination of blood and her.

Already high from her first kill, her own synapses instantly fired up a notch too. She returned his luscious tongue lashings.

She could taste blood on him too. He must have already made a kill. She languished in the sweetness mixed with his delectable freshness.

Their hands roamed over each other's torso, grappling as they searched in their need.

They were on their knees on the ground in the dark, feeling the full force of nature.

Kiera pushed Pryderi backwards forcefully, so he was on his back. She grappled with his trousers so she could get to her prize.

She hurriedly raised her skirt and quickly mounted him, impaling herself on his shaft, pumping up and down with a fierce fury.

Their minds were giving and receiving every intense, pleasurable sensation.

They were both panting and grunting as their bodies thrust together with a violent force. It was brutal. It was carnal. It was bestial.

Pryderi gave in to his nature and bit deep into his mate's shoulder, heightening the pleasure for them both.

The taste of her blood trickling into his mouth tipped him over the edge.

Kiera's face turned skyward as she yowled her orgasm as Pryderi screamed his.

He guided her down to lie on top of him, licked her lips and rubbed cheek to cheek.

He licked the wound he'd inflicted on her shoulder, sealing and healing it.

His hands swept through her hair, round to the back of her head as he kissed her deeply.

"Amazing," he muttered.

"Fang-fucking-tastic," she grinned.

They preened and kissed a little longer before realising they were still out in the open, and their noise may have been less than subtle.

They righted their clothing and headed back to the house together.

Pryderi paused and dashed back to collect his discarded brace of rabbits. He also picked up Kiera's discarded rabbit remnants as an afterthought.

He quickly caught back up to his mate and they entered the witch's house together. He slung their kill onto the kitchen counter.

"I didn't actually expect you to bring them in," Cerys smirked, munching on her aley, cheesy toast supper.

"But you asked," Pryderi replied, quite put out.

"I opted for a Welsh Rarebit in lieu of rabbit," she laughed at her own joke.

Relenting at his sulky pout she added, "But thank you very much. I'll make a proper stew for my dinner tomorrow."

"Well, out of two you will. Did you want to make gloves with the other?" he chuckled, nodding his head at Kiera's one.

Cerys picked up the limp body in question between her finger and thumb.

"Oh dear," she mocked. "Poor Thumper didn't stand a chance."

Kiera blushed crimson.

"Don't. I couldn't help it," she moaned, abashed.

"Oh, don't look so down. I told you you'd change your mind."

"It just ran towards me. I gave chase without knowing what I was doing. But then I pounced and it was in my teeth. And I tasted its blood."

Cerys held up one hand.

"Please. I understand your nature. I accept it. But truly, I don't need to hear all the gory details."

"But you said…"

"I know very well what I said. And I stand by it. I just don't share your excitement. It's a necessity not a sport."

"But it can be both," Pryderi interjected, stroking Kiera's cheek.

She looked back into his eyes and felt 'home'. She saw his reassurance and adoration shining at her.

"Aher, feel free to hop into the shower," she told Kiera, who blushed again but wandered in the direction of the bathroom.

"Alone," she admonished as she grabbed Pryderi's hand.

Her action earned her a curled lip, but he had the good sense not to hiss out loud.

"You can have one after, you randy tomcat," she teased.

He shook his head.

"No. Not like that. No more. Mate," he vowed.

"I know, Pryderi. I know," Cerys sighed sadly, feeling this pairing was doomed.

"Whilst we're waiting you'd best be chopping some branches so your leader doesn't think I lied to him," she added.

Cerys just wanted some time on her own to reflect and think. She was making no headway as to the identity of Kiera's father. Nor was she coming up with a plan to integrate her into Rhion's clan.

She munched her way through the rest of her Welsh Rarebit, mulling over thoughts which insisted on tumbling into each other.

She had one day left to come up with a genius idea. Problem was she still had no idea where to start. It was the proverbial catch 22.

Chapter 17 – Clean Up

Lily finally got through the long line of injured warriors needing additional help healing. She was exhausted and slumped into her armchair.

"Now you will listen," Dougal blustered as he barged in, speaking English to help avoid any eavesdroppers.

"No, not now. Can't you see I can't even keep my eyes open?"

"Like that is any of my concern."

"Not your concern? If you send me anyone else I couldn't heal them. I would've thought that would be a priority, if nothing else."

"My priority is stopping your insubordination."

"Insubordination? Is your ego really that fragile?"

Tiredness had only heightened her raw emotions. She was angry he'd put her through all of this. And now he was yelling at her like she'd done something wrong.

"You contradicted me in front of my warriors."

"I merely told you that you're pushing them too hard. And I shouldn't have to say it. It should be self-evident."

She'd risen from her chair as her anger also rose.

"And who are you to decide? Why are you the judge of MY army?"

"Army? So it's true. You're preparing for war," she gasped, taking a step back.

"What I do, or plan to do is none of your business."

"You make it my business every time your so called training gets out of hand. Elinefae are great self-healers. I am supposed to be here for protection. But you're forcing them to fight, to battle almost to death. You don't give them time to heal in between sessions and then they end up here when injury builds on injury and it's too much for them."

"I am doing it for their own good. Gargh, I'm not explaining myself to you," he huffed as he turned to walk out.

"What are you so afraid of?"

He spun around and faced Lily, drawing himself so close their noses almost met. His eyes were glowing in the darkness.

"I am afraid of nothing, witch."

"Could've fooled me," she muttered under her breath at his retreating back.

There was no chance of rest after that encounter. She whisked out of her den, grabbing her shawl as she went out the door.

Dougal was so infuriating. No, he was menacing, she grumbled to herself as her feet stomped on.

'Bloody bully,' she thought, 'Who does he think he is? War? I hoped I was wrong.'

Her feet took her onwards, spurred on by her inner turmoil.

There hadn't be tribal wars in Britain for over a century. Why now? They had all worked so hard to reach and maintain this equilibrium.

She strode forever onward as her mind dwelled on all the negative repercussions her clan leader would ignite.

She cursed her own kind for stopping their coven gatherings. They'd become complacent. They'd simply stopped needing them. The information exchange had dried up. There was nothing to tell. Well, there was now.

"Bloody men," she screamed out as she kicked a tree stump.

She'd wandered deep into the forest by now.

"Hey, stop that," squeaked an angry little voice.

"I'm in no mood for any more confrontation," Lily warned.

"Well don't hurt nature and we won't have to hurt you," the little voice shouted back.

Lily sighed deeply as she plonked herself on the ground with a thud. Her hands washed over her face as she groaned.

"You're right. I'm sorry. I'm hurt and I'm scared, and I don't know what to do."

A golden light flitted close to her face, and Lily found herself staring into familiar eyes.

"Frydah. How come you be here?"

"Well hello to you too," she grouched.

"Sorry. Hello. Greetings. I was just surprised. I did not intend on our meeting. I have no offering. Did I summon you?" she asked, confused.

"You're babbling. And no, you didn't summon me. I doubt you could from here, even if you tried," she sneered.

"Well, why did you come?"

"I'm starting to wonder that myself. I come all this way just to be met with rudeness."

"Frydah, I'm sorry. I said I'm sorry. I've had a really bad day," she said as she began to cry.

"Oh no. No. I didn't mean to make you cry."

"You didn't. Not really. It's just…this whole thing…is…such a mess," Lily blubbed out.

She felt a tiny hand smooth her hair, and she tried to force a smile and halt her tears.

"Shh…tell aunty Frydah all about it," the faery soothed.

"Well you know about Shakira, but we still have no idea what to do about her."

"Is she here?"

"No, she's with my sister Cerys. She's keeping her safe for now. But the elinefae won't want her. We don't know who her father is. She can't be with humans."

"Hmmm…"

"And I've come home to a whole heap of bodies to heal. And I fought with Dougal, and he's planning war," she blurted as tears threatened to emerge once more.

"This is quite a mess indeed. I sensed a darkness as I approached this place."

"It's all so hopeless," Lily bawled as her tears broke through her resolve.

"I'm here to help," Frydah said brightly, her wings flickering as she hovered.

"You are?"

"I couldn't before. We weren't alone. Do you know what he'd do to me if he found out?"

"I have an idea."

"Look, when you called to me, it wasn't just me. You said 'Little folk within this woodland dwell', that meant many fae were called. I just got there first."

"Oh, sorry. I didn't know who I was looking for."

"He has contacts everywhere," she said conspiratorially as she looked around her.

"Who?"

They both sensed around them and nodded as they agreed they were definitely alone.

"Threaris," Frydah whispered.

"Oh frack."

"Exactly."

Lily took a deep breath before saying with a sigh, "Well, I suppose it could be worse."

"It could be better too. I just thought you should know."

"Thank you," Lily said gratefully, knowing what a risk the brave little faery was taking.

"I need to get back before I'm missed. I don't want my wings clipped."

"Oh yes, go go."

"I'm sorry I can't help more."

"No, you've been a great help. I appreciate it. Now go quickly."

With that the faery's golden glow flickered and poofed into thin air as she transported home.

Lily swiped in front of her eyes to clear the evidence of her despair, and hurried back to her den once more.

Night had fallen, and most of the clan were going about their duties. A few of them saw her pass by and smiled their greetings. She barely acknowledged them in her haste.

She bolted her door and put up her sound barrier before she took the cover off her mirror. She waved her hand across it, and reached out with her mind to Cerys. She had to warn her.

But there was no answer. All she saw in the reflection was darkness. She couldn't raise her sister, no matter how long she tried.

"Oh good goddess, I'm too late," she muttered, raising her hand in front of her mouth.

She staggered backwards into her chair. Her shock rolled over her, turning her blood to ice. She sat frozen to the spot, her hands now in a prayer position, fingertips touching her lips, her eyes closed.

There was a hammering at her door.

"Not now," she shouted.

But the hammering continued.

"Oh right," she muttered as she dropped the sound barrier, realising her visitor wouldn't have been able to hear her.

"Not now," she repeated.

"Are you OK?" came a concerned voice.

Lily silently stood, and drew the bolt across. No sooner had she done so when Loth swept in and gathered Lily into his arms.

'I felt your panic, when you walked through the encampment,' he thought at her.

'I'm sorry I worried you.'

'It's not like you. What's wrong?'

Lily shook her head.

'Nothing.'

'This is not nothing. No lies.'

He still held her in his arms. He could feel her trembling.

'You helped me. Now I help you. I have honour,' he told her in no uncertain terms.

'You don't want this. You don't know what you're asking. I wish you no harm.'

'Now I'm really worried.'

'This is not for elinefae.'

He scowled at her. He took a step back and grabbed her face in his hands. He forced her to look at him.

'Tell me. I'll help.'

Lily's shoulders sagged, and her head hung down as he released his grip. She bit her lip as she closed the door and sealed the room again.

"I'm too tired for any more mind talk. And what I say cannot leave this room. Swear it."

The brave elinefae wafted his hand in a circular motion, and brought his clenched fist to his heart, bowing his head.

"I swear it," he promised.

"I have to tell someone," she sighed, worry wrinkling her brow.

The blonde giant led her to her chair and knelt in front of her. He looked earnestly into her eyes.

"I think my sister is in mortal peril," she started.

He grabbed both of her hands in one of his. It lent her the courage required to inform him of the situation.

Once she finished supplying the main points as quickly as she could, Lily started towards the door. She'd gathered some emergency supplies in a bag on her way. Not that she thought much would help against a sorcerer, but you never knew what may be useful.

Loth was at her side as he reassured her, "I'll take you to where you need to be."

She nodded gratefully, then they were walking out her door as quickly as they could without arousing suspicion.

They had just made it outside when a dark mountain of a man stood blocking their way.

'*And where do you think you are going?*' Dougal huffed angrily in her head.

Loth saw the ensuing battle rising in their eyes, so quickly showed Dougal an image of an injured warrior out on the trail, suggesting he required Lily's attention.

" *We've been training hard, Sir,*" he said aloud.

Dougal harrumphed but let them pass, quietly pleased at the hard training they were still undertaking. He was certain he'd succeed in his campaign.

Loth led Lily by the hand in the direction they'd go in to attend to the injured elinefae. It was only half a lie. There were many injured around, and one was even in the location he'd shown his Leader, he just didn't strictly require witchy assistance.

He made sure they were out of sight of all, then let Lily lead the way to her nearest portal. There was no time to lose. She hated using this one, it was too close to camp, and may draw unwanted attention. But she had no choice. Her sister's life may be at stake, and who knew what the sorcerer may unleash on all their kind.

Loth quickly held her close and wished her well.

Lily took deep breaths. She opened the portal her end. She knew she could do this. She'd done it before. With one more deep inhalation she reached out to the portal on Cerys' side.

She smiled broadly briefly as she saw Cerys' garden appear before her.

"Knew I could do it," she muttered as she stepped through, the portal closing behind her.

The air was crackling with magick, making all her hairs stand on end. She looked for shelter, so she could look around undetected.

She ran over to the bushes outside the lounge window and carefully peered in.

She could see nothing. There was nobody inside. But then she heard it. The cries.

She scurried around the outside of the house to the source of the screams. She peeked in at the window.

Her mouth dropped as she saw two naked bodies writhing together.

'Oh, cries of pleasure,' she thought to herself, blushing.

But she was puzzled. She turned back round to face the garden, and felt the magick. She crept towards the epicentre of the energy.

It led her through the trees. She skirted around the edge of the garden, cautiously nearing the origin of the magick.

She wandered across a small field, and into a wooded glade. Magenta sparks were flying around, making sharp cracks in the air.

"Cerys," she gasped, running towards her friend.

"Lily?" she replied, halting her savage sparks.

They ran into each other's arms and hugged their hello.

"Not that I'm not happy to see you, but why have you come? Are you alright?" Cerys questioned quietly.

"I messaged you, but I couldn't raise a response. Why didn't you answer?" she semi-accused.

"I wasn't close enough. Pryderi is at the house, and err, well they're umm…"

"Mating like rabbits?" Lily helpfully supplied.

Cerys smiled, "Yes. Honestly, as soon as he got out the shower they started playing tonsil tennis, and I fled my own home. It really ought not to happen."

"So you came out here?"

"I needed space to think."

"And sulk?"

"Oh, the crackles," she hung her head in shame. "I may have been taking my frustrations out on some dead wood."

"Dead now."

"No. What do you take me for? The log was already long past. It was just good target practice. And I couldn't bottle up my anger. I feel so helpless," she slumped down onto the charred remains as she said this.

Lily plonked down next to her.

"Well, I was trying to convey some news to you. It may help a little."

"Well spit it out."

"I had a visit from Frydah."

Lily paused to allow Cerys to take this information in before continuing.

"Yes, she came to see me. I probably looked as shocked as you do now. She needed to ensure we were alone. She fears the consequences of divulging the information."

"What? What information?"

"Thre=aris is Shakira's father."

"Kiera."

"Pardon me?"

"It's just Kiera now."

"Oh, that must be easier. But did you hear what I said?"

"Yes, but I'm struggling to believe it. Threaris? How can this be? Didn't he die years ago? Nobody's heard of him in…"

"About twenty years?" Lily said suggestively.

"Ooooh!"

"The penny drops."

"Yes, yes it does. But oh. Oh what now? Is he still really living?"

"Frydah certainly seems to think so, why else would she bother with the cloak and dagger routine?"

"Oh my. So where the bloody hell is he? And why hasn't he owned up to his responsibilities?"

"Now, that's the question."

Cerys sighed long and hard, "Well I suppose it could be worse."

Lily chuckled, "Exactly what I said."

Lily placed her hands on her knees and slowly rose up from her perch, stiff with the cold and damp air.

"Well, I best not dally. If you're not in imminent danger I need to get back before I'm missed."

"Oh sister. I've not even asked. I'm so sorry. How goes it?"

"Not well. The amount of wounded I had. You've never seen the like," the Scottish witch lamented.

"Oh Lily. What is he about?"

"War."

"Are you certain?"

"He admitted as much when we argued."

"That I'd like to see."

"Well, I was just so angry with him. And then he had the gall to moan at me, after all the healing I'd had to perform in his name."

"Gratitude!"

"So I told him exactly what I thought of his rough treatment."

"Oh oh oh, that went down like a lead balloon, I bet."

"He tried to hit me."

The merriment halted in a heartbeat.

"He WHAT?" Cerys raged.

"It's fine. He missed. Caught a good'un on my barrier though," she chuckled.

"Serves him right. How dare he? He goes too far."

"Yes, but I'm not taking any more. I'm trying to find out exactly what he's about. And Cerys, I will stop him. This cannot continue."

Cerys nodded in agreement and took Lily to the portal.

"Hang on. Nobody was here to open my end," Cerys said.

"There'll be nobody my end either, and I'm going straight home."

"But?"

"I thought you were in great peril. It was a great motivator. Turns out I can open them with ease," Lily bragged.

"Well, I suppose your greatest gift is finally revealed. Now, get going before you really do get into trouble."

Cerys watched in awe as Lily opened both ends of the portal. She made it look so easy. A witch with hidden talents, she mused.

She wandered back to the house and made some tea to mull over the news of Kiera's father.

Chapter 18 – Fear Him

Kiera woke up in the dark, her cheek against a firm naked chest and with a strong muscled arm around her. She nuzzled into Pryderi's chest as she came to. He was already awake.

He moaned appreciatively at her closeness and planted a kiss on the top of her head.

She looked up into his orange glowing eyes. She was still surprised how well she could see in the dark as she traced his facial features. She'd been able to before, but not to this extent.

She gazed at his black hair flopping down over his forehead and followed the trail around the pointy ear which was visible to her, and down his fine neck. His hair was long and flowed like a stream.

She snuggled back into his embrace as she hoarsely requested, "Tell me about your home."

He cleared his throat a little, "What do you wish to know?"

She loved his deep voice. It sent vibrations through the centre of her being. She couldn't place his accent. It wasn't like the Transylvanian vampires of films, but nor was it purely Welsh. It held a mystery all of its own.

"Everything," she murmured, just wanting to hear him talk.

He shared images in her head. He showed her the forest she was familiar with, and beyond. It was as if they were there, walking the forest paths.

She saw a clearing with people busying about chores. There were men and women and children all roaming about in the darkness.

"So you really do come out at night?" she queried.

"Mmm hmmm," he confirmed as he continued his image narrative.

"Why? I've seen you in daylight. Lily showed me I don't burn."

Pryderi chuckled, "I've heard Cerys tell of your vampires. We are not them, my love."

He showed her a deer hunt.

"They come out more at night," he explained simply, "The light, it hurts our eyes as we spend most of our time in darkness. I am more used to it than most. I like the day and spend more time in sunlight. But it is still shadowed by trees. Human fake light hurts me."

"Makes sense," she shrugged. "What's your house like?"

"Den," he corrected.

He took her through the encampment in her mind, and on towards a grassy hill. He felt her confusion until he took her through the illusion. To all outsiders they saw a grassy hill, but there was a concealed entrance which they walked through.

They travelled down some steps and through underground tunnels.

"Deep underground," she remarked, feeling a little fearful.

He frowned, but continued the journey until they reached his den. It was a simple dwelling with little furniture. There was a rudimentary bed and a chair and that was pretty much all there was from the view he showed her.

"Is that it?" she asked, failing to keep the disappointment out of her voice.

"What more do I need?" he replied, a little hurt.

"Sorry. I just didn't know what to expect. Is there no fireplace at least?"

"It is warm underground. And elinefae do not feel cold, not like humans."

"Oh, OK. Um, a kitchen?"

He pulled her closer and smiled into her hair.

In her mind he walked her through to the communal eating area. He realised she was worried about food, despite her hunting success.

She saw many elinefae gathered in a large room, eating from wooden bowls and breaking bread. He laughed as she let out a relieved laugh of her own.

"Not only deer," he assured her. "Deer help maintain our strength. But we eat all of it. We avoid draining all blood when we hunt. We have quick kills. We share its flesh with clan. And use skin for clothes. No waste."

Kiera was pleased to hear that and squeezed her beloved.

"The forest supplies. There are nuts, berries, and leaves. Cerys and farmers help. There are humans who supply grains, but know not where it goes. We grow vegetables."

"Who cooks?"

Pryderi showed her an outside area out the back of the dens. There was a large open fire where both males and females prepared meals.

"And drink?"

Pryderi was finding Kiera's questioning amusing. How did she not know all this? But he felt honoured to be her tutor.

"Water. It falls from the sky, and runs in streams," he smiled.

"Not blood?"

"Sometimes blood. Sometimes coffee."

"Oh of course. I forgot your coffee addiction."

"Cerys' fault. Not normal for elinefae. One of us was at her house and she fed him some, not thinking. He liked it and took some back and we liked too."

"Good. I may have to introduce you to tea too."

"Not same. Coffee does something to us."

"Something?" she queried, wiggling her eyebrows suggestively.

"Sexy? No. We don't need as much deer when we have coffee."

"Good news for the deer. Why do you need them at all?"

"Why do you need food?"

"As otherwise I'd die. Oh. But is it their blood or meat?"

"Both. The blood is in their flesh. And it is easy to find. Humans don't see us."

"Why not humans?"

He pulled a face.

"Have you smelled humans? Yuck. Even more bad now. Now more…chemicals," he struggled to remember the word Cerys had used.

"Not healthy?"

"No. Not at all. They are poisoned. We live with and of the forest."

Tired of talking he pulled her up to lip level and smooched her. She didn't argue. She couldn't anyway as his tongue filled her mouth.

She felt so right being with him. She'd never felt like she belonged anywhere until now.

She felt herself melt into the mattress as she gave herself to him again.

They couldn't help themselves. Their souls had been parted for so long and now they'd found each other they had to be together in every way possible.

As they lay together recovering Kiera whispered, "I want to come home with you tomorrow."

But Pryderi didn't hear her. He was fast asleep again.

Cerys popped into the coffee shop midway through the next morning, on a break from her shop.

Her mind was racing as fast as her heart, and that seemed to be trying to run a marathon.

Pryderi was supposed to return home that evening, but she didn't think Kiera would be able to separate herself from him.

She'd been driving herself crazy all morning. She tried to comfort herself that Kiera was unlikely to get harmed. The girl was half sorceress after all. But she barely knew of her powers, let alone how to control them.

And if the elinefae decided she should be executed who knew what would happen? They may even call upon Cerys herself. But she knew she'd not be able to bring herself to murder the dear girl. Not now. She shuddered at he thought.

Maybe they'd be alright with her. She wasn't human. Perhaps a touch of magick would benefit their race, and they'd welcome that. Cerys sneered at her foolish hope.

She continued worrying about all the worst case scenarios.

So, to calm herself she had come over for a cup of tea and a chat about anything else, the more mundane the better.

"Good morning. One tea please," Cerys said as brightly as she could.

"What's good about it?" Gwen grumbled as she began preparing the drink.

"Oh dear, someone got out the wrong side of bed this morning."

"Sorry. It's just I thought she was better than that."

Cerys gave one of her enquiring eyebrow looks.

"Shakira. She said she had flu. I was worried about her, wasn't I? So I stopped by her house last night to see if she needed anything. I felt sorry for her being poorly all on her own. Well, how stupid am I? She wasn't even there. Out raving no doubt. I was a fool to trust her. Well, I had to report it to Annie, didn't I? So here I am covering for a girl who's gone AWOL. I have better things to be doing, don't I?"

Cerys finally managed to interrupt the heavily Welsh accented tirade.

"I'm so sorry. Didn't I say? I was sure I told Annie. Shakira's at my house. I felt badly for her too, so went to collect her as soon as I heard the news. Young girl like that shouldn't be alone when she's so unwell."

Gwen rolled her eyes.

"Well you could've said. Now I feel bad for thinking badly of her. Eh, you're not giving her any weird potions, are you?"

"Potions? The very notion. Of course not. I'm feeding her healthy food, and giving her herbal tea. Or is that what you meant by potions?" she checked snidely.

"You're right. I don't know what's got into me today. I'm all up in the air," Gwen said raising her hands up along with her tone of voice.

Cerys reached for the woman's hands, and said softly, "You are just fine."

It had an immediate calming effect, and Gwen wiped her brow with the back of her wrist.

"I think I need to sit down a moment," she said, staggering over to a table.

Cerys followed her. She had reached into her bag and sprinkled some herbs into the takeaway cup before replacing the lid. She offered the spiked drink to the calmer yet still slightly flustered woman.

"Thanks," Gwen said as she sipped.

Cerys stayed with her until Gwen's eyes seemed clearer, and she had completely settled. Once she was satisfied, Cerys got up and walked out empty handed.

"Oh this can't be good. This can't be good at all," she worried under her breath and scurried back to her shop.

She bolted off to her private room and immediately called Lily.

"Lily, oh thank the goddess you're there. I've just come back from the café. Gwen seemed to be under some sort of spell. She's fine now, but oh goodness, this is not good. I'm sure it must be him."

"I don't know who else it would be. Oh dear. What to do? Should I come back?"

"No. Dougal would be angered, and it's best to avoid doing that at present. Try to keep him calm. We don't want more trouble on our hands."

"Where are you now?"

"In my shop. But I think I must go home. What if he's after her? Oh, but how can I stop him? Oh Lily. I'm truly scared."

"Calm sister. I've been thinking, and here's what you should do."

As the sisters spoke of their scheme there was a commotion at the cottage.

The young lovers had managed to get out of bed long enough to make some breakfast, have a shower and get dressed.

They were cuddling on the sofa, having a cup of coffee when a voice sounded behind them.

Pryderi sprang to his feet to face their attacker, hissing and snarling. The orange glow in his eyes looked like fire as they burned ferociously.

"Hello daughter," the stranger said, ignoring the hissing beast by the sofa in front of him.

Pryderi scooped Kiera round behind him with one strong arm, and arched his back further in defiance.

Kiera peeked around her defender and spat, "You're no father of mine. I don't know you."

The man, dressed in dark blue robes bowed his head in acknowledgement.

This man looked sort of middle aged, but with a deep wisdom in his green eyes. His hair was brown, like hers, but kept smartly short. Could he be her father?

He looked quite suave and sophisticated. But that didn't mean she liked him.

Kiera took all this in in a second as she too shifted to a defensive stance. Her father was unperturbed by the display of animosity.

"You are quite right. You do not know me. I am the sorcerer Threaris. And I *am* your father," he told her evenly, as he faced his palms down and forwards in a gesture of 'keep calm'.

"How did you get in?" she spat.

"Please. A witch's ward is hardly a match for a sorcerer," he sneered.

"What do you want?" she asked, slightly less aggressively.

"You."

That was more than Pryderi could take. He lunged over the sofa, and barrelled towards the man.

"*My mate,*" he roared as he leaped.

He cried in agony as he was repelled by Threaris' barrier of protection. He flew backwards and landed hard against the wall.

Pryderi was shocked but undeterred. He ran back in front of Kiera.

"She's mine. Not yours," he growled, shaking off the pain shooting up his arms.

"I really don't have time for this," Threaris stated as he wafted a hand in Pryderi's direction.

The gesture made Pryderi fly across the room and back into the wall. This time he slumped down, unconscious.

"What did you do to him?" Kiera screeched as she ran to her lover's side.

She stroked his cheek which was already starting to bruise. The bruise healed under her fingers but he did not wake up.

"Come quickly child," Threaris commanded as he gripped her wrist, dragging her to her feet.

"I'm not going…" she started, but as she finished, "anywhere with you," she found herself in a different room.

"Where the fuck am I?" she demanded.

"Home," was the simple response.

"Like hell I am. Where the fuck have you brought me? And where's Pryderi?"

"The male is still in that hovel I found you in. He'll be fine. And this *is* your home."

"He better be alright."

"Or what?"

"Or you'll be sorry."

Threaris actually laughed at her outrage. This just angered her all the more, of course.

"You'll be laughing on the other side of your face soon enough," she shouted, hitching up her sleeves.

Threaris calmly took a couple of steps backwards. He seemed to look shocked for a second as he breathed in, but he hid the expression in an instant.

"My dear girl, I hardly think so, do you? And I would so prefer to do this in a civilised fashion."

She charged at him, but she too fell flat on her arse, but not as forcefully as Pryderi had done.

"Now that wasn't very nice," he said drily.

The next thing she knew, she was stood fully clothed under a freezing cold shower, gasping in shock.

She grappled for the controls, turned the shower off and sprang out of the cubicle. She found a towel hanging up.

As she towelled herself off she realised she was alone. She had no idea where she was, but she was definitely alone.

Taking the opportunity, she wriggled out of her freezing wet clothes and shuffled into the fluffy white towelling robe she also found hanging up. She slowly took in her surroundings. They were certainly opulent. This bathroom was huge; easily as big as her lounge in her cottage. The walls were cream marble, and the taps appeared to be solid gold.

As she walked further into the room she noticed a small wall hiding a lavatory. There was also a freestanding bath on gold lion's feet near a picture window. She walked over and looked out over a sea. She could see the sea, not only in the distance, but directly below her too.

There were jagged rocks poking through tempestuous waves.

"No escape from this window then," she mused sadly.

Her heart plummeted. How was she supposed to get back to Pryderi? She missed him badly already.

She began to cry as the harsh reality of her situation hit her and panic set in.

She was being held prisoner in some undisclosed location far away from home. She just knew she was a long way away. She could feel the distance between her and her mate. She ached for him.

Pulling herself together she splashed some cold water on her face at the beautiful sink. The irony of more cold water did not escape her.

She hung up her wet clothes on the heated towel rail, hoping it would dry them off.

Still in the bathrobe, she ventured through the large white door and found herself in a gigantic bedroom. There was plush white carpet underfoot, with cream and gold wallpaper covering the walls.

And there was a window to her right, with a couple of chairs in front of it. Her heart sank as she saw the male figure in one of those chairs.

Threaris sat in an impeccable dark blue suit, one leg crossed casually over the other. His fingers steepled together at his mouth.

"Oh you have much to learn," he teased, "Lesson 1; do not answer back to your father."

She rushed at him, arms waving wildly. But she found herself back in the freezing cold shower, this time without any clothes on.

As she hopped out she saw the towel and dressing gown back on their hooks. As she grabbed for them she realised the towel was dry already. Her mouth gaped open, but she quickly closed it again. Her jaw was firmly set as she stomped back through to the bedroom.

"You have to stop doing that," she seethed.

"Only once you've cooled down," he said, plonking her straight back under the cold spray.

She put the robe back on and stormed out.

"It's really not funny," she shouted.

And promptly found herself back under cold water, with Threaris' voice telling her, "You're better than this, girl."

She sulkily put the robe back on yet again, and went back to face the tyrant, dripping wet. This time she kept her mouth closed.

"Well, the silence is better than the banshee impression, but why are you not dressed?" he said, looking a little perplexed.

"I don't know. Maybe because some maniac dumped me in a freezing cold shower fully dressed?" she scoffed.

"Aaaaargh," she shrieked as she was put under the cold shower again.

"What are you? Some sort of pervert?" she yelled as she came face-to-face with her tormentor.

He gently shook his head, barely concealing his chuckle.

"Get dressed," he firmly commanded as he dumped her back into the cold shower.

Kiera got back out of the shower and towelled herself off, wondering why she was bothering.

"Get dressed. Really funny," she muttered, looking over at her still sodden clothes.

She stomped back into the bedroom.

"Please sir, do you have some dry clothes, sir?" she mocked as she curtseyed sarcastically.

"Yes thank you," he said, a smile crinkling the corner of his eyes.

"Well, would you mind sharing them with your naked daughter?" she huffed.

"Before you accuse me of being a pervert again, which I don't appreciate by the way, there's some in the wardrobe over there," he said pointing in the right direction.

As he sauntered across the room he shook his head.

"I must say I'm disappointed, Shakira."

"Kiera," she said over her shoulder.

"Very well. I must say I'm disappointed, Kiera."

"I don't know what you have to be disappointed about. It's not like you've just been ripped away from your mate and kidnapped," she huffed.

He ignored her sentiments.

"I am disappointed that you cannot even dress yourself."

"I'm getting clothes. See?" she said pulling a plain white dress from the wardrobe.

"Which you could already be wearing."

"If I hadn't been repeatedly been subjected to the cold water treatment perhaps I would have got dressed by now."

"Girl, sarcasm really isn't dignified."

With that he vanished from the room, leaving Kiera to dress in shocked privacy.

Chapter 19 – The Truth Will Out

Cerys had closed her shop and immediately fled for home after speaking with Lily.

But she was too late. She arrived to find her protection ward vanished, her sofa in disarray and an unconscious Pryderi slumped against her wall.

She knelt down and felt the energy around him, wary of doing any further damage. Satisfied there were no barriers to her interference she grabbed some powder from her magick medicine cabinet and blew it into his face.

Pryderi shook his head as he came to. Cerys put a hand firmly on his shoulder to keep him from moving.

"Steady, tiger," she warned.

But it was of no use.

He leapt up anyway, crying out, "Kiera. Where is she?" as he glanced all around him.

He had to steady himself against the wall as dizziness threatened to sweep him off his feet.

Cerys gently took his hand and sat him in a chair.

"My money is on her being with Threaris," she said glumly.

"We have to find her," he cried urgently.

"Yes, of course. But right now you need to sit still. You were under a sleeping spell."

"Sleeping spell?" he asked, trying to shake the grogginess out of his head.

"If you sit there like a good boy I'll make you a tea to help speed up the recovery."

He nodded, but shifted uneasily in the chair as she brewed some 'wake up' herbs.

He gratefully sipped, and began to feel more alert.

"So, are you able to tell me what happened?" Cerys asked as the elinefae came to his senses.

Groggily, Pryderi managed to relay the few details he knew.

"Fine. It's at least her father, as I thought. So she's safe. I think."

"You think?"

"Pryderi, he's a sorcerer. There are no guarantees. You have to face that. But I don't think he'd hurt her. He had fae protection in place for her when she was young. I'm just not sure what happened in the interim. It seemed to just stop."

"Oh good," he muttered sarcastically.

"Pryderi, sarcasm is not an elinefae trait. I'd thank you to watch your tone."

She brushed out her skirts, where there were no wrinkles, but the action performed its job of calming her.

She continued, "But I'll forgive you in the extenuating circumstances. And because you're really not going to like what I have to say next."

His head and shoulders had been bowed over, his elbows supported on his spread thighs, but he now looked up suspiciously at the witch as she spoke.

"It's time to come clean to clan. I can't storm a sorcerer's residence with no backup."

"Oh no. No. Rhion will kill me. Really kill me."

"You or Kiera. Your choice," came the blunt response.

"Fine, me," he chose immediately.

"No time like the present," she said dragging the still dazed elinefae to his feet.

Lily had shown her the trick to opening both ends of a portal, but she was very nervous. If she got this wrong there was no telling where they'd end up. But there was no time to lose.

Cerys opened her own portal as usual. She closed her eyes in concentration she focussed on her destination, and waggled her hands in front of her. It wasn't strictly necessary, but it helped focus her intention.

She opened her eyes and saw the boundary of the elinefae camp. She brushed her hands in front of her.

"Piece of cake," she grinned.

Taking Pryderi's hand, the pair stepped through the magick portal. Cerys was careful to close both ends behind her.

They semi-jogged to Rhion's lair. Even in an emergency Cerys considered running undignified.

Rhion was just dispatching some orders to one of the Watchers as they approached, but he beckoned them over.

"Excellent to see you. Has he performed his duties well?" the leader asked cheerily.

"Well, yes, but can we go somewhere private, please, sir?" Cerys asked as she sauntered closer.

Rhion blustered a little in surprise, but agreed nonetheless.

"Stay here," Cerys commanded Pryderi.

The Leader and the witch walked together into the trees, beyond all possible earshot.

"What's all this about?" Rhion asked, a little more testily than he intended.

Cerys stepped in close, really close. Her hips were touching Rhion's warm thighs.

She reached up to twirl his long hair in her fingers. He had to duck his head down a little to look her in the eyes. He was so tall and she was really quite petite.

"Don't toy with me," he warned, already feeling a stirring in his loins.

Cerys bit her lower lip and twisted her hips very girlishly, but she couldn't help it. She was nervous.

Rhion put a large hand on her hip to stop the enticing motion before he lost all self-control.

"Tell me," he said more softly.

"I apologise. To my shame I have kept something from you."

This earned her a scowl, but she maintained their gaze, her eyes full of earnest apology.

"I needed to find the truth before telling, and things got out of hand."

She let her hand rest on his heart, her cheek rested next to it as she broke eye contact.

"I've messed up and I'm so sorry," she apologised, nuzzling into his huge chest.

"There's a girl. She's half elinefae," she began.

Rhion broke away, his anxiety growing.

"What have you done?" he asked angrily.

"Kept her alive."

"By the goddess," he growled. "You've let her live? You've protected her? Why did you not bring her straight here for trial?"

"There would have been no trial, and you know it. Not a true one. Your laws would have demanded her head, and I couldn't allow it."

"Couldn't *allow* it? Allow? You were the judge?" he barked.

"She's Pryderi's mate. And half sorceress."

"Mate? Cerys, this is too much. This defies all."

"But it is nature. It is a soul match. Please. She's a good girl. She's truly good. I've met her, spent time with her. She had no idea of who she was. She's been brought up by humans."

"Humans?" he bellowed, now pacing.

"They know nothing. I swear it. She is far away from them. She drove here, following her heart's call. As I was seeking information she ran into Pryderi and their fate was sealed."

"Pryderi knows her? He also has kept this secret?"

"Because I demanded it. Please do not take it out on him."

He started striding back towards the encampment, ready to throttle the insolent male.

"Please, Rhion. Wait. There's more," she pleaded, pulling on his arm, bringing him to a halt.

"She is the daughter of Threaris. She is now in his presence."

"Cerys. Words fail me. How could you let this happen? You have made me a fool. And now there is untold danger to me and all our people."

"He was in my cottage this morning when I was out. He just took her from under my nose. It is I who is the fool. Me who has brought all this upon us. And me who will rectify this. But I need help."

"You dare ask for my help? Now it's too late? I trusted you."

He stomped off, and this time there was no stopping him.

Cerys felt even more dreadful than she'd imagined possible. She'd injured this great elinefae. She had betrayed his trust and coerced one of his own to do likewise. She felt sick and sank to the ground in despair.

Rhion approached Pryderi, who had been pacing where he'd been left. Upon seeing the raging storm approach he sank to one knee and lowered his eyes.

"*I beg forgiveness*," he mewed quietly in their own language.

The reply he received was a boot in his chest, pushing him on his back in the mud.

"*You. Have you any idea what you've done?*" Rhion roared, unleashing a punch across Pryderi's face as he tried to get up.

He didn't fight back. He merely muttered another apology, bringing himself back to one knee, his face looking at the ground.

"*I can't even look at you. I trusted you with my life. And this is how you repay me?*" his Leader grunted.

"*I do not know the words to show you my regret. But now she needs my help.*"

"*And you think I will help? If Threanis kills her he will be making my job easier.*"

"*No. You cannot say this,*" Pryderi said, rising to his feet.

"*You dare tell me what to say?*" Rhion yelled, shoving Pryderi's chest.

"*She is my mate. I will do all I can to save her. I will lay my life down for her.*"

"*She is not even elinefae,*" he sneered

"*She is partly. I did not choose this. Do you think I would? That I have been happy hiding this from you?*"

"*Yet you did hide it.*"

"Unwillingly and to my shame. But I will fight for her," Pryderi raised his voice as he squared off to his own Leader.

Rhion looked the young man over from toe to head before shoving him out of his way as he stormed past.

A small group of onlookers crowded around Pryderi as their Leader walked off. They were asking questions, but he declined to answer.

Shock rippled through his companions. They hadn't heard the whole conversation but had gathered enough to know it wasn't good. That Pryderi had a secret half-mate.

Fortunately, Arwyn happened upon them and took Pryderi off on their own so his friend could update him in private.

Rhion had continued on to Cerys' den. She rarely used it, but knew this was where she would have fled to. He was correct in his assumption.

"We can all get to Avebury Rings within half an hour?" he heard her say.

"I'll be there to hold the way," she signed off.

"What are you up to now?" he grunted.

"Emergency coven. If you won't help then I need to call in the witches. We cannot leave that girl where she is."

"A girl should be with her father," he gruffed.

"Not this one. I don't trust him."

"Even if you survive this encounter, what then?"

"I have no idea. I've spent weeks trying to formulate a plan. I still know the same. The girl must live."

"Despite all convention?"

"Despite all."

"You seem so sure of that."

"I know you can't right now, but please trust me," she requested.

Standing on tiptoe she reached up and pulled his hair gently so he lowered his head. She risked quickly kissing his big full lips.

"I must go," she said, hopping away before he could react.

"Be nice to Pryderi," she added.

She scurried out before he could answer, and headed straight for the portal.

She had hoped to see Pryderi but couldn't find him, so was denied the reassurance she craved.

Cerys travelled straight to the stone circle of Avebury Rings, opening both ends of the portal herself. She was proud of herself for having the bravery to do so.

It was twilight and there was no one around. She had grabbed her bag on her way out of the den, and began to prepare the area.

She began by smudging (burning sage), to cleanse away any negative energy. She then held the space quietly, and set up protections around the circle.

Just as she was finishing, the first burst of light emerged, signalling a witch trying to arrive. She checked who it was, and let them through.

Lily appeared under her own power at the same time. They both helped open portals for all the other witches until they had a full house.

Witches had travelled from all around the globe for this gathering. They'd not held coven for years, and there was a buzz of excitement in the air. It could be held in any sacred space nominated by the witch calling the meeting.

They made a colourful crowd when gathered. Each witch tended to wear a cloak corresponding to their own colour. This was usually the colour associated with their magick; the one which shone at the edges of their sparks. Or matched the predominant colour of their aura, which was often the same. Cerys' own cloak was purple, but having taken an aversion to the colour, the reverse side was blue.

The witches called the corners, and opened up the circle officially. The sacrificial wine was passed around. The cup refilled itself when it became empty; a perk of being a witch at coven.

Chen was next to Cerys, much to her delight. She was still drawn to the male witch from China, and it had been far too long since she'd seen him.

They glanced across at one another in silent acknowledgement of the mutual attraction. But they had to keep infuriatingly focussed on the meeting.

Formalities completed, Cerys took a small step forwards.

"Merry meet. Thank you all for attending at such short notice. I know it's been a while, and I apologise."

Murmurs of mutual apology went around the circle.

"I wish we could meet under happier circumstances, but there is something urgent we need to address. There has come among us a halfling. She is half elinefae and half sorceress."

Cerys paused as gasps and similar noises of surprise erupted.

"She has found a mate within my clan."

Another pause as more murmurs travelled around.

"However, her father, Threaris has captured her and taken her away to an undisclosed location. I do not know what his intentions are, but this cannot be good. And it is torturous to the newly mated pair."

Sounds of agreement were added to the murmurings.

Heather and Rose were perhaps slightly less shocked than the rest. They had known something important was happening. But neither had been totally prepared for this revelation. It was unheard of. It was almost impossible to comprehend.

"I have alerted Rhion, my clan Leader. He was not impressed. Under elinefae law the halfling Kiera should be executed. I have let it be known that this would be unwise, and counsel you likewise. I feel deeply that she must live."

"But a halfling? It's unheard of," a brave witch ventured.

"I know, but I also know the truth in what I say. The circumstances of her conception were unconventional. She is no half human abomination. Great magick and healing run through her veins."

"But what can we do? Threaris is a powerful sorcerer," another dared to speak up.

"I was hoping we could all come up with a plan together. We need a locator spell, and a way of quietly neutralising a sorcerer, another to snatch the girl away and then a way of tethering her so he can't take her back."

"Oh is that all?" someone scoffed.

"You see why I needed your help," Cerys admitted.

They talked and drank long into the night. They were still trying to agree a solution as the sun started to rise.

They all paused to witness the beauty of a new day dawning. The golden light filled them with a sense of hope.

They closed the circle and agreed to go home. They needed to do some research before any ideas could be put into action.

Cerys worried they were taking too long, and she could only hope Kiera was OK.

Chapter 20 – Every Story Has Two Sides

Kiera was not having fun. There was no happy father daughter reunion. She had not expected or sought one.

Having met him, she had come to the conclusion her so called father was a sadistic bully. She was incredibly angry that he'd swooped in and stolen her away like he had some claim to her, as if she were mere property.

"Who does he think he is?" she huffed out loud to herself., "He's nothing but a sperm donor. What does he expect of me? He's ordering me around like a five year old. Where's he been all my life? Arsehole!"

She was still moaning to herself as she begrudgingly dressed for dinner.

Threaris had sent up a servant to command her to attend dinner with him. This had been the trigger to her current torrent of verbal abuse to thin air.

She hated the clothes in the wardrobe. They were all far too formal and girly. She had checked the clothes in the bathroom, but they were still too damp to wear. So she had resorted to searching the offerings in her room.

She pulled out the least offensive garment, plonked it on, but pulled a face as she looked at herself in the full length mirror.

"It's too big and way too fussy," she huffed as she wrinkled her nose and scrunched her eyes.

When she reopened her eyes her mouth fell open in astonishment. Her reflection was wearing a tan jumpsuit with a belted waist. Simple, classic and elegant. Her lush brown hair was caught up in a chignon. And was that makeup on her face?

Her eyes were shaded a subtle brown and a nude lipstick was on her lips, just as she'd choose.

"Much better," she declared at her mirror self.

She strode out of the room in her court shoes, with a defiant air. A different servant was waiting for her on the other side of the door. This one was female.

She was almost as tall as Kiera and had a willowy elegance about her. Her impossibly bright red hair was tied back in a ponytail, but looked as if it was trying to break free. Kiera decided she looked fearsome yet kind.

"Hello, I'm Zondra," she said sweetly, her intensely blue eyes shining brightly.

"Hi. I'm Kiera," she replied as politely as she could, feeling instinctively that this female commanded respect.

Zondra smiled, "Yes, I know, Miss. I'm here for you. Threaris said I am to be your maid."

"And you just accepted that?"

"Why yes. When the Master gives an order one doesn't argue," she replied simply yet with a touch of sadness.

"He's not my bloody master," she growled.

Zondra did her best to conceal her smile as she curtseyed her, "Very good, Miss."

Kiera eyed her sceptically before asking to be shown the way to the dining room.

She'd not been out of her own suite of rooms yet, and still had no clue as to where she was.

Her stomach was forcing her to comply with the dinner invitation. She suspected she'd be left to starve if she declined.

"That's not what I supplied," her father sniffed, regarding her outfit as she entered the dining room.

"If I'm to be kept prisoner I wanted to at least feel comfortable," she sniffed back.

"Well, at least you managed to dress yourself at last," he dismissed as he held his palm towards a chair, suggesting she sit in it.

Kiera flounced towards the table but chose to sit in a different chair from the one suggested.

A couple of the servants in the room seemed to have a coughing fit until the sorcerer glowered at them.

Threaris rolled his eyes, but wisely remained silent. He was hungry and in no mood to delay food by having an argument.

The sorcerer signalled to the head servant that he was ready for the food to be brought in.

Kiera turned her nose up as a plate of salad was placed in front of her along with some cutlery.

"What's wrong with salad?" Threaris asked grouchily.

"What's right with it?"

"Fine. Don't eat it. Starve," came the abrupt response.

He tucked in happily to the leaves, whilst Kiera stabbed at them with her fork.

She reluctantly put some lettuce in her mouth and chewed. And chewed. And chewed some more, all the time wishing there was a nice juicy steak on her plate.

Once her father had finished his entrée he waved impatiently to the servants to clear the plates. Kiera had only managed that one mouthful.

"I'm not trying to poison you. If I had wanted to kill you I would have done so at that hovel of a cottage. I would not have bothered with the effort of bringing you here."

"If it was so much bother then maybe you shouldn't have done it," she bit back.

"You are my daughter."

"So you keep telling me. But how do I know? You may be lying."

"Or just deluded," she added under her breath.

"You think there's many sorcerers wandering around becoming fathers, do you?"

"I don't know. There may be. I have no idea what you lot get up to. It's not like I had anyone to educate me in this crazy shit, is it?"

"There is no need for language."

"Oh no, it's perfectly acceptable to kidnap young women and rip them away from their mates, having ignored them their entire life. To just waltz in and claim fathership having never even bothered with so much as a birthday card. But swearing is taboo."

"You do like playing the victim card, don't you? Firstly, I sent someone to watch over you, but you rejected her."

"Pardon me?"

"A certain faery? And secondly, it's not like I volunteered to become a father to an elinefae halfling. But I don't suppose you've thought of that, have you?"

"I don't care. I'm sure you have some 'poor you' sob story. But nothing excuses kidnapping me."

Kiera covered her mouth and nose as their next course was served. The stench of the stilton and broccoli quiche made her heave. She waved hers away, and the server complied.

She looked pleadingly at her waiter and asked, "Please may I have a ham sandwich or something instead?"

The servant looked up at his master, who nodded almost imperceptibly. Her plate was taken out of the room and a few minutes later a plate loaded with sandwiches arrived.

The bread was cut thickly like doorsteps and was deliciously warm and crusty, as if it had just been baked. The ham was also thickly cut. Kiera licked her lips and gratefully took a big bite.

"Thank you," she said around her mouthful of sandwich.

Threaris looked askance at her appalling manners, and shook his head. But the servant gave a slight bow as he proceeded to pour some red wine.

Kiera took a grateful gulp, but she could still smell her father's stinky food. It was almost enough to put her off her own meal.

She looked at the table between them and wished there was something sweeter smelling. A bowl of potpourri popped into view.

Her father grimaced. The bowl of sickly dried flowers disappeared but he was good enough to put a shimmering misty shield between them to keep the smell from wandering over her side.

"So, there's nothing wrong with your elinefae senses then," he stated.

Kiera glared, but let it fade into the hint of a smile as she realised what he'd done.

"Thank you," she said quietly, the words catching in her throat.

"You're welcome," he said, inclining his head before continuing to eat.

They ate in silence after that.

As the servant approached to clear their empty plates Threaris asked if Kiera would like dessert, which she declined.

"We'll take coffee in the drawing room," he ordered.

Kiera bristled, but gulped down the rest of her wine before following her father out of the room. She didn't fancy another cold shower, and he had shown an inkling of kindness with the anti-smell thing.

The drawing room had an open fire lit in the hearth, and was dark. The thick damask curtains had been drawn, and the walls were covered with dark red wallpaper.

The only light in the room was provided by candles.

"I wasn't sure how your eyes would react to brighter light," Threaris supplied.

"I've been brought up by humans," she told him tersely.

Feeling sorry for her bad manners she added, "But thank you."

A silver tray was brought in and placed on the low wooden table beside the fire. There was a silver coffee pot and china cups on the tray, along with a silver bowl of sugar cubes and a small silver jug of milk.

"How do you take your coffee?" her father asked, picking up the pot.

"Black, one sugar...please," she replied, feeling awkward.

"Do feel free to take a pew," he told her.

She sat down in one of the high backed, dark leather chairs opposite him.

"Alright. Out with it. I know you want to tell me your side of the story, and I suppose it's only fair. I just know my mother's side from a second hand source. I never knew my elinefae parents."

"Are you certain you're ready to hear it? It's not pleasant."

"Well, up until recently I thought I was a human girl. Then I discovered my vampire mother somehow seduced you when she was in heat, and she was subsequently slaughtered along with her husband and supposedly me with them. Does it get any worse?"

"I suppose not. Not when you put it like that."

He sat back in his chair and took a sip of his coffee. Kiera made herself comfy too.

"I was on a sort of pilgrimage, a mission. The destination is unimportant, I didn't reach it. I knew there was an elinefae encampment nearby but I thought I was far enough away not to be in their presence. They don't take kindly to my kind."

"Because sorcerers are evil?"

"Well, some have a certain reputation, yes. Evil is a harsh word though."

Kiera absorbed the confession, and felt uneasy. Had he just admitted he was malevolent? Just as she had begun to feel slightly more at ease she was suddenly on her guard again.

"I hadn't bargained for a stray elinefae wandering outside her territory. I still don't know why she was so far away, but she was. I hadn't even detected her presence when I found myself pinned under her. Her musk overpowered me before I could even gather my thoughts."

"So she raped you?"

"That's putting it a little strongly. A female in heat is pretty hard to resist though, and I'd not err…had relations in a very long time."

"You were horny."

"Really, I shan't continue if you're just going to be crass."

"I'm just trying to understand."

"Just be silent and listen. We had our encounter, which I confess was pleasurable…"

"Eww!"

"Hush. Until she sank her teeth in. It's quite normal in elinefae mating. But as she drank from me I was," he cleared his throat before he could continue, "In the throes of passion and well, she drank too much. I was rendered senseless and she drained me dry."

"She killed you?"

"If I'd been human yes, she would have killed me."

"Wow, talk about black widows."

"Her husband came upon us, and rightly dragged her from my seemingly lifeless body. Everything went black as I truly lost consciousness. I suppose they assumed me dead. When I awoke it was with the power of the dawn. The rising sun re-energised my body, but I was still weak."

"Wait, so the sun reincarnated you?"

"No. Are you listening? I didn't die. I may be saying it wrong. The sun and moon have their own magick. With the new day my cells were powered up, like solar energy powering up my magick. But my body needed fuel. I dragged my body to a nearby stream and drank."

"Shit."

"Please stop using profanity. It's most unpleasant. The sun and water sustained me enough in order for me to get myself home."

"The puffy vanishy thing?"

"Yes. It takes quite a lot of energy and concentration, but fortunately I am well practised in it, so just about managed. My butler found me collapsed in the hallway, and helped nurse me back to health. I woke up a few days later in my bed. Now listen, this bit is important. I had no idea I had sparked life. I didn't even remember what had happened at first."

"Convenient amnesia," Kiera muttered.

"Most inconvenient. But it seems your mother had wiped my memory as she bit me. It's a useful throwback from when they used to dine on humans. Not that they were ever their favourite prey, but it sufficed when food was scarce."

"So they really were like the vampires of horror films?"

"No. They'd seldom kill the humans. They'd sip enough to sustain them, but send them on their merry way, none the wiser as to what had happened."

"Oh God, I'm related to an evil magician and psycho blood drinkers," she moaned, putting her face in her hands.

"I am a sorcerer thank you. Pah, magician," he scoffed.

"Sorry. Elinefae not vampire, sorcerer not magician. Got it. But what's the difference?"

"Quite a lot. Magicians are cheap human conjurers of illusions. Sorcerers *are* magick. It is the essence of our being, and we draw energy from all around us."

"Like witches."

He rolled his eyes, "I suppose a little, but we're far more powerful."

Kiera stretched her arms out above her head and yawned.

"Well, thank you for the bedtime story, but I'm very sleepy."

"It is quite a lot to fathom. We have much to catch up on."

"Well, goodnight," she said, rising to her feet.

"Goodnight," he replied, letting her go.

Zondra was waiting outside the room, ready to guide Kiera back to her suite. Once safely inside, she turned down the bed, and pointed out the silk pyjamas awaiting her charge.

"Will that be all, Miss?" the maid asked.

"Yes thank you, Zondra."

The maid curtseyed and started to walk out.

"Zondra?"

"Yes, Miss?" she queried, turning back round.

"Am I truly a prisoner here?"

"I think Master just wants to be sure of your attention, Miss."

"What's he like?" she asked, sleepily.

"Oh, much like all powerful men used to getting their own way I suppose, Miss."

"Thank you, Zondra. Goodnight," Kiera said with a yawn.

"Night night, Miss. Sweet dreams."

Zondra disappeared from the room, and Kiera got ready for bed.

"Well, no need for a shower tonight," she mused to herself as she got changed.

She really did feel very tired, and climbed straight into bed.

Threaris had remained where he was and effortlessly changed his clothes, confident that the sleeping draught in the girl's coffee would soon take effect.

Chapter 21 – Predators

Chen had loitered behind at the end of the coven meeting to assist Cerys with the clear up. He stepped closer to Cerys, and brushed her hair out of her eyes.

"You look worn out, if it is not too impertinent to say," he commented kindly.

"You're just full of compliments, Chen. Thanks."

"Relax. I was just saying I am concerned for your health."

"Sorry. I've not had much time for rest lately."

"It must be difficult with so much on your mind," he consoled whilst stroking her cheek.

She drank in his delectable Chinese accent and breathed in his exotic scent. She leant her cheek into his touch further, feeling both comfort and excitement.

"We used to be good together," his soft voice melted her middle.

Cerys looked into his intense, rich, dark brown eyes. Her breath hitched as their stares collided.

"Chen, I don't have time for this," she said regretfully, forcing herself to look away.

"Oh, I think you do," he whispered into her ear, making her wriggle.

"We need to find Kiera. Fun later," she demurred.

"You cannot blame me for trying to ease your stress," he said sadly, taking a step back.

"Blame you? Don't talk nonsense. I'm very tempted, dear boy."

"Maybe I can still be of assistance?"

"Oh?"

"Might I join you when you return home? Two heads are better than one."

Cerys smiled her thanks and agreed most readily. She was only too happy he was able to accompany her. He'd been detained far too long.

She opened up both ends of her portal, and took them both back to her home.

"You're completely unprotected here," he uttered in astonishment as they approached her cottage.

"Oh right, that. Yes, I'm afraid it was no obstacle for Threaris."

"Would you like some help making a sorcerer proof shield?"

"You can do that?"

He smirked and rubbed his chin.

"In my land it is always best to be fully protected."

"Yes, I suppose it is," she giggled shyly, "But I can't help thinking it's shutting the stable door after the horse has bolted."

"Better to be prepared."

"You're right," she conceded.

They both raised their hands and started building a barrier together.

"There. Sorcerer and unwanted guest proof," Chen chuckled as he completed his task.

"Amazing," she breathed, carefully noting exactly what he'd done.

They continued walking through her garden.

"Go in," she invited her friend.

She paused at her vegetable patch to collect some vegetables and herbs, before joining Chen in her home. It had given her some valuable time to calm herself.

She was drawn to that man like a moth to a flame, but she couldn't afford to lose any time. Kiera may be in terrible danger. Or worse, she may be being corrupted by that sorcerer.

"Make yourself at home. I won't be a moment," she told the man standing in her sitting room as she entered her home.

She remembered the rabbits which were still hanging in her pantry, and collected them. She took out a pot in the kitchen and placed all the ingredients on the table.

"Time is money," she muttered, regretting she couldn't cook this the proper way.

She chanted as she waved her hands over the raw ingredients. Within moments there was a steaming hot rabbit stew bubbling in the pot.

She made some herbal tea and took a tray loaded with her offerings into the sitting room.

Chen had already found some books and was sitting cross legged on a soft chair, reading.

"That was quick work," he smiled up at her as she approached with the delicious smelling stew.

Cerys laid the tray down and took the seat next to him.

They ate from trays on their laps as they both started looking through her books.

Chen only spoke to admire her food and to give his thanks. Neither had eaten since breakfast, and were hungrier than they had realised.

Pryderi was more thankful than ever of his Watcher status. He was running around the clan's boundary, trying to run off excess nervous energy whilst checking for any intruders.

He wondered if the sorcerer would come after him. He hoped he would. He wanted to be taken to wherever Kiera was, no matter what happened to them.

She was alive at least. He could feel her life force deep within himself, and sense her far off echo.

He was slowly going insane with all this waiting. He'd promised Cerys he wouldn't try anything on his own. Not that he could really; he wasn't able to open portals and he had no other way of travelling great distances at speed.

So he was serving out his time, beating his feet against the earth. Trying not to think how much he missed her. His body felt truly cold for the first time without her presence.

He sniffed in, and could almost smell her scent; her yellow flower signature. It almost brought the adult elinefae to his knees and tears to his eyes, not being able to nuzzle into her neck, her hair brushing his face.

Arwyn finally caught up with his friend.

'*Slow, my friend,*' he thought at him.

'*Arwyn, do not ask the impossible of me.*'

Arwyn grabbed Pryderi's arm, forcing him to a halt. He was taller and broader than Pryderi and blocked his path.

'You do not think it wise to conserve your energy?'

'For what?'

'For her. When Cerys does come up with a plan do you not think she will take you with her?'

'Yes.'

'And will you need to be at your best for Kiera?' Arwyn gave Kiera's thought signature name as Pryderi had shown him it to be.

Arwyn and Elan were his two best friends, and the only two he had divulged his secret to. They were all Watchers; brothers of clan and brothers in arms.

As a large, well-built male with piercingly pale blue eyes, sexy shaggy dark hair and designer stubble along his hollow cheeks, Arwyn was quite in demand. He knew what it took to satisfy a female. Many females. And males; he wasn't fussy.

His comment was intended as a lurid one, but Pryderi took it seriously.

'And my best is not good enough. I failed her,' he whined.

'And who among us would be able to defeat a sorcerer? Who would even try what you did? My friend, you did more than you could.'

'And it wasn't good enough,' Pryderi spat his self-hatred as he punched the air.

'It was not a fair fight.'

'And I have failed clan. Rhion is still angry as is his right.'

'You forget I agreed to your secrecy.'

'Thank you for keeping it. I am sorry you had that burden.'

'You would do the same for me.'

'Argh, my brother, what will we do?'

'I have no answers. But we will get her. I vow this to you.'

The two males brought their foreheads together in recognition of the sacred vow.

Pryderi just hoped his longed for answers would come sooner rather than later.

Arwyn bumped shoulder to shoulder with the elinefae he truly saw as a brother as he challenged him to a hunt. It had been their distraction technique for as long as they could remember.

They ran through the forest, racing to be the first to catch the stoat which fell into their path.

Arwyn considered that the benefits of the blood feed would outweigh the energy exerted in the kill. And it always cheered them up; the thrill of the chase.

The two elinefae were not the only predators stirring that night.

Threaris had changed into dark clothing, and grabbed an empty jam jar. He pulled the penknife from his pocket and manually jabbed holes in the lid.

He stuck the jar into a leather bag which hung at his hip, and transported himself to a woodland in Surrey.

"Frydah," he called out. "Fryyydaaaah."

There was no response, so he became more forceful.

"I demand your presence you pesky pixie. Frydah show yourself."

There was a rustling of leaves, and a golden glow flitted its way towards the sorcerer.

"Why did you not come when called?"

"Apologies, Master Threaris. I was in the middle of something. I am here now."

"What were you up to?" he sneered.

"Nothing as important as you," she tried avoiding answering him directly.

"You wouldn't be up to mischief, would you?"

The poor little faery was distracted as she tried to justify herself. The sorcerer quickly captured the fae in his jam jar and took them back to his home.

"Let me go, let me go," the angry little faery buzzed as she banged her fists on the enchanted glass.

"All in good time. But first you will answer me. You have been dabbling where you should not."

Frydah stood with her fists on her hips, glowering.

"Well…?"

"Well what? You've not asked anything. Just accused. An ugly accusation I am not at all happy with."

"When I tracked you, I thought you had been visiting my daughter. I overlooked the matter."

"And?"

"Don't try to wriggle out of this. What have you been up to?"

"Hello Frydah. How are you Frydah? Looking well," she mocked.

"Answer me, you infuriating creature."

"Creature? Oh even nicer. Why don't you try being nice?"

"Because I don't stay friends with traitors."

"Traitor? That's a strong word sorcerer. I discovered your daughter had gone missing. Who told you? Me. Did I then not have a duty under contract to try to locate her?"

"You were innocently just trying to discover her whereabouts? How did she evade us in the first place?"

"She wished it, I think," Frydah replied simply.

"Just like that?" he asked, snapping his fingers.

"I know of no other explanation. And I don't like your tone. Now let me out," she demanded, stamping her foot and pouting.

"So why did I not hear of her whereabouts?" he said, ignoring her demand. "I had to enchant a human in a common coffee house to tell me her whereabouts. Even then I had to search as she was not where the human had said she'd be."

"Well maybe you would've heard from me if you'd not pounced in and snatched her before I could say agra..abra...acra...oh that stupid human word."

"Abracadabra?" he actually sounded amused.

"Whatever. You apparently needed no assistance from me, so I might as well have not bothered."

"Perhaps. But I think I have a use for you now," he sneered as he lifted the faery up by her wings.

She was powerless to stop him. He'd cast his freezing spell before he took off the lid.

Threaris mercilessly produced a board, and pinned the faery to it by her wings as if she were no better than a butterfly corpse.

Frydah screamed in pain. As soon as the freezing spell wore off she tried to wriggle but the motion just tore her wings and hurt all the more.

"I'd advise you to keep still," he taunted her.

"Why are you doing this?" she asked through agonising breaths.

"Because you lied to me," he shrugged.

"And because I can," he added with an evil look.

"But I've not done anything wrong," she cried.

"I'm in a forgiving mood," he declared, ignoring her protestations.

"I'm giving you another chance," he said as he took them to the library.

He hung the faery on her board next to actual butterfly specimens.

"You're a monster," she wept.

"You have no idea," he jeered. "Now be a good girl and do not fail me."

Not wanting the faery to tear through her wings entirely he popped a pushpin into the board so she could stand on that.

He gave Frydah her instructions, and left to get a restful night's sleep.

Chapter 22 – Friend or Foe

Kiera was awoken the next morning by Zondra opening her bedroom curtains, and delivering a breakfast tray.

"If you don't like it, I can get something else, Miss," she told the girl in the bed.

"Err, no. Croissants are fine. Thank you."

"I neglected to ask what you'd like. I'm sorry, Miss. I have a lot to learn."

"As do I," Kiera said glumly.

"I'm not entirely sure what elinefae eat," the maid apologised.

"I'm not really sure myself yet. I've not had the chance to get acquainted," she replied more sternly than she intended.

Kiera sat up properly and started breaking off a piece of warm croissant.

Zondra's amiability was a small relief amongst a whole pile of anxiety. Kiera felt alone and scared and pined for Pryderi with a pain she couldn't even begin to define.

"So, should I expect another summons today?" Kiera asked around a mouthful of pastry.

"Master has urgent business to attend to today."

"So, that's a no?"

"Would you like a guided tour after breakfast? I can show you around, Miss."

"I don't have any other plans. I mean, that would be nice. Thank you."

"I'll just be right outside the door when you're ready, Miss. No need to rush."

Kiera was left alone to finish her breakfast in peace.

She looked around the room, trying to familiarise herself with her surroundings. She resented being held prisoner. She was determined to find a way out of here.

She just couldn't shake off her lethargy this morning though. She felt really heavy. She decided to have a shower before she got dressed.

"Hmm, so there is hot water," she smirked as she stood under the warm jets.

It helped revive her somewhat. When she was finished she found her own clothes dried and ironed back in the wardrobe in her bedroom. She hurriedly put them on, and went to meet Zondra.

True to her word, the trusty maid was just outside the door to her rooms. Kiera couldn't help thinking all that lurking was a bit creepy.

There were several servants she'd come across already, and she wondered why they all worked for Threaris. Their amusement over her verbal assault hadn't escaped her. She got the feeling they didn't like him very much.

Trying to put all negative thoughts aside, Kiera followed Zondra through the halls of the large abode. She'd not seen the outside, she didn't even know if it was a mansion, or a castle, or something else.

She wasn't sure how much she could really trust Zondra yet, and kept her questions to a minimum.

They went from room to room, floor to floor, with Kiera trailing in Zondra's wake. The maid was quite happy to have someone to show off to. Kiera smiled and nodded politely, not really taking it all in. She peeked behind curtains to see nothing but an inescapable threshold.

'How am I going to get out of here,' she wondered to herself, biting her lip.

"Are you OK, Miss?" Zondra asked, noticing her charge was looking nervous.

Kiera nodded, but her sadness didn't escape the maid.

"All this must seem very strange, Miss. You being so far away from home and all."

"Where am I?"

"I'm afraid I can't say, Miss."

"Oh. I wouldn't want to get you into trouble."

"I see what you're thinking. Even if I somehow managed to escape he'd only find me and bring me back. And I'd lose all privileges. Nobody eludes the Master."

"What hold does he have over you?"

"I...I..." Zondra stuttered.

"Pardon me. I didn't mean to pry. Forget I asked."

Kiera promised herself to find out though. This young lady seemed far too nice to be trapped here.

It occurred to Kiera that Zondra was as much a prisoner as she was. And if that were true, perhaps it applied to the other servants too.

"How dreadful."

"Pardon, Miss?"

Not realising she'd spoken aloud Kiera tried to cover her blunder.

"Err, the outlook. Out of all these windows along here all you can see is rough sea and jutting rocks. Simply dreadful."

"It is a bit dreary," Zondra agreed.

They were now standing in the library. Kiera felt an odd buzz and thought she heard a squeak and looked to see where she thought the noise came from.

There was a small glow on the far wall. Zondra seemed not to notice.

"So many books," Kiera exclaimed.

"Oh yes, knowledge is power, Miss. At least, that's what Master says."

"Might I be allowed to sit here and read on my own? You can stay in the hall, make sure I don't escape?" Kiera dared to ask.

"Very good, Miss," Zondra curtseyed and left as she was bid.

Kiera went to a bookshelf and selected a book and watched the maid leave the room. Ensuring she was alone she went over to the glow on the wall.

"Oh my frickin'…what the?" Kiera exclaimed in shock as she approached a teary faery.

"Oh, so now you see me," Frydah said grumpily.

A memory stirred.

"Have we met?"

"Yes we've met," came the huffy response.

"What are you doing up there?"

"Practising for Christmas. What the bloody hell do you think I'm doing?"

"Well, I don't know. Why does everyone expect me to know what the hell is going on? It's not every day I discover my whole life has been a lie. I'm human. Oh no, I'm not. I'm part elinefae, but oh no, it gets better, my daddy dearest is a bloody sorcerer. But that's not the best bit, he shows up and kidnaps me, just to leave me alone in this hellhole. But sure, I know all about this fucked up world you lot live in."

"Alright. No need for hysterics. Or swearing."

"Sorry. No. No I'm not. What am I apologising for? I didn't ask for any of this."

"OK. You have a right to be upset. But would you please get me down?"

"Of course," she said reaching for one of the pins.

"Ouch," Kiera exclaimed when she felt a sort of electric shock.

"They're enchanted, dummy," Frydah pointed out.

"Well, how am I supposed to get you down then?"

"Carefully."

"Oh, yeah, that helps. Thanks."

"Oh the sarcasm again. I'm presuming you can break the enchantment, having the same blood running through your veins as the man who stuck me here."

Kiera shuddered at the thought.

"Eurgh, don't remind me."

"You can do this. Hold your hand near the pin, but not too close."

Kiera did as instructed.

"Now, think 'free'."

"Free? Is that it?"

"Yes, but imagine the spell dissipating too. Like drawing back a curtain."

"Free. Curtain. Got it."

Kiera concentrated. She felt a tingle run through her, and to her amazement a shimmer appeared in front of her eyes and started to fall.

But then it re-emerged. The tingle stopped as her attention wavered.

"Focus. Keep your concentration on freeing the spell until it completely disappears."

"Right. Sorry. I just was surprised."

"Surprised?"

"Yes, I saw a shimmery thing."

"Hmm, well that would be the spell. Get used to it. Quickly."

Kiera took a deep breath and repeated the process. This time the shimmery curtain fell completely then vanished from existence.

"Good girl. I knew you could do it."

Kiera reached for a pin.

"Carefully," Frydah cautioned.

Kiera held a hand cupped beneath the faery as she slowly pulled a pin out of one wing.

Said faery grimaced and shuddered a little, but was able to reach around for the second pin. She let her feet rest on Kiera's hand.

"Owww, I can't quite get it," the faery moaned as she twisted awkwardly, hurting herself in her escape attempt.

"Here, let me," Kiera said, removing the second pin.

Frydah collapsed into Kiera's hand with a moan of both pain and relief.

"Are you OK?" Kiera asked, concerned.

"Mmm, I will be," the faery grimaced.

Kiera carried the little figure over to a chair, and placed her gently on a cushion.

She spied a wooden globe, and hurried over to it. Her shoulders sagged in relief as she pulled the lid open, and found a small selection of alcohol inside, as she'd suspected.

She poured a measure of whisky into the bottle's cap, and took it back to Frydah.

Kiera dipped her little finger in and ran it along the holes in the faery's wings and propped the remaining liquid in the cap in Frydah's tiny hands.

"For the pain," she said softly.

Frydah had winced as the sticky fluid was applied, but flapped her wings as she sipped.

"Thank you," Frydah said gratefully.

"You're welcome. So, why were you there? And is Threaris not going to notice you're missing?"

"Oh don't worry about that. I'll fly myself back up and pretend to be still pinned like a museum exhibit when he returns."

"But aren't you going to escape?"

"Escape? From here? Have you not felt it? This place is impenetrable."

"Oh, so what now?"

"Now we get revenge," Frydah said with a slightly evil chuckle.

The faery cast her own magick to fully heal herself, and flapped her wings excitedly.

"Ahh, that's better."

She flitted up to Kiera's eye level, and got close to whisper in her ear.

"Nobody traps a faery and gets away with it," Frydah confided.

"I should think not."

"Your father told me what I should do with you. And to some extent I will need to comply so he doesn't try to hurt me again, but he didn't specify what I'm not to do. In thanks for freeing me, I shall assist you. Besides, my first edict still stands. I've always been your protector."

"You? It was you, wasn't it? When I was little. You were my imaginary friend."

"Not quite so imaginary."

"Oh right, I suppose not. Sorry. It's just my mum…"

"Yes yes, I know the human corrupted your mind. Believe it or not I was sorry to lose contact. But you stopped believing and then you could no longer see me. I was still there though."

"Thank you. But why can I see you now?"

"I suppose being subjected to elinefae and witches and sorcerers reopened your mind somewhat?"

The girls giggled.

"Yes, that would do it," Kiera admitted.

The two became reacquainted and chatted for a little while. But Kiera soon became quiet again.

"How do we get out of here?"

"You're thinking like a human," Frydah said sadly. "Do stop that. First we have to neutralise the foe."

"My father?"

"Yes. And no, I'm not sure how yet. He's very powerful. If you just escape he'll come after you, and you'll be worse off than ever."

She flew closer to Kiera again and whispered conspiratorially, "But you know what? With your elinefae magick in the mix, I think you could become even more powerful than him," Frydah said with glee.

"Speaking of which, are you ready for your first lesson?"

"Lesson? What are you going to teach me?" Kiera asked, full of curiosity.

"What I was instructed to do," the fae winked. "Magick."

Kiera's eyes went wide in surprise.

"Well, I'm not going to teach you exactly what he wanted, but let's start with the basics."

"But the maid is still outside. Will she not get suspicious?"

"She will pay no heed. Besides, I'm doing what was expected, in a roundabout sort of way. I'm sure she has orders to leave us be, thinking you are being bent to his will."

"Right," Kiera nodded. "So where do we start?"

The faery rested her chin in her hand as she thought for a moment.

"Hmmm, well you need to be able to escape. How's your teleporting?"

"Teleporting?"

"Vanishing. Zapping from one place to another."

"I can do that whoosh thing too?"

Frydah hit her forehead with her hand.

"Oh boy, this is going to be harder than I thought."

The faery was as patient as she could be whilst she instructed the girl on how to take herself to where she wanted to go.

They started with her going from one side of the library to the other at first.

It took several attempts, but she got the hang of it.

Patience is not something often associated with faeries, and Frydah was almost bursting with steam by the time Kiera managed to take herself to her rooms and back.

Upon returning she saw the sad and grumpy look on Frydah's face, so she vanished again.

Frydah was still huffing when Kiera returned with some sugar cubes she'd stolen from the kitchen.

"I heard somewhere that your kind like sugar. That's correct, isn't it?"

This earned her a smile from the less fraught faery.

"Thank you. Yes, we have a sweet tooth," Frydah confirmed, already munching on a sugar cube.

She was sitting on the edge of a coffee table, her legs kicking with glee as she consumed her treat.

"Right. Next we vanish."

"Didn't I just do that?"

"Teleporting. You just learned teleporting. Do try to concentrate," Frydah gruffed, now frowning again.

"I'm trying. I'm sorry. So, what's the difference with vanishing?"

"Teleporting you actually go somewhere else. Vanishing you just hide."

"Right. Disappearing hiding," she thought out loud.

Frydah nodded before showing her this new trick.

Kiera learned this one a lot more quickly, and couldn't help but think it would come in handy when hunting.

She caught herself mid thought, and shook her head at herself, wondering what she'd become.

"Right, that's hiding and escaping taken care of. You need to protect yourself too, in case you can't run away."

Kiera yawned, "Can it wait? I'm very tired."

They had spent hours together already, but the faery was relentless.

"Just this last one. It's just a very brief introduction. You have much to learn and I don't know how much time we have."

Kiera looked so forlorn that Frydah took pity on her.

"Please don't be upset. You're doing very well."

"You're just saying that."

Frydah stamped her foot and glowered.

"I don't say things just for the sake of it. I am not a human."

"OK, keep your hair on."

"My hair? Where would it go?" Frydah said, looking genuinely puzzled, clutching her golden locks.

"It's just an expression. It means calm down. Oh dear, it is a bit odd, isn't it?"

The pair giggled again before beginning the next lesson.

"OK, you have my own protection around you, but you may face situations where you need more. I won't always be there to lend my strength. So, imagine a ball of light around you," Frydah began.

Kiera imagined a ball of light all around her; a big fiery red ball. She smelt smoke.

"No no no, light not fire," Frydah shrieked.

Kiera saw flames on the rug she was standing on.

"Stop. Stop what you're doing," Frydah yelled as the flames grew.

Kiera screamed and tried to let go of her magick, but she was panicking and couldn't release it. All she ended up doing was releasing more fire balls.

Hearing the commotion Zondra burst into the room. Her bright blue eyes widened as she yelped, "Oh goodness, this will never do, Miss."

She called the water from the pitcher on the sideboard and dowsed the flames as Frydah helped Kiera stop creating further damage. Kiera finally managed to stop the energy flow, and thus stopped fuelling the fire which was now quenched.

All that was left was a smouldering patch on the rug. A large hole had been burned in the ancient heirloom.

"I think perhaps we had better get you back to your rooms now, Miss," Zondra suggested.

"Good idea. I'll clear up here," Frydah commented, surveying the damage and beginning to magickally dry and repair the rug.

Kiera was exhausted and followed Zondra out of the room, promising Frydah she'd return the next day. She knew exactly where she was going, but didn't dismiss her maid. She felt her presence strangely comforting.

Zondra stayed silent until she saw her charge comfortably settled back in the sitting area of her rooms.

"Can I get you anything to eat, Miss? You must be hungry," she asked calmly as if nothing out of the ordinary had transpired.

"Just a snack, please. Cheese and fruit will do."

"Very good, Miss."

The maid disappeared and soon came back with the requested snack and a pitcher of fresh water.

Kiera was left alone to mull over her lessons and to mope over her situation.

Chapter 23 – Aching Hearts

Cerys and Chen had read late into the night, and had fallen asleep atop their books.

Chen was first to awaken. He took a moment to gaze upon the beautiful witch by his side. The morning light was peeking through the curtains, illuminating her lustrous brown hair which had fallen across her soft cheeks.

Chen's heart skipped a beat as he tried to catch his breath. He wondered how he'd ever managed to part from her, and knew he didn't want to do so again.

Duty had got in their way. They'd had what can only be described as a love affair in the distant past. Chen sighed as he thought how distant that all was.

He had been called back to China urgently, and had remained there ever since. There had been a war brewing between clans, and they had called all native witches home to help create peace.

They had finally achieved peace, but at what cost? There had been battles, and lives had been lost. But none of that had felt as painful as the loss of this woman. And now he was back at her side.

He wondered whether the precarious peace was stable enough for him to return to this place of serenity. Would he be allowed to stay where he felt he belonged? He wasn't sure he could tear his heart out again.

As he was agonising over their possible future Cerys fluttered her hazel eyes open. The light showed the golden flecks in them to their full glory.

Chen smiled, one of those full boyish smiles that creased his eyes and showed his teeth.

"Good morning, beautiful," he whispered breathily.

"Chen," she exclaimed, puzzled as she struggled to fully come to.

Then she remembered the night before, and smiled as she brought her aching shoulders up so she was sitting properly in her armchair.

She circled her shoulders, trying to ease the ache, but Chen came to her rescue. He stood behind her chair and massaged her aches away, much to her delight. She groaned her pleasure at his ministrations.

It felt good to have him here, in her home, to feel his touch. She allowed herself a moment to wallow in what was dangerously close to happiness. Afraid she may get too fond of this remembered closeness she stood up.

"Thank you, but we have work to do. Would you like coffee?" she asked, sounding more abrupt than she meant to.

Chen looked like a puppy whose nose had just been snapped. Looking at the floor, he replied in the affirmative.

Regretting her harsh words she walked over to Chen and stroked her hand across his cheek, making him look at her.

Electricity zinged between them as their gaze met.

"I'm sorry. I just can't…"

"I understand," he said glumly, pointing his gaze back to the floor.

"No you don't. What happened, our parting, I don't know if I can go through that again."

"Then don't."

"What?"

"Don't let me go. Whatever happens, promise we won't part. Not again."

"Chen, I can't have this conversation now. Please. We have more important things happening than you and me."

"Isn't there always?" he retorted bitterly.

"I shouldn't have let you come here."

"No, you shouldn't have let me leave here."

"I don't remember having much choice."

Chen shrugged his shoulders and sighed, "You're right. But it wasn't my choice either."

His dark eyes were staring straight at her again, and she saw his years of pain echoing her own. She hugged him to her, and they both wept, sharing their agony all over again.

"I missed you," Cerys confessed through her tears.

"Me too," was all he could manage to say around the lump in his throat.

Chen grabbed her face in his hands and kissed her. He kissed her with all the power and passion that had built up in those long lonely years.

Their mouths collided and their tongues slid together, as if they too were searching for what had been missing for so long. Chen's hands gripped onto Cerys' sides as he drew her closer, making her groan into his mouth.

Their fire had been lit, and it was burning with a blaze so fierce that nothing could extinguish it.

Last night he had been playful when he suggested a night of passion, but now Chen was committed with his whole mind, body and soul. It took them both by surprise.

They ran up to Cerys' bedroom. Chen tore off Cerys' clothes in a wild frenzy, needing to get to her body. He barely paused long enough to undress himself as they continued their ferocious kiss.

Cerys inhaled his sweet sweet scent as he moved them over to the bed and covered her with his body.

Their need was intense and demanded immediate satisfaction. They couldn't bear any preamble. They were both trembling like trees in a storm.

He slid inside her immediately, and Cerys felt like a desert being quenched by rain.

She had been alone for so long, had dreamt of them reuniting every night of their separation, without any hope of it ever happening. But now he was here, and she could breathe again. She'd never felt so alive as their bodies writhed together.

Cerys came within moments of their union, but still she needed more.

They gripped onto each other where and how they could, clutching flesh in desperation.

They were gasping and moaning in sheer ecstasy. And still their bodies thrashed, seeking satisfaction.

Her back arched as she climaxed, this time taking Chen over the cliff with her. They screamed out as they were drowned by their pleasure, overcome by their delight.

Chen shuddered as he found his release, his very core was shaken by the force of their passion.

They held onto each other tightly as they stilled, as if they were clinging to a rock in a turbulent sea and their lives were in peril.

Chen finally managed to take his face away from nuzzling her neck as his lips sought hers.

Both his hands raked through her hair as he looked deep into her eyes.

"My beautiful woman," he breathed.

"By the goddess I missed you," she sighed.

"I think you can tell I missed you too," he replied breathily.

She stroked her palm across his cheek as she kissed him.

"But we really do have work to do," she admitted regretfully.

"I know," he groaned, moving to get up.

"So much for keeping focussed."

"Oh, I was focussed," he grinned.

"On Kiera, not me," she chided, but smiled despite herself.

He bent down for one more kiss before actually getting up. Cerys shooed him into the shower whilst she went to make coffee.

She sighed wistfully, wishing they could spend all day in bed, but knowing they had to formulate a plan.

She sighed even harder as she thought of how Pryderi and Kiera must be suffering. Then she felt guilty for allowing herself to be distracted.

"Hey, I wasn't that bad, was I?" Chen mocked as he cuddled up to her back and nuzzled her neck.

"Don't fish for compliments. I was thinking about the task ahead if you must know."

"Mmmm," he moaned as he kissed her neck.

"But now we're thinking as one. We'll think of something," he comforted as he wrapped his arms around her waist even tighter.

"I hope so, Chen. I hope so."

Kiera woke up to an empty bed. She'd eaten dinner alone as her father was still "out on business", which was a relief.

And she'd gone back to her room to worry the evening away, crying herself to sleep.

She felt reassured by her protector faery's presence, but she was still trapped and away from Pryderi. Oh, how she ached for him. It physically hurt to be so far away for so long.

She was curled up in a ball in her bed when Zondra came in with her breakfast tray. She instantly put it down on a table and ran to her mistress, fearing she was ill.

"Whatever is the matter, Miss?"

"Pryderi, I need Pryderi," she screamed.

"Pardon Miss, but who is that?"

"My mate," Kiera wailed.

"Sorry, Miss. I did not know," she soothed as she stroked the girl's hair.

Kiera was inconsolable and just wailed all the louder, clenching her middle still huddled in her foetal position.

"Shh, calm yourself. I am here."

Zondra began to sing a haunting song. It was like nothing Kiera had ever heard before. It calmed the waters in the depths of her soul. By the time the song ended Kiera had managed to stop crying.

"That was beautiful," Kiera said in stunned admiration.

"Thank you, Miss," was the simple response she received, but it was accompanied by a curious smile.

"You're not human are you?" Kiera blurted.

"That, Miss, is a tale for another day. Your breakfast will be getting cold. Please eat."

Kiera felt compelled to find nourishment, and found herself alone once more.

Left to herself however, her discomfort slowly started to creep back in. But she managed to shower and get dressed before heading to the library.

Chapter 24 – Soothers

"Oooh, you look dreadful," Frydah remarked.

"Gee thanks," Kiera replied sarcastically.

"Have you been fed?"

"Yes," an irritated Kiera replied abruptly.

"Very well. Let's start with some healing this morning. Seems appropriate."

It turned out that this was Kiera's forte, she was a complete natural. She even managed to help heal some of her own inner turmoil.

There was a knock on the library door at midday.

"I brought you some lunch, Miss," Zondra chimed breezily.

"Thank you," Kiera smiled genuinely.

She still didn't trust the maid entirely. She was under her father's control, after all. She liked her, but could she really rely on her to keep her silence over what she'd seen?

"Will you sit with me, Zondra?"

"Oh no, Miss. It wouldn't be right."

"But I want to hear your story."

"Not yet, Miss, if you please. Some tales are too sad to tell when there is no happy ending. Not yet, at least."

"But why are you trapped here? You do have magick, don't you?"

"Same reason as everyone else here, Miss. I can only do so much as he allows."

Zondra's hands went unconsciously to the silver necklace around her neck as she said this.

"I'm sorry. I'm prying again, aren't I?"

Zondra's response was merely to curtsey as she left the room.

"Now she's a curiosity," Frydah mused as she flew close to her protégée.

"Do you know what she is?"

"I'm not sure yet, but I have my suspicions."

"She seems nice. She comforted me this morning when I was upset. She seems to genuinely care. And she did help put the fire out. She feels sad. I think she'd escape if she could."

"Stupid. Of course she would. Everyone here would escape if they were sure they could and not be caught again. Once you've been ensnared by a sorcerer there's a bond that's hard to break."

"Hard but not impossible?" Kiera asked slyly.

"Now you're talking. Right. Next lesson; breaking bonds."

This lesson was harder as it involved having to make a potion, and they didn't have easy access to all the ingredients, so they had to satisfy themselves with the theory. But Kiera thought she grasped the concept at least.

Frydah managed to find some books in the library which looked like they may be helpful in their scheme. She carried on researching as Kiera was called in to dinner.

"Change," Frydah reminded her.

Kiera grinned as she magickally changed her clothing, realising this is what her father had meant for her to do her first day here.

Her first day. How long had it been? It felt like she'd been here for years. And like a black cloud, her sorrow enveloped her once more.

Kiera went to have dinner alone. She gulped down her red wine, hoping it would help numb her pain. She picked up the bottle as she wandered back to her rooms.

Having drunk more of the ruby liquid, Kiera gazed into the mirror on her dressing table, and tried to picture Pryderi. She missed him so much, and the pain was becoming almost unbearable.

Whilst she was with Zondra she seemed to be able to quell the agony, and Frydah distracted her. But now she was alone she felt the full force of her pain.

Pryderi's image started to blur into view in her mirror. Tears began to fall down her cheeks, making the image blur further.

"Oh Pryderi," she cried.

The image vanished as she let her arms fold down onto the dressing table so she could rest her head on them.

Her body shuddered as she burst into a flood of tears. With her head still on one arm, she reached out with the other for the bottle of wine.

She didn't even bother pouring it into a glass, she drank straight from the bottle.

"Pryderi," she screamed to the ceiling, as she slid off the stool onto the floor.

She was clutching and clawing at her body now, leaving red scratches in her wake.

"Pryderi," she wailed.

Pryderi had made his way to Cerys' cottage, unable to remain at home any longer.

He burst through her door, making the two witches inside jump up and cast an additional protection barrier.

"Pryderi, what the bloody hell do you think you're doing coming in here like that? I could've vaporised you," Cerys shouted.

"I need her, Cerys. I need to be with her. I need to help. What can I do?"

"What can you do? What can you do? Not give me a heart attack would be a good bloody start."

"I can't concentrate. I got sent home from the hunt. Me. I was stumbling and falling like a fool youngling."

This was shocking news indeed. Pryderi was one of the most highly skilled hunters she'd ever seen. It was why he was assigned as a Watcher; any potential threats would be swooped upon within seconds.

He suddenly let out a cry as he clutched his stomach. The pain brought him to his knees.

Chen pushed his arm across the front of Cerys, pushing her back a couple of steps.

"Careful. Look at his eyes," Chen warned.

Pryderi's face turned full to them as he leered at them on all fours. His eyes were dull and cloudy but focussed on the witches.

Cerys stood her ground, and drew herself up to her full height.

Pointing her finger towards the still open door, she commanded, "Out in the garden with you. Feed. NOW."

He felt compelled to do as instructed and wandered out to the rabbit warren.

He started pouncing without restraint, and soon had three rabbits dangling from his leather waist cord.

The two witches watched from a safe distance, trying to ensure his blood lust was appeased.

"What in the name of the goddess just happened?" Chen asked.

"I have no idea. I've never seen him so savage nor a thirst take hold so quickly."

Chen risked a quick peck on her mouth.

"You handled him brilliantly."

"Well, I had my doubts for a second. A raw elinefae is not something to be messed with. And I never thought I'd have to speak to him that way."

"You like him a lot."

"Are you jealous?" Cerys smirked.

"Should I be?"

He just got a gentle slap across the side of his head in response.

"Wait. Where is he?"

The pair crept closer, but they couldn't sense him.

"He's vanished," Cerys exclaimed.

"Don't be ridiculous. He can't just…huh."

"Huh? Don't you huh me."

"Don't get grumpy. It just occurred to me. Who is his mate?"

"Oh crippity crap, he can just vanish, can't he?" she said, her mouth falling open.

Pryderi found himself in a sumptuous cream carpeted room.

He was dazed, and started to look around him. It didn't take him long to see the lump on the floor that was his mate.

He rushed over to her, but her body was lifeless.

"Kiera, Kiera," he called, gently shaking her and tapping her face.

"Kiera," he called more anxiously, as he struggled to revive her.

"What the hell is going on here?" Frydah screeched as she popped into their presence.

"Who the fuck are you?" a rather protective Pryderi growled.

"A friend," Frydah said, keeping her distance.

"Some friend. How did she get like this?"

"She said she'd been fed."

"Clearly not."

He returned his attention back to the girl in his arms.

"Kiera, I'm here. Please come back to me."

"She's not fed," a meek voice said from the doorway.

"She told me she had," Frydah fired back.

"Not blood. He was keeping her weak," Zondra muttered.

They'd all felt the massive burst of magick when Kiera had called her mate to her. It had taken the last bit of energy she'd had in her though.

Her need to feed had equalled her need for her mate.

"Make sure we're secure," Pryderi commanded the two females.

He grabbed one of the rabbits at his belt.

"It wasn't *my* hunger," he muttered as he bit into a rabbit carcass.

He held the dripping corpse to Kiera's lips, allowing the rabbit blood to trickle onto them.

"There's weak and there's dead. She's only just turned. She's not fed properly at all yet. Do you people know nothing?" he cursed.

Frydah let the comment go. He was angry, and he had every right to be. She was angry with herself. She'd failed the girl.

"Come and help me," he instructed.

Frydah flew over in a panic.

"What can I do?"

"Pry her lips open."

Frydah did as she was told, and Pryderi squeezed blood into Kiera's now open mouth.

"Come on, baby. Drink for me," he urged.

A song drifted into the ears of the two helpers on the floor.

"What the fuck?" Pryderi exclaimed, but not looking away from his task.

The song carried on, unperturbed by the gruff elinefae.

The music was so beautiful Frydah felt tears pricking her eyes, and she struggled to hold Kiera's mouth open.

They all held their breath as they heard Kiera groan.

"Well don't stop," Pryderi yelled at Zondra. "Whatever you're doing, keep doing it."

The song started up again, and Kiera gulped.

She stirred a little in Pryderi's arms.

She licked her lips. Frydah relinquished her hold.

"That's it, my love. Drink," Pryderi said softly.

"Get back," he warned Frydah.

She needed no second warning, Frydah flitted across to Zondra who was still by the door.

Kiera's eyes rolled in her head as she tried to open them.

"Steady. It's here."

Kiera gulped again, the glistening red fluid reviving her senses.

Before he could react, Kiera snatched the carcass and sank her teeth in. Pryderi sat back on his haunches and rubbed his mate's back as she sat up.

She shot him a feral look, and he jumped up to his feet and backed off. Kiera growled as she carried on sucking on the rabbit.

Pryderi took another quiet step away.

"It's OK. It's all yours," he assured her, laying his hands out flat in front of his crouched body.

With gnashing teeth and lioness like snarls the famished girl devoured the entire rabbit. She sucked the marrow out of its bones before crunching those down too.

She sniffed the air and sat low on all fours. Her shoulders rocked from side to side as she honed in on Pryderi.

The singing had stopped as the horrific scene had played out before Zondra's eyes. She was frozen to the spot.

Frydah however was no stranger to elinefae, and flew between the pair.

"Kiera. Kiera, hear me."

The beast on the floor cocked her head to one side, shifting her glowing gaze to the golden light in front of her.

"Kiera, we do not eat our husbands."

Frydah thought she saw a sadistic smile just as the girl pounced.

With a cry Kiera leapt to the side of Frydah and straight for Pryderi. He didn't know what to do. He wouldn't hurt her, but would she hurt him?

He was stunned. Never before had an elinefae attacked another in this type of situation, especially not a mate.

He was knocked off his feet, and his arse thudded against the floor.

Kiera ripped another rabbit from his belt and began to ravage it.

There was a joint gasp of relief from the other three in the room.

Pryderi let out a nervous chuckle as he righted himself.

"I'm sorry," he apologised to Kiera. "I forgot I had more. Enjoy."

He stroked her head as she carried on with her meal. Her eyes closed at his touch. She let out a noise, which would have been a mew of contentment if her mouth hadn't been full.

"Don't speak with your mouth full," he joked.

Kiera grinned around rabbit fluff. Her eyes were sparkling with joy as she devoured her meal.

Zondra made her way to the nearest chair and collapsed into it. Her hand wiped the sweat from her forehead.

"Not used to the sight of blood?"

"I don't think I was prepared for the savagery," Zondra said in hushed tones to Frydah.

"Well, if she'd been fed you wouldn't have had to."

"And how was I supposed to know? I gave her what I was told to. I even asked what she wanted. Not once did she say she wanted a whole flipping animal."

"Hush you two," Pryderi called over his shoulder. "Time for that later."

"Hello. You must be Pryderi," Frydah greeted.

"Greetings. Yes. You are?"

"Frydah. Time for introductions later, though," the faery deferred, feeling slightly ragged.

He shifted on the floor and pulled Kiera close, in between his widened legs. He sighed heavily as he felt her body against his. He had missed this with every fibre of his being.

Kiera was calmer, but didn't stop eating.

Pryderi breathed a massive sigh of relief through his mates' hair into her neck. He was grateful she was alive, and he was here, wherever here was.

Zondra heard her master's voice in her head.

'I felt a disturbance, yet you have not reported anything unusual.'

'It's nothing, sir. Kiera was hungry.'

'And this disrupted the shield why?'

'She err...conjured some rabbits.'

'She's not supposed to be able to do that.'

'I think it was born of necessity. She'd become too consumed by her need.'

'Duly noted. We'll have to give her just enough blood to stop her doing that again.'

'Very good, sir.'

Threaris' voice disappeared.

When Zondra looked up she saw three pairs of eyes staring at her. Even Kiera had paused in her feeding frenzy.

"What was that?" Pryderi asked.

They had all felt the buzz of electricity, but hadn't been able to hear what Zondra had heard.

"You disturbed the shield. He felt it."

"And?"

"Oh, and he was checking what had happened."

"And you told him..?" Pryderi's patience was growing thin with this woman.

"Relax. He doesn't know you're here. I told him Kiera brought some rabbits across."

"Very nice," Frydah admired the ingenuity.

"What?" Pryderi asked, the subtlety clearly lost on him.

Frydah explained, "Threaris is her Master. She is bound to him. He would detect a lie and I am sure she'd be severely punished if she tried. So she told the truth. Just with some details left out."

"You trust her?"

Zondra stood up and glowered down at him.

"Well, you don't see him here, do you?"

He look abashed and shook his head.

"And I did just help save her life, didn't I?"

He nodded and humbly said, "Sorry. Thank you."

"Hmm, that's more like it."

"Careful there Pryderi. You don't want to upset a nereid."

Kiera had finished rabbit number two and tugged on his shirt.

"Sorry, here you go," he apologised. "This is the last one though. I was unprepared. I'm sorry."

Kiera shrugged off his apology as she tucked into the final rabbit.

Zondra winced at the squelchy sound.

"A nereid?" Pryderi questioned.

Zondra blushed.

"Your friend is wise. Yes, I am a descendant of the nereid. A sea nymph."

"Your song gave you away," Frydah excused herself.

She was embarrassed she'd outed the maid. She blamed the stress of everything that had happened.

"Yes, our song has its own power. It is one of the few gifts I retain in this dungeon."

Pryderi looked around the room.

"Dungeon?"

Zondra's deep blue eyes darkened.

"A dungeon has many forms. I am trapped here, elinefae. As are you now."

"Apologies. You should meet Cerys," he smirked.

Frydah couldn't help but let out a giggle.

"You mock me?"

"No. Cerys is my clan witch. Her temper is short too."

"Spend as much time here as I have, and see how happy you are," she seethed.

"Sorry. Sorry."

Kiera was wriggling in his arms, having finished feeding.

"Better?" he asked her.

She was unable to speak past the lump in her throat.

'Just glad you're here,' she thought at him.

"Me too," he whispered as he bent his head down to kiss her.

Frydah beckoned to Zondra to follow her out of the room. The two vanished into the library to talk.

The mated pair had their privacy to do what came naturally to them.

Kiera was still recovering, so Pryderi was as gentle as his desperate passion would allow.

He carried her over to the soft bed and delicately undressed her, before disrobing himself.

He saw the need in her eyes. Her blood lust may have been satiated, but her Pryderi lust was far from it. She needed him every bit as much as he needed her.

They needed confirmation this was real, that they really were together again.

He nipped playfully at her lips, and licked the remnants of blood away. And she soon lapped back.

Pryderi started with slow tender strokes as he entered her, but got spurred on by the woman underneath him.

He thrust ever faster as she wrapped herself around him, clinging to him like her life depended on it.

His skin tingled as he neared his climax. His hairs were standing on end, the sensation pushing him over the edge as she burst into her own release. A golden glow shone all around them.

'Together forever,' she said in his head.

He licked at her lips and rubbed his forehead to hers in loving agreement.

Chapter 25 – Evil Machinations

Threaris had not been idle. He was in disguise and in conference with Dougal.

"*The time to deploy your men is now,*" he told the elinefae Leader.

"*And your clan will meet us there?*"

"*Yes. My own Leader has confirmed you shall have support.*"

"*And their barriers?*"

"*Will be taken care of. You have my word.*"

"*I do not mean to question your clan. I just have not heard how such a thing can be done.*"

"*Oh, there are ways. And it shall be done.*"

They each beat their heart with their right fist and bowed their heads as they parted company.

Dougal summoned Loth to him.

"*Gather the troops,*" Dougal commanded.

"*Yes sir,*" Loth accepted with a bad feeling he tried to keep hidden.

Loth did as instructed but dropped in to Lily's den along his way.

"Lily, I don't have much time, but we're being gathered. I think he plans to attack another clan."

"Very well. Go Loth. Goddess keep you safe," she said, waving her hand above his head.

Loth quickly continued on his way before anyone could notice. He hoped the goddess would forgive him the indiscretion of divulging the secret to the witch. He felt it was the right thing to do, and heavens knew they needed divine intervention.

His Leader had always been focussed on strength and force, but their training had intensified greatly over the past year, and he couldn't shake the feeling it was not for the greater good.

He didn't understand it. Nobody had openly threatened them, and there were no rumours of attack. They were supposed to be a peaceful race. They wanted for nothing.

But Loth was a loyal elinefae, so he continued summoning the fighters.

They all congregated in a clearing on the edge of their encampment.

" I'm sure you've all been curious what you have been training for," Dougal loudly announced to them all.

" Well, today is the day of reckoning. Today we set out on our mission. Our peace is threatened, and we shall not wait like sitting ducks for our enemy to strike. I see you all have your packs. Follow me now to glory."

He strode with purpose out of the clearing. His troops, both males and females amongst their rank, could do nothing but follow their leader.

Threaris had walked far enough away so as not to be noticed. His butler was by his side.

"Hm hmmm, now we have some fun," he said with a sinister smile whilst rubbing his hands together.

"Yes, my lord," the subservient butler placated, but feeling sickened by what he was witnessing.

"And now to deal with the other thorn in my side."

"Sir, might I remind you she still has a purpose?"

Threaris struck the man across his face.

"You think I had forgotten? Why do you think she is even still alive? Cretin. She is proving to be troublesome though. She must learn her place."

"Yes, sir."

Threaris transported them both back to his lair, and set the servant about his duties.

The sorcerer stormed into his daughter's bedroom.

She barely had time to vanish Pryderi and his discarded clothes out of sight.

"What do you mean by still being abed at this hour?" he growled.

"I was close to death, thanks for asking," she sniped back.

"Don't be so dramatic."

"You starved me of blood."

"You shouldn't need it."

"Shouldn't need it? I'm part elinefae, as people keep reminding me. Of course I bloody need it."

"And your better part is a sorceress. Try listening to that side."

"Did you want something?"

"Not really. I was just checking you were still here."

"Where else would I be?"

"Hmmm, yes, where indeed?" he said snidely on his way out.

'That was close. He didn't see me though?' Pryderi thought at her.

' I think it's safe to say you were undetected. Your head is still attached to your body.'

'But how?'

'Part sorceress,' she winked.

'You have been busy.'

'What? I was supposed to just sit here waiting to be rescued?'

'I'm just impressed,' he thought whilst kissing her.

'We have to be careful. With him back at home we're in more danger now than ever.'

'But of what? He's your father. He wouldn't harm you, would he?'

'Well, he almost killed me through lack of feeding. You heard Zondra, he's been keeping me deliberately weak.'

'But why? What's he afraid of?'

'Me. Frydah thinks I could be more powerful than he is.'

'Have you learned anything of his plans?'

'No. He's barely spoken to me. I'm like shit on his shoe.'

'We really need to find out.'

'No shit Sherlock.'

He frowned at her.

'Um, you were stating the obvious.'

'Fine. But I'm right.'

'I'll try to speak to him later. Right now I ought to get out of bed before he comes back.'

'*He won't be right back,*' Pryderi said, wiggling his eyebrows.

Kiera slapped his arm.

'*Really? Now?*'

'*It's stress relief.*'

'*Well find another way. It's not happening. Not now.*'

Her mate pouted, so she kissed his gorgeous lips but made it clear she meant what she'd said.

"Even pinned to the wall you can still meddle, can't you?" Threaris seethed, his face close to the faery.

"How can I? I'm pinned like a butterfly."

"And just how did my daughter get rabbits through my barrier, pray tell?"

"How should I know? I imagine they were dead before they came through."

"Don't get smart with me."

"I don't know. I wasn't there, was I?"

"How did she know how to do it? It's not what I told you to teach her."

"Instinct needs no instruction. I heard she was starving to death. It seems like a sheer act of desperation to me."

The sorcerer glared at her from the corner of his eyes.

"Hmmm, perhaps. But you will regret it if I learn you had a hand in this."

"You need her alive, don't you? Maybe you should be grateful she found a way?"

"You're dangerously close to impertinence, faery."

"Funny what immense pain will do."

"Just make sure you stick to your instructions."

"Yes sir."

He glanced back at her hearing her insolent tone.

"And watch your smart mouth."

He stormed out of the room and headed to his own suite, where he sealed himself in. He slumped down in a chair, and summonsed his butler along with a glass of whisky.

"More trouble than they're worth," he grumbled, sipping his amber liquid.

"Oh surely not, sir."

"Dangerously close," he said, pinching the top of his nose.

"But sir, the rite."

"Yes yes, I know. I'm so close I cannot give up now. Not after all these years."

"If I might be so bold sir, perhaps the carrot is better than the stick?"

"Well she is certainly as stubborn as a mule. What do you suggest?"

"A little tenderness? The girl has been ill-treated, I fear. Perhaps more carrot less stick would help calm her spirit?"

"Her spirit. Argh, her spirit. She's so damned stubborn. Sheer pig-headedness."

"I can't imagine where she got that from, Sir" the butler smirked.

Threaris shot him a stern look, making the butler scurry away whilst suffering another coughing fit.

Cerys and Chen however were lost. They had been left dumbfounded by Pryderi's disappearance.

"I was relying on using him as a compass to locate Kiera," Cerys whinged.

"It is an annoying setback, granted."

"Annoying? I'm going to have to tell Rhion his best Watcher has vanished. I'm already in his bad books. This is not going to go well."

"It's impressive though," Chen admitted.

"Yes. Even Threaris had to be here in person to kidnap his own daughter."

"How did she do it?"

"She must have been pushed to her limits. She'd denied magick so long I can't imagine she'd knowingly do it. Oh, how she must be suffering."

Chen stroked her hair soothingly as he told her, "But she'll be stronger now she has her mate by her side."

Cerys smiled at him.

"Yes, it's always better when the one you love is nearby."

She stepped into his arms and felt grateful for his comforting embrace.

The two decided they needed to go to Rhion straight away. Darkness had fallen, and he'd be awake.

They quickly travelled to the encampment. Cerys was getting used to this zipping between portals.

Rhion was indeed upset by their news, and ranted and roared at them, so they beat a hasty retreat back to her cottage to come up with the ever elusive solution. The goalposts kept getting moved.

"Without Pryderi, you know we don't have a key to his barrier," Chen said, stating the obvious.

"Yes, we have no trace of her blood now. He'd swallowed enough during their mating, I could sense it. You don't need that much for this type of blood magick."

"Do you have anything else? She's been staying with you."

"Wait. Wait a minute. Haha, I *do* have her blood. When she transitioned she bit her lip."

Cerys ran straight to the spare room and rummaged in the bin. Things had been so chaotic she'd not had a chance to clean up properly.

She pulled out a cloth with a small trace of blood on it, and waved it in the air.

"Thank the goddess for the girl's clumsiness," she sighed with relief.

She zoomed to the kitchen to get a freezer bag and put the cloth inside it. She then tucked that bag into her hip bag.

"See, things are looking up already," Chen announced cheerfully.

"Fabulous, now all we need to do is find a way of overpowering a sorcerer," she replied acerbically.

"Your glass is always half empty," he sighed. "Come on, back to the books then."

There was precious little information to be found. People seldom wrote about sorcerer's weaknesses, it's not like they have many.

But it didn't deter the duo. They pawed over their books all night, until once more they fell asleep in the process.

Chen conjured up a marvellous energy giving breakfast the next morning, and Cerys ensured they had a steady supply of coffee as they continued their search for a glimmer of hope.

Chapter 26 – A Lesson in Potions and Motions

It was midmorning when Kiera tore herself away from her bed.

She magicked herself clean and dressed, knowing the temptation of Pryderi joining her in the shower would be too great for them both. And they could not afford to be distracted. She felt her father's net closing in.

Keeping Pryderi hidden from sight, the mated pair strode into the library. Frydah greeted them, and asked Zondra to keep guard.

She usually stood at the door, but today she'd be protecting the occupants in the room rather than merely indicating Kiera's location. She was to give them a signal if Threaris was approaching.

"Morning Pryderi," Frydah nodded towards him.

"Hey, how did you know I was here?"

"Who taught your girlfriend the trick? It's faery magick, and I am a faery so I can sense it."

"Hey, that's cheating. You didn't tell me that," Kiera complained.

"It didn't seem important," Frydah shrugged.

"Frydah, we need to find out what my father's really up to," Kiera brought them back to their important mission.

"Agreed. He seems more agitated now. He doesn't want you dead, otherwise you would be. But keeping you weak? It's not a good sign."

"Right. So, how do we discover his plan?"

"Luckily for you, I've been thinking about that. I like keeping things simple. Zondra told me how he drugged your coffee the first night?"

"He what?"

"He was paranoid you'd escape, but seeing how useless you were with magick."

"Hey!"

"Remember the shower?"

"Something I should know?" Pryderi interjected.

Kiera blushed as she dismissed his query.

"Knowing how useless you were," Frydah continued, "he didn't feel the need to do it again. We need him to remain ignorant."

"But he knows I at least brought rabbits through."

"Yes, but happily Zondra and I convinced him it was pure instinct, which happens to be true. And he thinks I'm only showing you enough to change your food and clothes. You know, things that would otherwise annoy him."

"Gargh," Kiera let out an exasperated yelp at how manipulative her father was.

"So, we let him think that. The element of surprise is ours. Anyway, like I was saying. He drugged your coffee, and it gave me an idea. We can do the same to him."

"We can?"

"He takes you to the drawing room for after dinner coffee. He dismisses the servants at that point?"

"Yes, he seemed to want to be alone to talk."

"Right, so you need to repeat the scenario. Pour the coffee and slip the little medicine ball into his cup."

"You make it sound so easy."

"Well it can be. We can hide it in your bracelet so you can just release it at the right time."

"And just what do we make this magickal ball out of?"

"Lunch," Frydah sniggered.

She got Kiera to call her maid into the room, and they issued their special lunch requirements.

"Err, where do you think you're going?" the cook stopped Zondra in her tracks.

"The kitchen garden?"

"To feed the girl?"

"Yes, she still needs iron," Zondra replied semi-honestly.

"So give her some beef."

"Master says that's too much. She's to have just a little."

The cook harrumphed but allowed her to pass and enter the small courtyard garden. It was actually a balcony, and the only outside space where they could go to.

Zondra had committed the list of herbs to memory and carefully placed them in her little basket, covering them with baby spinach, to keep her cover story accurate.

She headed back to the kitchen and put the ingredients in a bowl. She took care to put the dressing in a separate jug, and even put a few flowers in a small vase next to the pitcher of water. As an afterthought, she put some bread and cheese on a plate too.

"Pah, precious little princess, that one," the cook huffed, seeing the preparations.

"We're to make her feel at home until Master says otherwise."

Zondra made a swift exit from the kitchen and headed back to the library.

Frydah quickly picked out her ingredients, and Zondra coaxed Kiera into eating the salad.

"You really do need some more iron. You still look sickly. Besides, I've told cook this was all for you, so you need to eat up."

Kiera scrunched up her nose, but started to chew the leaves.

"It's what my food eats, not me," she whinged.

"Haha, you've changed," Pryderi scoffed, picking up a leaf and devouring it.

"I brought this for you. Sorry it's not much," Zondra apologised, shoving the plate of bread and cheese in the direction she saw the leaf travel to.

"Many thanks," he said, grateful for anything.

Zondra resumed guard duty whilst Frydah started tearing the herbs and one of the flower heads into tiny shreds.

Kiera watched with fascination as she carried on chewing the leaves, which she'd drowned in dressing to make them palatable.

"You will learn to like this," Pryderi told her.

Not for the first time, Kiera wondered about the feasibility of living like a wild animal in the woods. She was unsure it sounded like the life for her. But she put the thought to the back of her mind as Frydah scrunched up the shredded herbs into a little ball.

"*Dehydro*," the faery whispered into the ball.

Kiera gasped as the herbs all shrivelled and dried in front of her eyes.

"Eurgh, your bowl's all greasy," Frydah said indignantly.

"Sorry, my leaves needed lubrication."

"May I use this?" Frydah asked Pryderi as she flew to his plate.

"Of course," he agreed, picking up the last of his breadcrumbs.

The faery dropped the dried herbs onto the plate, and started to rub them with her hands. A few minutes in, she paused in her task to mop her brow. It was hard work for the tiny being.

"May I?" Pryderi checked, poised with his unused knife.

Receiving permission, he crushed the herbs with the back of his knife until they were reduced to a fine green powder.

"My thanks," Frydah acknowledged as she scooped the powder together, once more forming a ball.

Kiera couldn't quite hear what the faery said next, but the powder turned white as it formed a small ball shaped tablet.

"So, he won't taste or detect it?"

"Not with the flavour taken out, and the hiding spell," Frydah winked.

"OK, so say I manage to get him into the drawing room, pour the coffee and drop this little thing in there, and he spills his deepest darkest secrets. Won't that make him angry?"

"Ah, it would if he could remember. That's what the flower was for. Forget-me-not can have the opposite effect than its name suggests when used correctly."

"Clever faery," Kiera praised her little friend.

Frydah wiggled her wings and giggled shyly.

"We just wait for dinner now?" Pryderi asked, with a tone of suggestive hope.

Frydah flew up to his nose and smacked it. The elinefae barely felt it, but received the message loud and clear.

"Please keep your thoughts away from your trousers. There is still much to learn."

"Fine," Pryderi pouted.

Kiera sucked on that tempting bottom lip of his.

"Maybe later?" she told him, hoping they could fit in more snuggle time.

Frydah rolled her eyes at the incorrigible pair.

"Hmmm, a little compulsion next I think may be useful," the faery mused, drumming her fingers against her lips.

The girls concentrated on their lesson, and Pryderi tried to amuse himself browsing books in the library.

Hours later, Kiera was becoming really quite good at compulsion, and poor Pryderi seemed to be her guinea pig, much to his chagrin.

"Oh flip, my parents. I've not spoken with them for ages. They must be worried sick," Kiera suddenly exclaimed.

"What that human detritus?" Frydah huffed.

"I'm sorry about what she did to you, Frydah. But they raised me. They care for me. And I don't have my phone. I don't think my father will let me communicate with the outside world somehow."

"Ohh, two birds one stone. I think a certain witch may be worrying too. You can get her to contact them."

"Yes, but how do I contact her?"

"Ahh, next lesson coming up. Let's go to your room for this one."

All four beings transferred to Kiera's beautiful rooms. She was made to sit at her dressing table.

"You remember what you did the other evening?" Zondra asked her.

"You saw that?"

"Yes. Sorry, Miss. I was trying to keep an eye on you. I was concerned," the maid blushed.

"What did she do?" Frydah asked.

"She called up this one in her mirror," she nodded at Pryderi.

"Ah, that's how it started," Frydah mused.

"OK, so look into the mirror," Frydah instructed, "And picture Cerys."

Kiera could hear a ringing noise, similar to that of a telephone.

Cerys skidded across the floor and into her bathroom to connect the call coming through, thinking Lily was calling.

Her mouth dropped open in shock as she saw Kiera's image in her mirror.

"Kiera, dear. How wonderful. Are you OK?"

"Oh Cerys, I don't know where to begin. But I'm fine. Frydah and Pryderi are here. And my maid, Zondra."

"You have a maid?"

"Well, more of a friend really. Long story."

"It sounds like you're in good hands. I'm glad Frydah is there," she said waving as the faery flitted into view next to Kiera.

"Look, we're formulating a plan here. I've got to get some answers out of my father at dinner tonight first. Just stand by, and we'll contact you again, all being well."

Cerys smiled, and her worry lines disappeared from her forehead.

"Oh thank the goddess. We've been drawing nothing but blanks here," she admitted.

"We?"

"Oh, Chen is here with me. He's a witch too, and is ready to help."

"Oh. Well, good. Cerys, please can you do something for me?"

"Just name it, dear."

"Can you do that impersonation thing again, please? My mum and dad must be worried about me."

"Oh but of course. I should have thought of that already. Sorry, dear. I was a bit distracted. And don't worry. You're still recovering from flu as far as work is concerned. Although I suspect you may be going home once this is all over." Cerys put the word home in air quotes.

"Thank you. I must go. I don't know how secure this is."

"Your father is nearby?"

"In his rooms, I think."

"Yes, we should keep this to a minimum. Don't worry. I'll put word around and we'll all be ready when you are."

"Thank you."

And with that the image went fuzzy until all Kiera saw was her own reflection again.

"Very good," Frydah nodded triumphantly.

"That felt easy compared to what we've been doing."

"Good, so it should. Right, time for a rest before dinner, I think. You still look tired."

The faery and nereid started to leave the room. Frydah pointed over her shoulder.

"And I mean rest," she added towards Pryderi.

He spread his hands out in an innocent 'what else' gesture.

Chapter 27 – Wheedling Out Truth

Kiera received her summons to dinner, and she conjured herself into the sort of dinner dress her father would approve of, and fixed her hair and makeup smartly.

She had been told to win her father over as best she could under her own merit, and was doing her best.

As she walked into the dining room she saw his smile of approval, and laughed as she noticed his more casual wear. He was clearly trying to impress her too.

She quickly changed her clothing to black smart jeans and a silky top. Still smart but far more comfortable, and matched his level of casual attire.

He smiled at her.

She curtseyed as she asked, "You approve?"

"Very much."

She walked over to the chair around the corner from his, rather than the seat at the opposite end of the table.

The servant quickly moved her place setting to her chosen location.

"I feel we got off on the wrong foot," she stated.

"You took the words right out of my mouth. I am not used to guests."

He actually sounded apologetic, and Kiera looked askance.

"Oh, don't look so shocked. I'm not a bad person really," he said smoothly.

He clearly didn't know she knew otherwise, so she tried to keep the scepticism out of her looks.

He raised his glass of wine to toast, "To a fresh start?"

"To a fresh start," she chimed as they clinked glasses.

Kiera tried to subtly scan her glass for traces of narcotics. Her father noticed, but said nothing. He accepted he had probably earned that.

"Kiera, I am your father. I have not acted as one. For that I apologise."

Kiera gulped.

"Did that hurt?" she said before she could stop herself.

"Are you going to remain this difficult?"

"I'm sorry. But like I said, we got off to a bad start."

"And I am trying to make it up to you."

The servant brought out a steak, cooked rare and placed it in front of her.

"Thank you," she acknowledged his thoughtfulness.

"I had not allowed for your, shall we say, mix of genetics. I heard what happened. I did not mean for you to get so sick."

"Is my elinefae side so abhorrent to you?"

"I confess I struggle with it. It is not your fault."

"Oh?"

"Enough dreariness. I shall try to accept you as you are. So, have you had a pleasant day?"

"Yes, thank you," she said, unsure of how to respond knowing he'd detect any lies.

"Is there anything you require?"

"I suppose my freedom is out of the question?"

He banged his fist on the table.

"I am trying to be nice, damn it," he exclaimed through clenched teeth.

Kiera had jumped a little at his outburst.

"I'm sorry. But it's hard to feel fondly for someone who is my jailer."

"It is for your own protection. I need to keep you here safely. And being as you are, I do not think you can be trusted not to run amuck."

Kiera took a deep breath to calm herself. She was supposed to be winning him over, not rubbing him up the wrong way.

"OK, OK. I'll be good. I apologise, again."

"I'm not used to being spoken to so freely."

'Perhaps you should try hiring free people not captives,' she thought to herself, but held her tongue.

Pausing, she tried to explain herself.

"You're really not seeing the best of me. But I'm a little stressed. You must understand what a shock I've had. Up until recently I thought I was a human being, one that didn't fit in perhaps, but a human all the same. Suddenly this whole new world has been shown to me, and my father kidnapped me, and it's all just a bit much."

Threaris paused to reflect, to try to see the truth of her words.

"It must have come as quite a shock."

"Just a bit," she said with a nervous laugh.

"And I didn't help, did I?"

"Not really, no. Why don't you tell me about yourself? Help me understand?"

"What do you want to know? You didn't like my story before."

"Hearing the horrors of my conception was really…unpalatable," she struggled to find the right word.

"It's not exactly the stuff of romance novels, is it?" he chuckled wryly.

"Not quite. So, tell me something nice. Your choice."

"I wasn't always this way. Life has made me a little sour. I was in love once."

Kiera's eyebrows rose in surprise.

"As I said, I wasn't always this way."

"What happened?"

"She was killed," he said sadly.

"Oh, not so nice."

"Kiera, she was killed by elinefae."

"Oh, that would turn you against my kind, I suppose."

"You claim that heritage more than mine?" he questioned, more out of curiosity than crossness.

"Both," she replied simply. "How did it happen? If it's not too painful for you to talk about."

"Her name was Azi. She was a witch, and tied to a clan. It was in the time of battles. I had tried to bring her to my home, but she refused, feeling her duty was to protect the clan. She was in the wrong place at the wrong time. An enemy clan attacked them and she got caught in the crossfire. No, I'll be blunt. They targeted her so the clan would not be protected."

"That's awful. I'm sorry," she soothed, dropping her cutlery to reach her hand across to cover his.

He almost withdrew his hand at her touch, but he thought better of it. He struggled to accept her simple act of kindness.

"Oh my poor father. Are you so unused to concern?" she sympathised, noticing his reaction.

He took his hand away, and coughed away the sentiment gathering in his throat. He ate his food in silence, avoiding her tearful gaze.

The silence was deafening as they both finished their meal.

"Please don't shut me out. I feel like I was just getting to know you," Kiera pleaded as the servant took their plates away.

"You're, you're not what I expected," he said more meekly than she'd heard him sound before.

Internally, he was warring with himself. He was beginning to like this girl. But he couldn't afford to let his guard down. She may die at his hand, and he didn't want to lose anyone else he loved. She was supposed to be incidental, a pawn in his game of life. He shouldn't be allowed to care.

"I just want to know you. Please, come and have coffee with me," she pleaded.

Against his better judgement he agreed. He ordered coffee to be taken to the drawing room. The servants were dismissed as before.

"I'll be mother," Kiera said getting up to pour.

The damaged sorcerer didn't seem to have the energy to argue. His eyes were closed as his head fell onto the back of his chair. He looked so hurt.

She found herself feeling sorry for him. But she also knew wounded animals could be the most dangerous.

Feeling guilty, she slipped the herb ball into his cup, knowing he'd never fully open up to her otherwise.

She tried to not look too eager as she watched him start to drink.

"We should have some conversation," she said as she sipped her own coffee.

"I'm not good company, I'm afraid. Too many sad stories," he admitted, swiping his free hand down his face.

"Like your girlfriend, your lost love?"

"Yes."

"And my mother?"

"Yes, but you know she wasn't intended to be your mother?"

"You intended to create me?"

"Oh yes. I wasn't really on a pilgrimage. I can't. I'm not allowed to leave this place for long. You see, I'm a prisoner too."

"You're being held prisoner?" Kiera was aghast. She hadn't expected this.

"When Azalea died I was filled with anger. I wanted to tear the world apart. Being a sorcerer this is not advisable. I really could have. I went on a killing rampage, striking down all who stood in my way, and yet it was never enough."

"You killed those who killed her?"

"Both entire clans. I hated them all. Those who targeted her, and those who failed to defend her. They were all guilty by association."

Kiera gasped at the enormity of this new horror.

"I would have wiped out the entire species, but I was stopped before I went too far down that road."

"How?"

"A sorceress was called in. Elinefae don't normally like us, but they find us useful in a crisis," he sneered.

"What was her name?"

"Althea. She was a good sorceress, or so I thought. But she bound me to this lair."

"So you couldn't harm anyone?"

"To stop me, yes, but more to teach me a lesson. But that was over a hundred and fifty years ago. I've been trapped here so long," he moaned.

"That is a long time," Kiera agreed.

"Oh, I can nip out here and there, but not for long."

"What? No, but hang on, you've been out on business the past two days," she stammered, confused.

"Mostly I was locked away in my room."

"But why?"

"Because it hurts too much to be near you."

Kiera was momentarily stunned into silence, wounded to her core. It took every ounce of her strength to bury her feelings and to remember the reason for this charade.

"What is the purpose of the curse that keeps you here?"

"I'm supposed to have learned some lesson or other."

"But you don't know what?"

"Some ridiculous thing about happiness and forgiveness. But the dead do not forgive, so it's useless."

"Do you remember the wording of that curse?"

"Oh, there's even a scroll of it up on the wall of the library. It amused Althea to put it there, I think. I've stared at it for hours on end. But it doesn't matter. I'm going to break the curse anyway. That's why I brought you here."

"Me? I can help?"

"Your blood can."

Kiera gulped and stammered, "My blood?"

"My blood. The rite needs more than I can give and survive so I need more."

"Oh. You're going to kill me?" she gulped.

"Maybe, maybe not."

"Well, that's good to know. Thanks."

"You have to understand, it's what you were bred for. It's the only way."

"I was bred like a lamb to be slaughtered?"

Threaris smirked, "Yes. Your bitch of a mother interfered though. I was on my way to mate with a witch, one of suitable lineage. But that thing attacked me."

"A witch? Near...oh my God, you were going to Lily, weren't you?"

"Not that she knew, of course."

Kiera felt like she was going to throw up.

"You were planning to...rape her?" she asked, bile rising in her throat.

"I'm not proud of it. It was necessary. I was going to compel her. I wouldn't have harmed her."

"No, just impregnate her against her will."

"I would have taken care of her. It wasn't a pleasant scenario even to my own mind. I had a few drinks before heading out to steady my nerves."

"You were drunk. You ended up in the wrong place."

"Only slightly out, but it was in the direct path of that monster."

"You're the monster, and you got what you deserved," Kiera yelled at him.

"You're angry. Don't be. You don't know what it's like. I was desperate. I am desperate. I had a vision. I saw Lily holding you as a baby. I knew what I must do. Lily was too good for the likes of me," he groaned.

"Damn right she's too good for you. The vision didn't lie. She did hold me. She rescued me. She carried me away from the elinefae who killed my mother and her mate because of what you did. You doomed my life."

"I didn't know. I found out some time later that you'd survived. You'd been concealed. But I found out. And I sent Frydah to protect you as soon as I knew. I couldn't do it myself."

Tears had begun to fall from his eyes as his inner turmoil brewed.

"You couldn't be my father?"

"I couldn't stay in your world. And I wanted you to have a life. A good life away from this hellish prison. So you wouldn't be condemned by the darkness which enshrouds me."

"So you could pluck me out of happiness to kill me when the time was right? Oh, how considerate," she spat.

"I don't want to kill you."

"Then don't."

"I'll try not to. I'll do everything I can not to. Especially now."

"You disgust me."

"I disgust myself," he cried.

Kiera couldn't listen to any more. She was amazed she'd stayed as long as she had, but she'd been frozen to the spot with each revelation. Her father was vile on so many levels.

She ran to her rooms, right past her mate and Frydah and into the bathroom where she promptly evacuated her stomach of all its contents into the loo.

Frydah flicked to the drawing room to check on Threaris, he was crying himself to sleep in his chair. She let sleep take him fully before taking hold of him and transporting him to his bed. She magicked his clothes into pyjamas and left him.

Kiera was heaving and crying, her hair held back by a very concerned Pryderi. He was rubbing her back trying to console the distraught girl.

Zondra having heard the commotion had gone in and run the cold water tap to soak some flannels.

Kiera sat back at long last.

"Finished?" the water nymph checked.

Kiera nodded slowly, and found her face being wiped with the cool flannel. Zondra tossed it aside and applied another one to the back of Kiera's neck.

"Did he poison you?" Pryderi asked.

Frydah popped back in just as he was asking his question.

"No," she sobbed, "That would have been kinder."

In amongst sobs and shaking, she relayed what she'd learned. Her friends were all as disgusted as she was.

Zondra dragged her hand down her face and rested it on her cheek.

"What do we do now?" she wondered out loud.

"Get this girl a glass of water," Frydah suggested.

"Oh, right you are."

Zondra scurried to the adjoining room to pour some water and returned as quickly as she could.

Still sitting on the cold tiled floor, Kiera gratefully sipped the cool refreshing drink.

Zondra ran the shower for Kiera, and Pryderi helped her get clean. The hot water ran over her skin, and made her feel human, or elinefae again, she corrected herself.

Pryderi wrapped her up in a warm towel and dried himself then her. He grabbed the towelling robe and put that on his mate before carrying her over to her bed.

She sat upright against the plumped up pillows, and Zondra offered her some red wine.

"I hear it has iron in it," she winked.

"Good for fraught nerves too," Frydah chipped in.

Once she'd drunk the offered wine Kiera let her head fall to Pryderi's shoulder next to her. He lifted his arm and wrapped her up in a proper cwtch; the most comforting type of hug you can find anywhere.

"Are you OK?" he whispered, kissing the top of her head.

"I will be," she responded, still a little vacant.

Frydah transported her and Zondra to the library.

"She needs rest, and we need to find that scroll."

Chapter 28 – Curses

It didn't take Frydah and Zondra long to find the scroll. It was right above the fireplace. Frydah hadn't paid it any attention before. It was written in Latin, and she'd assumed it was some family motto. Far too boring for faeries to bother with.

Frydah now translated out loud, and Zondra transcribed onto a clean sheet of paper.

Threaris' Curse

Threaris' tyranny is at an end.
Here he must remain, his heart to mend.
With humility his knee he must bend,
And forgiveness seek, to make amends.

His lesson he must learn well
Should he ever wish to break this spell.
Within these walls he must dwell,
Until with love, his heart brims and swells.

When finally his happiness is near
I, Althea shall then reappear,
His bonds to break and his unrest to shear
To set him free, far away from here.

"Well, I don't know what's so difficult about that," Frydah muttered, "He must truly seek forgiveness and find happiness."

"Because that's so easy to do," Zondra said quite heatedly for her.

"Touch a nerve, did I?" the cheeky faery quipped.

"Have you met the sorcerer? He's not exactly sweetness and light."

"But for over one hundred and fifty years, don't you think he would have tried?"

"What makes you think he hasn't?"

"Because he's not free?"

"I think he tried and failed. Have you sensed his bitterness? I can taste lemons just being near him."

"Hmm...his anger and resentment has only increased."

"Exactly. What did Kiera tell us he said? 'The dead do not forgive'."

"And he killed so many."

"That would leave scars on anyone's soul. And his feels dark indeed."

"Well, she clearly cursed him in a hurry, it's very sloppy and wide open to loopholes."

"In what way?"

"For a start, it doesn't limit his powers. And he must dwell here; that leaves him able to leave, even just for short periods. As long as he lives here he's able to roam about."

"Yes. Any time he goes out it's basically to capture someone, and he does that as quickly as possible."

"Is he capturing folks just to be his servants, I wonder?"

"Well it's not to make friends."

"But you're all a curious mix. Take you, for example. Nobody in their right mind would capture a nereid. Forgive me for saying, but your wrath is fairly widely accepted as something to be avoided."

Zondra blushed as she confessed, "That may have been a little bit my fault."

"What did you do?" the faery asked accusingly, hovering with her hands on her hips, her toes tapping.

"I was curious. One day I was swimming past and sensed the magick here. I felt drawn to this, and kept coming back day after day. I think seeing me swim so freely annoyed him."

"And that's reason to capture you? That makes it your fault?"

She cleared her throat and blushed a darker shade of beetroot.

"Fine. When I actually saw him I became more intrigued. I swam to shore."

"Oh yuck, eww, you fancied him," Frydah sneered with disdain.

"He's good looking. I didn't know how awful he was. I started talking to him. He was charming at first. But then he started to get sad as he opened up more. Realising he'd said too much I think, he got angry, and before I could make a break for it back to the sea he ensnared me."

"Why did you not tell me before?"

"It's a little embarrassing."

"Well yes, but he told you something, too much you said. And those mood swings? Lady, we need to talk."

*****

Dougal and his troops had reached shore and boarded the sea going vessel he'd been told would be waiting to carry them to their enemy.

*****

There was something hard and warm under Kiera's cheek as she woke up in the morning. She took a deep breath in and let her nostrils fill with the scent of evergreens and woods.

She sighed as she snuggled closer to Pryderi's bare chest.

'*Good morning,*' he thought at her, showing her an image of a glorious sunrise.

She let out a purred moan of satisfaction in response.

He shrugged her up his body and bent his head down to swipe nose to nose.

'*OK?*' he asked her silently in her head, aware of not waking up Zondra who he suspected would be at her post.

"Hmm hmmm," was the dreamy reply.

The sun had not yet risen, and the room was still dark. When Kiera managed to open her eyes she looked up into a familiar orange glow.

She took a moment to fully focus, but when she did she saw her mate clearly. Her own glowing white eyes meant the darkness posed no problem.

She traced the outline of his gorgeous form. She raked her fingers through his long dark hair, trickling them along his temples, and down his chiselled cheeks.

His breath hitched as her wandering fingers feathered across his luscious lips, closely followed with a quick swipe of her tongue.

Her mouth journeyed down his neck, pausing to suck on the throbbing pulse point at his jugular. A groan of wanton pleasure escaped his mouth.

His eyes were glowing with intensity when she glanced up into his adoring face.

She pecked kisses down his bulging pectoral muscles, down the well in the centre of his torso. Her mouth was halted by the presence of the top of his trousers, making her mewl in surprise and frustration.

When she fell asleep last night he was still partially clothed, and not having her magickal abilities, he'd not wanted to disturb her by moving.

He chortled playfully at her, using one strong arm to gently guide her back up on top of him so his mouth could meet hers with tender desire.

She pulled her knees up so she was better able to rub herself against the bulge in his trousers.

She'd already used her powers to remove her own clothes, and was about to do the same, when her hand brushed against something at his hip.

A licentious look sparked in her eyes as she tugged at the leather straps she'd found there.

Taking her meaning he released the leather strapping, traditionally used for dangling captured prey when hunting.

Kiera rolled over onto her back, allowing her mate to pull her wrists up to the bed posts. Pryderi took his sweet time tying her in place.

By the time she was fully ensnared, Kiera could barely withstand the spreading heat in her loins.

Pryderi found his trousers had been removed, as he looked down with surprise. He hadn't noticed, he'd been preoccupied with securing his mate to the bed. He was poised near her feet and shot her a disapproving glance.

'Uh uh, not yet,' he admonished.

Kiera's knees lifted and her bum wiggled, pleading for satisfaction.

With one last cheeky look into her eyes, he ducked his head down and planted a kiss on her ankle.

That ankle was nudged in his face as she showed him how far away he was from where she needed him.

He sucked on one of her toes, which made her moan in both pleasure and annoyance.

His eyes narrowed at her as he looked up.

'Not what you want?' he teased.

She shook her head vigorously, no.

He started an agonisingly slow trail of kisses up her leg, behind her knee, coming to a stop on her inner thigh, which he suckled on.

Kiera was crying out for him to get to her sweet spot.

Pryderi nuzzled the apex of her thighs, then skimmed up to her stomach, making Kiera grizzle and her hips buck.

Skipping her enflamed nether regions, he licked up her stomach in one long stroke, all the way up to her breasts. His lips surrounded her nipple as he sucked softly at first, before intensifying the pull, making Kiera thrash in her bonds.

Her legs were trapped by the weight of his body, but that didn't stop her trying to bring her hips up more.

He pulled himself up further to reach her mouth. His tongue brushed her lips before delving inside to find hers.

With his weight lifted a little she brought her legs up to wrap around him, grinding herself against his large, erect cock.

He instantly pulled back, shaking his head at her naughtiness.

Drawing himself back down the bed, he planted her feet wide apart, back on the mattress.

He took pity on her and brought his head back down to her glistening pussy. He licked up the edge of her fleshy folds, making her draw in a sharp hissed breath.

His tongue lapped at her swollen nub. Kiera moaned aloud, only now fully appreciating the coarse texture of his tongue. The rough abrasion catapulted her into a long awaited orgasm, her hips thrusting her further onto his tongue.

He paused just long enough for her to recover her equilibrium, before shooting her a look full of pride and promise as he began lapping once more.

Each pass of his tongue shot intense tingles through Kiera's core, making her muscles clench.

"Please Pryderi," she begged out loud.

He bobbed his head up, putting a finger to his lips, reminding her to keep quiet, but winked as he did so.

'What do you want?' he silently questioned his prostrate mate.

'You.' Even in his head she sounded breathy.

'Where?' he asked with a sexy smirk.

Her feet wrapped up behind his back to draw his body to her. He didn't really need the encouragement, he couldn't contain himself any more.

He let his body lower to hers, and slowly entered her silky opening. She groaned and tried to take him in further, quicker.

He languorously buried himself deep inside her, making her muscles cling onto him tightly. They both exhaled loudly at the contact.

He wrapped one arm around her and reached up to the top of the bed with the other as he started building up momentum with his thrusts.

Not being able to reach down with her hands was incredibly frustrating for Kiera. She was not in control at all. But her frustration added to her excitement.

Her hips bucked to meet him thrust for thrust. They were both sweaty and panting as they built up steam.

With her hands out of action, she sank her teeth into Pryderi's shoulder, taking them to a whole new level of ecstasy.

It was too much, they both exploded into a cacophony of a climax, as they howled out their fulfilment.

The noise woke Zondra, but she quickly realised what it was, and stayed her hand on the doorknob, just before entering.

She had quick reflexes, and had jumped up instantly, fearing for the girl's safety. She blushed as she realised the true nature of the cries. She settled herself back into her seat, hoping Threaris hadn't heard.

The mated pair inside were blissfully unaware of the maid's near blunder.

Pryderi untied Kiera's wrists, which she quickly flexed before wrapping her arm around him, forcing him down onto his back, so she could cuddle up to his side.

Her knee hitched up and over his legs, so she could pull her body in tight. They both purred as they lay there, with the sun now starting to rise.

The golden glow was no longer provided by his eyes, but by the beautiful morning sun. For a brief moment they felt they didn't have a care in the world.

With his arm wrapped around her, Pryderi rubbed his thumb up and down Kiera's upper arm.

'Good morning,' he softly repeated in her mind.

Kiera stretched and preened before responding, *'Very good morning.'*

He kissed the top of her head.

'Why did you not untie yourself?'

"Would've spoiled the fun," she whispered, not having the energy to use her mind's voice.

'No, after.'

Kiera suddenly sat bolt upright.

"I felt like I couldn't. I was restrained. The bonds stopped me," she said, amazed.

Chapter 29 – The Thong Is

Kiera rubbed at her wrists with a thoughtful expression, and silently called Zondra and Frydah to the room.

"Oh, oh, did not need to see that," the faery winced, shielding her eyes with her hands.

"Oops, sorry," Kiera apologised. "We don't feel the cold. I didn't think."

She quickly magicked themselves dressed and out of bed. She wrapped an arm around Pryderi's waist, and he did likewise.

All three ladies were blushing, whilst Pryderi was just grinning. He wasn't shy, and certainly had nothing to be embarrassed about. He found their shyness highly amusing.

Frydah cleared her throat before demanding, "I assume you had a good reason for calling us here."

"Yes, yes I did. The leather strapping. It blocks things, doesn't it?"

"Leather is a poor conductor of magick."

"Jack had a leather collar."

"Jack?" the other three chorused, Pryderi most vehemently as jealousy reared its ugly head.

Kiera rolled her eyes as she clarified, "Jack. That nasty little Jack Russell dog my family had."

"Eurgh, don't remind me. Yes, I could stop him attacking you outright but not totally. Especially when you went into the elfin woods; their own barriers stopped my interference. Stupid humans. Only they could make a cat and dog live together."

"Ooohhh," realisation dawned a little late in Kiera's head.

Frydah flew in front of her face as she let out her full sarcastic charm.

"Yeeees, that's right. Cats and dogs do not get on. You are a sort of cat person," she said slowly and deliberately.

"Alright, lay off," Kiera bristled. "Look. My point is leather has an impact."

"Hey, I wear leather clothes," Pryderi interjected.

"Just imagine what you'd be like without them," Frydah mused.

Kiera clicked her fingers to bring their attention back.

"It numbed me. The leather stopped my magick tingle. So we can use it on my father too."

"Kiera. It is a poor conductor of magick, not a block on it," Frydah stated the obvious.

"If you let me finish, and stop thinking like a faery" she said, irritably, "It can be used in conjunction with something else to stop him, can't it?"

"Like a slave chain," Zondra added, fingering her own necklace.

"Exactly."

"Great. So where do we get a slave chain?" Frydah asked, pessimistically.

Kiera looked at her maid's neck.

"But it's bonded to her."

"By his blood?"

The lightbulb in Frydah's head finally lit up.

"Yes, that's right. Oh, I knew you'd be useful."

"As long as I'm good for something," Kiera huffed.

"No. Oh, you know what I mean," Frydah harumphed, feeling embarrassed at what she'd said.

"But you need a replacement. One that's still enchanted so he doesn't notice," Pryderi said, not wanting to burst their bubble, but needing to point out the flaw in the plan.

Zondra looked slightly crestfallen as the promise of her long awaited freedom seemed to die as quickly as it had risen.

"It won't be a true slave chain though, will it? Otherwise we'd just make a new one," Kiera thought out loud, noticing her friend's demeanour.

"No. It'll just appear to be one," Frydah explained.

Zondra visibly brightened. "So, how do we make this fakery?"

"It can't be a mere mirage. I need some silver," Frydah told them.

"Candlesticks," Zondra interjected, going to the fireplace, holding up the named items proudly.

"Pryderi, can you make a fire for us, please?" Frydah requested.

She wanted to reserve her magick energy for the task in hand.

Thanks to Pryderi's skill, there was soon a roaring blaze in the fireplace.

"We need to seal the room, so nobody senses our actions," Frydah had turned to Kiera, who then sealed the room from prying eyes.

Frydah smiled her thanks at her student, proud of how far she'd come in such a short space of time. Maybe the few lessons in her youth hadn't been wasted after all.

"If this doesn't work, I will have to put this back on," Kiera looked apologetically at Zondra, as she worked to remove the slave chain.

Zondra grimly nodded her understanding. But as the silver necklace was removed she breathed in deeply. Her fingers felt the now vacant space at her neck.

It was as if the weight of whole worlds had been lifted from her. She beamed with joy at sensing her freedom. After so many years she was herself again. She felt like dancing for joy.

A cloud darkened the former maid's face. Her thirst for vengeance fell over the nereid like a veil.

"He will pay for his sins," she said as she summoned the power of the winds, and blew into the fire to increase its heat.

Pryderi balanced a candlestick on the end of a fire iron, as Frydah started to chant. He held the silver in the hottest part of the fire.

Zondra blew into the flames again.

The silver began to melt. As it started to drip, Frydah waved her hands in fluid motions whilst continuing her chanting. Small silver links formed together, and floated in a golden light away from the fire.

Frydah completed the formation, and Zondra blew on the delicate necklace as it lay on the hearth, cooling it enough for the faery to continue the transformation from candlestick to jewellery.

Kiera held up the original offensive item, and the faery made an exact copy, persuading the silver to take the same shape.

With one more cool blast from Zondra, the fake chain was completed. Frydah waggled her fingers over, so there was enough residual magick to throw people off the scent.

"Kiera, over to you," the exhausted faery told her.

Kiera added a drop of her own blood onto the chain, mingling it with the magick, so to all intents and purposes it was exactly the same as the original. She even sealed it as she put it around Zondra's neck.

"I'm sorry I even have to do this much," she apologised.

Zondra placed a hand gently on Kiera's as she told her, "It's OK. You're nothing like him."

Kiera gave her a rueful smile as she turned her attention to the truly offensive chain.

"So, how do we make you small?" she asked the inanimate object.

"You don't. You just make people see it differently," Frydah explained.

"Pryderi, do you have a knife on you?"

Her mate smiled at her, insinuating the 'of course' he was thinking. He pulled his penknife out of a small pouch on his belt.

He tossed it in the air cockily before catching it then throwing it towards her.

She caught the folded blade, and fetched the leather straps from beside the bed.

"Hold this end," she commanded Pryderi.

She began to slice the leather into thin strips. She spoke softly over the chain which glimmered and glamoured into a thin chain. She threaded one link of it onto one of the leather thongs. Being careful to conceal any metal with the leather, she plaited the material into a makeshift bracelet.

"I used to make friendship bracelets at school," she announced before adding, "not that I had anyone to give them to."

She looked so sad as she spoke that it made Pryderi stretch out with his free hand to stroke her cheek.

"You do now," he told her softly.

She smiled at him as her fingers nimbly continued the threading, humming all the while.

"Directly or indirectly, the wearer of this bracelet shall harm none," Kiera enchanted the leather and silver in her hand.

"Frydah, please can you help me make this stronger?"

"I'm not sure you need my assistance, looking at that," she complimented.

"Really? You think it will work?" she asked, biting her lip.

The faery flitted to her side, and hugged the girl's arm as best she could with her tiny hands. She even kissed her cheek.

"I'm so proud of you," Frydah informed Kiera, wiping at her eyes.

Kiera was taken aback at this show of emotion from the otherwise stern faery.

"What? I have feelings," Frydah huffed.

"I know, and thank you," Kiera chuckled.

Zondra had been busy putting the fire out, seeing how much the two elinefae were perspiring. But she'd looked up and smiled softly at the exchange, brushing away her own tears.

*****

Dougal's troops had landed, and had hunted enough to replenish their energy.

They were advancing on their enemy with renewed vigour.

Their quarry would soon be within their grasp.

*****

Chapter 30 – For Her Next Trick

Making the bracelet, effectively a slave bangle, was the relatively easy bit. Getting Threaris to wear it would be the tricky part.

Frydah had in fact secretly lent her own powers to the bracelet, just to ensure Threaris' tie to Kiera would not break the bond.

They had some time in the afternoon, so Frydah took the opportunity to continue teaching Kiera what she could.

Already Kiera was exceeding expectations, and her confidence in her abilities was growing daily.

But today Kiera couldn't apply herself fully. She was worrying her lip and fidgeting, concerned about the task ahead. How would she be able to ensnare a sorcerer?

He'd captured so many other powerful beings. She knew he had great powers himself. Her only hope laid with him still not realising her ability.

He had consented to upping her blood intake a little, just to keep her alive really. It had become obvious he still wanted to keep her in a weakened state.

Fortunately, Zondra had been able to sneak in more nutrition for the newly transitioned elinefae.

Zondra's main difficulty was in keeping herself from tearing that man's head from his body. As Frydah had correctly pointed out, one does not cross a nereid and get away with it. Zondra had promised Kiera that she would leave justice to her. But her temptation now she was freed was great indeed. She was trying to avoid him.

Frydah was also struggling with restraint. Threaris had hurt her. He'd actually pinned her wings. The devil didn't deserve to live.

Pryderi was pacing like a caged tiger. He'd also been hurt and humiliated. But worse than that, the sorcerer had kidnapped his mate. In his eyes Threaris should not be drawing breath. And he would not be were it not for the fact that the sorcerer was his mate's father. This was her fight. He trusted her to do what was right.

All this tension led to a very unhappy afternoon for them all. They were all tetchy, and likely to snap at the slightest word out of place.

Kiera went to have a long hot soak in the bath on her own. If she went to dinner in that tense state he'd know she was up to something. If she was discovered none of them would escape with their lives.

She missed her iPod. She wished to play some soothing music as she immersed herself in the soapy suds.

No sooner had she wished for music, a soft gentle song could be heard. It was drifting through the adjoining door to her bedroom. It was Zondra.

'Sorry, I thought you needed some assistance,' she said directly to Kiera's mind, sensing her alarm.

'I can hear you,' she exclaimed.

'Yes, I am no longer tied to only your father. I have access to all my powers.'

'Please go on. That song was lovely.'

'Very well, my friend.'

Tears welled up in Kiera's eyes as she realised she'd gone from "Miss" to "friend". These droplets soon got washed away with the soft flowing song.

Kiera felt every muscle in her body relax as her eyes closed, and she was taken away to a happy place in her mind's eye.

Her meditation took her to a forest, her forest, the place where she'd first bumped into Pryderi. But now they were running side by side in the moonlight, laughing and free.

It was nice to feel happy. She couldn't remember the last time she'd truly felt the emotion, but now she snuggled into it as if it were a duvet, allowing it to envelop her.

She physically smiled as she sank a little further into the hot water in the bath, and a contented sigh escaped her lips.

She let her attention wander back to the 'dream' of her and Pryderi.

They escaped from everyone else, and wandered alone. They went to a body of water, where the moon reflected in its dark depths.

Trees were all around them as they laid on the ground. They began kissing each other fervently, their hands roaming over the other's body.

As their bodies drew closer and their need increased Kiera heard a cough at her ear.

She sat up suddenly, splashing water over the top of the bath.

She was about to launch herself up and out, but realised at the last second it was Pryderi in person.

'Having a nice bath?' he asked amusedly.

Her desire was still high and she beckoned him down to her. She planted a deep, longing kiss on his mouth.

He knelt down on the floor and touched his forehead to hers.

'I want you. But you must get ready,' he told her with deep regret.

Kiera sighed wistfully, but stood up anyway, letting the water pour off her lithe figure.

Completely naked, she sauntered past Pryderi and into her bedroom. Clothes appeared on her as she walked further along.

Pryderi took a moment to steady and adjust himself before joining her.

"You sure this won't affect me?" Kiera asked as she twirled the bracelet in her fingers.

"Like I told you a thousand times, it's not activated. It's just storing the magic until you will it into action. It needs your intention," Frydah replied.

"I know. It's just I can't help but worry."

Pryderi wrapped his arms around his mate's waist.

' I don't like you doing this alone.'

She turned around in his arms so she could look up into his electric blue eyes.

' You're always with me,' she said silently as she ran her fingers along his cheek.

"At the first sign of trouble you let us know," he said aloud.

Kiera nodded and put the bracelet on herself, wincing as she did.

"See," Frydah smiled.

"Alright smarty pants," she smiled back.

"You can do this."

Kiera took a deep breath and gave one slow nod to the trio who were all counting on her.

She took big strides as she crossed her rooms, and went out into the corridor, making her way to her doom. Dinner, she made her way to dinner.

"Good evening," her father welcomed her into the dining room

"Good evening," she replied, trying to sound breezy.

"Did you sleep well? Have a good day?" he asked a little too quickly.

Kiera thought he was really making an effort. The bits he'd remember from the evening before had been awkward, but had seemed to go well. It's just the bit after that which had her stomach churning at the very sight of him now. How could she be nice to this monster?

'He's my father,' she thought to herself, like that made everything OK.

"Fine thank you. You?" she managed to vocalise.

"Like a light. I don't even remember getting to my room, I must've been more tired than I'd thought. But it was the best night's sleep I've had in ages. Must be your positive influence."

Was that sarcasm? She wasn't sure, but it made Kiera want to squirm, whatever it was. She managed a smile, even if it didn't reach her eyes.

"I'm pleased to hear it."

Yeah, conversation was even harder than ever between them. Neither one seemed to know what to say.

They both had their secrets. Neither could divulge their future plans, or even what they'd been doing since their last meal together.

"Look, I know it's hard," Kiera began. "But I'd really like to be friends."

His returning smile almost seemed genuine.

"I think I'd like that."

"After all, you are my father."

"Yes, indeed I am," he said, with perhaps a touch of pride.

"As a sign of my good intentions, of turning over a new leaf, and giving us a fresh start, I made this for you," she said as she removed the bracelet from her own wrist and held it out.

"Oh, that's very sweet of you. It's not precisely my taste though," he said politely refusing the offering.

"It would really mean a lot to me if you wore it. It would show you felt the same way," she said, forcing a massive wave of compulsion over him as she spoke.

It caught him unawares, and without realising it he held out his arm. In a flash, Kiera fastened the leather around her father's wrist, setting her intention to cut off his magick supply.

As soon as it was fastened Threaris felt the numbing effect of the bracelet. He stood up, rage flooding through him. His heavy chair clattered to the floor.

"What have you done?" he roared.

"What should have been done before," Kiera smiled smugly.

A wry smile crept over Threaris' own face.

"Nice try," he sneered, holding the fastening between his finger and thumb.

But try as he might to release it with his own magick, the bracelet held fast.

"Tried, succeeded," Kiera goaded.

Threaris' face fell. He had been ensnared. This simply could not happen. Not to him.

"You have no idea what you have done," he shouted, taking steps towards Kiera.

She simply vanished herself out of his path, and reappeared the other side of the dining table.

He was no longer able to do the same. But he tried. He felt completely immobile.

Shock returned to anger again.

"You dare enslave me?"

"Would you not have done the same to me?"

"You stupid little girl. I don't know why I didn't just lock you in a dungeon until I needed you. I had begun to think we may manage to be amicable. That I may not need to kill you. But now?"

"But now you cannot kill me. You cannot kill anyone."

She strode over to him and gripped his arm and took them both to his rooms.

She willed him to sit down in a chair facing the fireplace. Frydah had already brought in the picture Kiera had pointed out to her in the library, which had been obscured from view there.

"What would Azi think of you?" Kiera asked, pointing to the painting she'd correctly guessed was of his girlfriend; the one whose death had started all this.

He couldn't look. His eyes were directed at the floor by his chair.

"Look," she demanded. "Look at the one you loved. Look and feel the shame that should threaten to overcome you."

"I feel nothing," he declared, still not looking.

"LOOK," she compelled.

He was unable to resist her compulsion. He had no powers, not even to protect himself.

"You're too late anyway," he bit out.

"The dead may not be able to forgive, but they still hold lessons. You will not move from this chair, you will not look anywhere but at that beautiful, innocent face. You will sit here and consider all you have done."

Tears were already forming in her father's eyes as the painful truth started to seep in. His anger was still holding it at bay, but that anger was weakening with each passing minute.

Kiera callously left him where he was, her spell remaining in situ.

On her way through the corridor she raised the fire alarm, forcing the entire household except her father to evacuate.

She transported herself to the edge of the barrier, and connected to the energy flow of her own magick. She carefully touched her fingertips to the barrier, and whispered her chant.

The barrier shattered into thousands of pieces, as if it were glass, before dissipating.

Crowds of servants came running towards her. They had felt the barrier's demise as they poured outside.

"Come everyone. Stand behind me."

She needed no compulsion. They all gladly went to her, able to fully feel the fresh air for the first time in many years. The sun was shining, and they basked in its glow, shielding their eyes.

They were unused to the bright light and they felt cold, but they cared not. They could feel. And it was glorious.

Pryderi was by her side, and had quickly nuzzled her cheek, letting her know just how proud he was of his mate. She squeezed his hand before returning her attention to the dazed servants.

She walked along the long line, and released the slave chain from each and every one.

The sudden release brought a torrent of emotions; some just breathed deeply, but most cried. Some actually fell to their knees in gratitude.

"None who mean harm shall remain," Kiera whispered as she held her hands up.

The air in front of her started to shimmer as she continued to murmur quietly. A dark cloud passed over them and the wind began to rise.

The newly freed servants began to look nervous. Had they just swapped one master for another?

"Please be at ease," she announced to them all, sensing their concern. "You shall remain free. You may return to your homes and families, to where you wish to be. But know this. None shall enter this place who mean Threaris harm."

Gasps and murmuring rippled around her.

"I know," she began, but her voice faltered, her own emotions were running high.

She cleared her throat, and took a deep breath to keep her tears at bay.

"I know he has done you all wrong. I know he has committed many atrocities. I apologise to you on his behalf."

"Why does he not apologise himself?" one of the crowd piped up, his newly regained freedom making him brave.

Kiera shot a warning glance in the direction of the voice.

"Because he is trapped in his room at the moment, and will no longer be able to harm anyone."

That seemed to appease the people gathered by her.

"He will atone for his sins, I assure you. I will personally make sure of it. But nobody else must interfere with the process."

This caused more murmurings, as they all wanted at least a pot shot at him. They needed to release their anger.

Kiera held up her hand to silence them.

"I hear your thoughts, I feel what you feel. But you must let go of your anger quietly. You must release your anger here and now. Put aside your resentment for what has gone on here."

Shoulders sagged, loud sighs could be heard and eyes were closed as they had no choice but to follow Kiera's instruction.

"I do not know where you all need to go to, but we shall assist you. If you wish no harm, and want to remain here you may do so. I am sure Threaris will need some assistance still. But this assistance will be voluntary."

Only the butler and head cook stepped forwards. Kiera had half expected this.

Frydah and Zondra had questioned many of the staff, finding out what each of them knew, trying to uncover the reasons of their capture and perhaps clues as to how to overpower him.

The two servants who had stepped forwards had been in Threaris' original employ. They had served him under their own volition.

They had not approved of his new servants and how he'd come by them, but had been powerless to help. They had done all they could to ensure their safety though.

They wanted to help their Master become the man he once was. Having Kiera in charge now, they were hopeful this may happen.

The butler and cook were allowed to cross through the barrier unharmed, and they returned inside.

"We need help getting everyone else back home," Kiera confided to Frydah.

"Perhaps a friendly witch or two?"

"Oh pants! I've not even told Cerys what we're up to."

She looked back round to the former servants.

"Please stay here whilst I arrange some transport for those who need it. If you can get home under your own steam then please do so."

There were some pops and flashes of light as the more magickal amongst the crowd took themselves away, having shouted a quick thank you as they went.

Kiera turned and crossed the barrier, but heard a thunk behind her. She looked round. Three sorry faces looked through the shimmer at her.

"I am sorry, my mate," Pryderi apologised, looking guilty.

"I'm sorry too," Frydah added.

"I'm not. He deserves to be torn limb from limb," Zondra seethed.

She shrugged and pointed at the ex-servants as she added, "She told *them* to let go of their anger, not us. Nobody crosses a nereid, remember?"

"Right. Um, I guess I'll just go and make this call on my own then," Kiera muttered, rolling her eyes.

Chapter 31 – Eruption

Kiera stomped along to the front door, needing some time to shrug off her annoyance. Her own team had let her down.

She could understand their feelings, of course. Pryderi and Frydah were very protective of her, and would obviously want to seek vengeance. Frydah had the added bonus of her own torture at the hands of the sorcerer to add to her pile of fury. And Zondra was indeed a nereid. She was the fiercest of all in her thirst for revenge.

Kiera promised herself to repeat the anger release process with her friends when she returned from her call.

She stopped by her father's room on her way, just to check her spell was holding. He was sitting where she'd left him, still staring at the painting. Despite the threatening storm, the room seemed lighter. Threaris wore a curious expression; it was mixed with the stare of compliance thanks to the spell, a sort of serenity and great sadness.

Kiera couldn't put her finger on it, but he seemed different somehow.

She backed away and raced into her room. Kiera opened her mirror connection to Cerys. There was just a misty haze for a while but eventually she saw Cerys' image appear, looking slightly windswept.

"Kiera dear, at last."

"My father is neutralised. Is everything OK there though? I can barely hear you."

"I'm mid-air, dear. Must be the wind noise," Cerys tried speaking louder.

"You're in the air?"

"Long story, Kiera dear. I'm on my pocket mirror here. We're in Ireland."

"Ireland? We?"

"Chen and I. We're riding on the back of his dragon."

"Oh tell me that's not a euphemism."

"It's not. I'm actually on a dragon. Not much time to explain. Lily called. Dougal's waging war."

Smoke billowed, obscuring the image in the mirror.

"Sorry. In the middle of it here. You must get here as soon as you can. We're trying to halt his progress, but so far we're only herding your mother's clan towards him. Seems they're more scared of this dragon than him."

"You can hardly blame them."

"We're trying to light a ring of dragon fire, so Dougal's forest fire doesn't reach the encampment. It's working, but it's also scaring the elinefae. We need your assistance."

"OK, things are sort of under control here. I'll be right there."

"Must go," Cerys shrieked as the reflection tilted and Kiera was left looking at smoky air.

"Just as I thought it was all over," Kiera grumbled, ending the connection.

She transported herself outside to her friends.

"We need to get to Ireland, there's a clan under attack," Kiera began as she quickly relayed her conversation.

"But what about these people?" Zondra asked.

"Can you stay here? Can you call help?" Kiera asked back.

"I'll think of something. You go."

Kiera held onto Pryderi and Frydah as she concentrated on 'Cerys'.

She squeezed her eyes shut as they shifted to their destination.

When Kiera opened her eyes a scene reminiscent of a war film confronted her.

They were a short distance away and could see flames and smoke. The cries of battle seemed to be all around them.

Kiera could smell the blood, the charring, the fear, the anger. The smell was so strong she could taste it.

Elinefae were head to head in battle. Teeth were clashing. Her sensitive hearing picked up the sounds of ripping flesh.

There were no weapons, only hand-to-hand combat, and it was brutal. Arms and teeth were everywhere, gnashing and colliding.

Noises reminiscent of a cat fight carried through the battle, only it was louder with more resonance.

Hisses, snarls and growls echoed all around.

A long, gut wrenching, shrill howl split the night as an elinefae was mortally wounded. The sound was carried on the wind and made Kiera's blood turn to ice.

She saw the wounded elinefae fall to the ground, clutching his gaping wound, blood spurting out of him. His attacker moved on, but the victim remained writhing in agony.

He was howling with pain, and began to convulse as his life force left his body in a torrent of red.

His howls were excruciating to hear, but the clans were too involved in their own combat to go to his aid. And it was too late. His body stilled as he went eerily quiet, his eyes glazed.

The trio were horrified.

"I'm too late anyway," Kiera whispered, realising the truth of her father's words.

She felt sick to her stomach.

Pryderi stood toe-to-toe with his mate, and gently clasped her shoulders. Bright blue met emerald green eyes.

"Not too late."

"Look at it."

"It is not over. We can stop thisss," he hissed, his own revulsion threatening to overpower him.

Kiera looked on at the scene in front of her. How could one person stop all this bloodshed? The elinefae clans were fully engaged in battle.

"I hate to admit it, but he's right. You can stop them," Frydah interjected, flitting at eye level.

"How?"

"Are you a sorceress?"

Kiera nodded.

"Well, act like one."

An image flashed into Kiera's mind. Before she had time to think too hard about it she breathed deep and transported herself.

It wasn't hard to find the Leaders of the clans. They were the loudest and were clashing violently, roaring out their battle cries.

Kiera appeared in the air above them, a forest green cloak and her long hair fluttering as if caught in the wind. A white glow shone all around her. Her eyes glowed with the same bright white light.

"STOP THIS!" she commanded, pushing her hands from her heart centre outwards.

A deathly silence pervaded the whole area as the two warring sides parted like the proverbial Red Sea.

A snarling Pryderi ran up the channel, staring down any elinefae who looked as if they may defy his mate. Nobody challenged though. They were all frozen to the spot by her spell. But he remained in situ, just in case.

Kiera hadn't seen his proper battle face before. He looked incredibly scary, yet in a sexy way. She pushed her arousal to one side.

"Ahem, that's better," she said a little too brightly as she levitated down between the Leaders.

She hadn't even known she could hover like that, and she was suffering a little with the shock of that as well as the battle. Her voice had risen in pitch as a result.

She inwardly calmed herself, and in her most scornful tone asked the female Irish Leader, "Is there somewhere we can talk?"

"Y…yes. This way," she stuttered.

"I'm not going anywhere with her," Dougal started to object fiercely.

"Oh, I think you will," Kiera sneered, beckoning him to follow, glaring at him.

Dougal's feet propelled him onwards until they were in what could be called a meeting hall of sorts.

"This is her territory. It's not neutral ground," he complained.

"Oh, I think you relinquished the right to make demands when you attacked, don't you?" Kiera dismissed.

"I attacked before she could."

"Ah ah ah, there will be time for explanations. First you will both sit," she compelled, waggling her finger.

Kiera had been momentarily surprised that the Irish clan Leader was female. She'd assumed they were all male. She squashed the thought down though, as now really wasn't the time to get to grips with sexism or the happy lack thereof.

Kiera banished negative energy from the room as she set up the privacy shield. She needed to clear the air between the Leaders.

Both Leaders were silenced as Kiera told them, "You will speak only when spoken to."

They both bristled at the command, but had no choice but to comply.

Kiera smoothed out her oddly acquired green dress as she sat between the feuding pair. She happened to quite like the outfit which had appeared with her intervention, but again, now was not the time to dwell on such matters.

"Right. Dougal. Perhaps you can begin by telling us why you felt the need to wage war?" She thought she sounded like a school teacher telling off naughty children.

"A messenger told me of their plan to attack us."

The other Leader made a squeaky noise, but was unable to vocalise her denial.

"A lone messenger?" Kiera continued to quiz Dougal.

"Yes."

"Did you know him?"

"No. He told me he was from another clan, and had come across the news via their communication network, and felt it fair to give me warning."

"Is this normal?"

"It's unusual. But I couldn't ignore the warning."

"So you took it upon yourself to train your men, to push them beyond their limits to wage a war based on hearsay?" she drew him out.

Dougal, hearing it put that way looked slightly embarrassed, but maintained he was in the right.

"You didn't think to check via your own network?" she probed further.

"I didn't want to expose ourselves. I needed the element of surprise."

"How convenient. And if this news was false?"

"There has been animosity between our clans for many years. I had no reason to doubt."

"And upon what is this animosity based?"

Dougal was visibly struggling against her compulsion.

"Oh, you will tell me," she added, reinforcing her will.

"They killed my sister. She went across to marry into their clan, but she didn't make the journey, or so they told me," he snarled.

Kiera turned to the female Leader.

"I'm sorry. I don't know your name. Please tell me now."

"Ailene."

"Thank you. Ailene, is what he says of his sister true? You will only speak honestly."

"It is true. She was sick when she was sent away from her clan. She died before she reached us. It is we who should seek vengeance. You dishonoured us by sending her in that condition. She could have infected us all. Then you dare accuse us of killing her," Ailene spat at her attacker.

"Dougal, why would you send your own sister when she was sick?"

"It was my parents who sent her, but she was not ill."

"Dougal, are you certain of this?"

"She was not ill," he confirmed more vehemently.

"Ailene, what was her ailment? I didn't think elinefae could get sick?"

"There are some illnesses. Not many. She must have been made weak first."

"You mean her parents did it deliberately?" Kiera was disgusted.

"It would appear that way."

"But why would anyone to that? To their own child?"

"To create war?"

"So what happened?"

"We gave her an honourable funeral. We refused to retaliate. We had pledged peace. Too much blood was spilled in the time of battles."

Kiera turned to Dougal, "See. They were not at fault."

"But then they sent the slut Sinead to us. She infiltrated our clan. We accepted her as a peace offering. But she was there to cause grief. She spawned a human. Her betrayal forced me to kill my own brother."

Kiera paled as she heard her own story emerge once more.

She was hurt, angry and tired. This day had been the worst of her life, and now she was the cause of all this destruction. It was all too much. Her last nerve snapped. Her anger had been triggered as her mother had been insulted.

Kiera launched herself to her feet and slapped Dougal across the face.

"You moron. That baby was not human. It was part elinefae."

Dougal rubbed his face. "But the other half was not elinefae."

"No, but it wasn't human either, you fuckwit," she spat at the arrogant Leader.

He looked alarmed. He was unaware of why she should be so angry about it.

"That baby was part sorceress."

"How do you know of this?" he asked, stunned.

Kiera looked him in the eyes, staring him down, refusing to be the first to look away.

Dougal conceded defeat. He cast his eyes downwards as he saw her for who she really was.

"Yes, I'm the baby you tried to kill. Not so funny now, is it?"

"It was never funny. I had no choice."

"There's always a choice," she yelled.

"I was upholding the law. I was protecting the line."

"You demolished the line. You killed my parents. You almost killed me. Luckily for you you didn't succeed in the last."

Both Leaders were staring at her.

Ailene was waving her hand frantically.

"Argh, you may speak," Kiera granted.

"But how can this be?"

"Ever hear of a sorcerer named Threaris?"

Ailene's gasp was all the answer she received.

"Yes, that arsehole fell into my bloodline. Don't ask me for details. It's all quite vile. But here I am. Daughter of him, and your two clans apparently. And I suppose that also makes me his niece," she explained, nodding towards Dougal.

Both leaders were still staring at her, wide eyed, open-mouthed.

"Hi," she said, waving.

Ailene managed to shuffle off her chair and onto the floor. She bent one knee and bowed her head low.

Dougal, not wanting to be left out managed to copy her actions.

"Oh please don't," Kiera moaned, "Back to your seats."

Of course they obeyed.

"This feud stops now," Kiera commanded.

The Leaders were both more than willing to comply with that.

Kiera led them back outside, where both Leaders announced the truce. The witches were allowed to start healing the injured.

There were elinefae who had given their lives in the fighting, and their bodies were carried away, and funeral pyres were prepared.

Fifteen of the fifty warriors on Dougal's side had been lost, whilst Ailene lost only four thanks to Loth's strong sub-leadership.

Kiera asked Frydah to return and help Zondra with the rehoming process at her father's house.

Pryderi was back at her side. She kept surprising him. And he kept falling in love with her a little bit more.

"Where do we get tea around here?" Kiera asked, taking the Leaders back inside.

They were now accompanied by their Seconds. Kiera healed the injuries of the four who hobbled beside her with a wiggle of her hands.

Tea was brought in, and Kiera acquainted the new additions with the details they needed to know. She left out the fact that Threaris was currently defenceless in his home. Probably best not to advertise that, she thought.

"So you see how ridiculous this all is?" Kiera asked as she finished.

Four heads nodded at her.

"There never was to be a second force to join this fight, was there?" Dougal thought out loud, feeling stupid.

"I highly doubt it. Threaris wouldn't command a whole clan. Given what he told me, his aim was always to eradicate elinefae. He too blames them for the loss of a loved one," Kiera replied sadly.

"He has wiped out whole clans before. Your two are connected with me. Seemingly, it was his revenge for my birth. For my dirty blood."

"So much anger. So much death," Dougal muttered. "It cannot continue."

"Right, shake hands then," Kiera suggested. She didn't need to compel them any longer.

She turned to Loth, Dougal's Second.

"Is he still fit to be your Leader?" she asked him.

"No," Dougal answered before Loth had a chance to respond, "No, I'm not fit. I stand down. I was blinded by hatred. I let a sorcerer fool me into battle. Lives have been lost. I am to blame for my error. I am shamed by it. I name Loth my successor."

"You," Kiera acknowledged as she looked at Loth. "You were badly injured, yet I did not see you kill."

Loth bowed his head, and went to kneel until Kiera stopped him.

"My Leader gave the order to attack, and fortunately not to kill. I did all I could to injure any of the opposing clan, and not kill."

"That must have taken great control."

"I did what I felt was right."

"Which put yourself in the greatest danger. I see a great Leader in you."

Loth did kneel down upon hearing this. His own humility would not allow him to stand under such high praise.

"Same question to you," she asked, turning to Ailene's Second. "Is she still fit to be your Leader?"

But she received a very different response.

"Without question, she is still our Leader. No wrong has been done by Ailene."

Ailene accepted the praise with a slow nod of her head and a slight smile, feeling proud of her Second.

"Very well. I shall leave the rest to you."

"What will you do now?" Ailene asked.

"I have no idea, if I'm honest."

"You are welcome to stay here. We shall find you a bed, at least for today. You must be tired."

"You would welcome a halfling?"

Ailene smiled a big toothy grin. "Halfling and half sorceress are two different things. I welcome Kiera, the peace maker and daughter of our clan."

Kiera glanced at Pryderi who was asking her in her head to accept the generous offer. It would be rude to refuse, and he saw his mate needed rest.

"Then we gladly accept," Kiera agreed, smiling at Ailene.

It was a massive relief to be accepted somewhere.

When she entered this place, Kiera had feared that should she survive the attempt at stopping the battle that they may turn on her instead. She hadn't held much hope for coming out of the situation alive either way.

She had her own protection powers, and Frydah had added her own, of course. But still, she had worried her own kind may give chase. Visions of torches and pitchforks had been at the forefront of her mind.

But here she was, being accepted. By a female Leader, no less. She was very pleased that there were such things. She'd begun to think of elinefae as overly fuelled by testosterone males. She didn't think she could live with that.

Kiera checked on the clean-up progress as she went back out into the night. There were lines of wounded still awaiting the witches attention. Kiera started to make her way over to them.

As she walked she realised the tang in her nostrils was the scent of elinefae blood. It ran across the land still. She waved her arms and called it all to her.

The spilled blood pooled at her feet. She instinctively released her cleansing magick, and it turned to water. She let it trickle away, down to the nearest stream.

She trudged over to where Cerys was tending to the injured, but Pryderi pulled on her arm.

'*Enough*,' he told her quietly in her head.

'*I must help.*'

'*No, you have helped enough. Rest now.*'

' I am still needed.'

'Please rest.'

Cerys had sensed their presence and made her way over to the pair as they stood silently conversing.

She hugged Kiera to her.

"You look ready to drop, dear."

"I'm fine, really. What can I do to help?"

"You can rest."

"Not you too."

"Me too?"

"Pryderi was trying to convince me."

"Well, he knows what he's talking about."

Cerys gave Pryderi a conspiratorial look as she nudged Kiera. Caught off balance, she fell into Pryderi's waiting arms.

He picked her up and carried her to the sleeping quarters. One of the clan was already waiting and guided them to a private den.

"Bully," she simpered sleepily as Pryderi carried her through.

He placed her down on the cot and released her cloak, letting it fall to the floor. He tackled her dress, but eventually managed to relieve her of that too.

With much self-restraint, he let her ease down on the bed alone. She wriggled, feeling the harshness underneath her backside.

"Here you go, princess," Pryderi teased, folding up her discarded cloak and putting it underneath her.

He laid down next to her, which made her wriggle in a different way. But nestling into his warmth she soon fell asleep. The exertions of the day had completely exhausted her.

Kiera woke up as she heard the ear splitting cry. She gasped and kicked out. But it was only in her nightmare, a mere memory from the battle.

She felt a strong arm wrapped around her. Pryderi was lending her his strength, and she took it. She nestled her back to his front a little tighter, and tried to calm her breathing.

"Shh," she heard him whisper into her ear.

Pryderi's thumb was rubbing her upper arm.

"That sound. I'll never forget that cry," she began to sniffle.

He twisted her in his arms, and shuffled down the cot so his face was against hers. He nuzzled cheek to cheek then forehead to forehead, making soft purring noises.

The actions and soft sounds combined together to ease her tension.

'*It's OK, Gone now,*' he thought to her.

He gently kissed her lips whilst stroking her hair.

Kiera wrapped her arms and legs around him, needing to feel his comfort. She nestled into his neck, and he held her close. Pryderi grazed her neck with his lips, and breathed in deeply.

He knew when his mate fell back to sleep as her tight grasp relaxed. He let her ease back onto the bed, and rested an arm over her so she'd know he was still there if she awoke.

Chapter 32 – Regroup

"What the hell did you think you were doing?" Lily shouted at Dougal as she held the portal open at their home encampment.

Cerys had opened the other end, and they took the warriors home as soon as the battle had ended and all had been healed who could be healed.

Loth held up a hand to stay the witch's anger.

"Now is not the time," he said, ending her tirade.

Lily stepped back and let Loth lead the former Leader to a holding cell. It was more for his own safety than punishment. There would be a lot of angry people fuelled by their grief upon their return, who would become angrier still when they realised the pointlessness of the battle. They lost loved ones for no reason.

Loth, as Second easily took control. He instantly gathered all the clan in the meeting hall. He informed them of what happened, emphasising Dougal had been duped by a sorcerer. He wanted to try to allay blame from the former Leader.

It wasn't entirely Dougal's fault after all. Threaris had seen the Leader's resentment and used it to his own advantage.

Loth also divulged the existence of Kiera, and her mixed blood. He told them how she saved them from further losses, and had begun a peace process, uniting the clans. He called for acceptance of their relative; she was a daughter of their clan.

Of course, his clan wanted to meet such a wonder.

"She has promised to visit as soon as she can," he appeased them.

Of course, there were those in the clan still devastated by loss, and there was much crying and wailing. Clan always sticks together though, and they received a lot of support from their 'brothers and sisters'.

"Dougal has stood down, and named me Leader," Loth said finally. "If any disagree come forward now. This is your chance to challenge."

Nobody did. They all respected him, even if he was a little younger than most Leaders.

Once the mourning period was over Loth would have to hold a ceremony making it official.

They all agreed not to turn Dougal away from the clan, but he would be punished as well as suffering the humiliating demotion. He would be flogged, and put on latrine duty. His main punishment though was to be shunned. Nobody would talk or even look at him for a fortnight. To elinefae this was akin to torture.

Ailene had ensured Kiera and her mate would be well cared for, and breakfast was taken to them in their guest den.

Kiera was incredibly relieved at this kind gesture. It only really hit her that morning that she was actually in an elinefae encampment. She had no idea on the correct etiquette, and she didn't even speak their language. She felt rude forcing them to speak English. Yes, most elinefae could speak some of her language, as they occasionally came into contact with humans, but it was limited and clearly a struggle for them.

If she'd had to go into the big dining area as Pryderi had described she would have struggled. It was hugely daunting. So she gratefully tucked into the warm fresh bread and honey, and gulped down her coffee in the privacy of the den.

'Hungry?' she heard in her head.

She smiled at Pryderi.

' I had no dinner.'

She grinned as she witnessed him ravenously eating too.

Kiera resorted to magickally cleaning their clothes. The room they were in was every bit as basic as she'd feared. There wasn't even a shower.

She felt better for freshening up and having eaten, but she was still tired. She'd used more energy than she'd ever thought possible, and effectively fought two battles. The one with her father being the more costly emotionally.

Pryderi rubbed his fingers over her cheek before touching his lips to hers. She could taste honey and coffee as well as his own delicious flavour.

Eventually they had to face the clan though. They made their way out of the den. A Watcher had been placed at their door, and Kiera almost tripped up over him as they walked out.

"*Pardon,*" he said in Eline.

Pryderi silently translated for her, and she smiled and nodded at the guard.

"*Please, this way,*" their guard indicated with his hand whilst bowing.

' I think Ailene wishes to speak with us,' Pryderi explained.

Kiera felt like a complete foreigner in this strange environment. She followed the Watcher through a maze of tunnels. It was dimly lit but she could see perfectly well. She sort of wished she couldn't. She couldn't hide her shudder from her mate who was following behind her.

'*Cold?*' he asked.

'*Just not used to dirt wall tunnels,*' she replied in his mind, feeling claustrophobic.

He shrugged, not fully appreciating her problem and encouraged her to continue onwards.

Cheers erupted as they entered the meeting hall, making them both jump. Pryderi stepped a little closer to Kiera, ensuring she was protected.

They walked down a long line of elinefae who had gathered, all wanting to meet the strange halfling who had helped save their clan.

Kiera tentatively reached out and shook the hands of some who stretched out to do so. She even received a flower posy from a little female. She brought the flowers up to her nose and inhaled the beautiful scent, which made her smile. The little female beamed back at her.

"My apologies. I could not stop them," Ailene called to them, spreading her hands out wide.

Kiera and Pryderi made their way quickly to the leader.

"I just wanted to check you were happy with your stay, but my brothers and sisters talked, and this crowd gathered."

"It's OK," Kiera lied, feeling like fake royalty.

She was terribly embarrassed, and the Leader was aware of her discomfort.

"They are thankful for your assistance."

"I am just glad I could help, and sorry it wasn't soon enough."

"They are grateful," Ailene repeated, trying to reassure Kiera she had been immensely helpful.

"I was going to offer you a tour. I am aware you have not seen homes like ours before."

Kiera was surprised at her command of the English language, her generosity and her understanding all at once.

Ailene smiled, "Cerys and I spoke before she left."

"She's not here?"

"No, she and Chen took his dragon home before they could scare anyone else."

The two females smiled at one another at this, merriment shining in their eyes.

"I didn't even know witches could ride dragons."

"I don't think Cerys did either," Ailene laughed.

"It seems Chen had hidden his creature from her. They have been hunted almost to extinction, but there are still some dragons in China and a few other places, I understand."

Kiera made a knowing 'hmm' sound, not quite sure what to say. She hadn't even known dragons actually existed before she spoke to Cerys whilst she was riding one.

"I am afraid the tour will not be possible," Ailene brought the conversation back around. "My people will swarm, making progress difficult."

"We had best get going anyway."

"Please, there is no rush."

"There are still things I must do. And I need to speak with Cerys myself."

"Very well. Do you require assistance from our witch to travel?"

"That's very kind, but I think I'm fine, thank you."

With a wave to the crowd the three made their way outside, where Kiera and Pryderi could find a clear space.

Kiera looked upon the charred parameter with deep regret. There were burned remnants of trees all around; the only visible sign of the battle from the night before. They stood like shadowy ghosts haunting the scene.

She shuddered as she took it all in, reality hitting her. She could smell the burned wood, and the faint remains of funeral pyres filled her nostrils, making her gag.

'*This will heal*,' her mate told her privately.

She gripped onto his hand and steadied herself.

The clan gasped as the pair vanished into thin air.

Kiera and Pryderi found themselves in Cerys' garden, as Kiera intended. But she was startled by some steam coming off the pond.

Chen and Cerys had been alerted to a magickal disturbance in their barrier and had rushed outside, but were glad when they saw their friends had returned safe and sound.

"He's a water dragon," Chen explained, pointing to the pond.

They all walked over, where they saw a small, thin red dragon happily swimming around.

Kiera was mesmerised by the ripples caused by the tiny creature's slinky sideway movements.

"He's so small," Kiera exclaimed.

A puff of smoke rose up towards them.

"Oh, I'm sorry," Kiera quickly apologised, noting his scowl.

"He shrinks to fit his surroundings, and grows as needed," Chen shrugged.

"Kiera, meet Shui," he carefully pronounced Shw-aay for her, exaggerating the up tone at the end.

Kiera reached out a finger as the dragon padded up onto a stone. He graciously allowed her to stroke him in apology before diving back in to continue his swim.

"He flies that way too. With him you have to sit just behind his head. His body sways from side to side, flying between realms. It is most difficult to stay on, and it makes you feel sick even if you manage to, so his neck is best."

As she stood up Kiera found Cerys wrapping her arms around her in an unusual display of affection.

"I'm so glad you're here," she told the girl. "You were marvellous."

Kiera stepped back as she blushed, dismissing the compliment. She didn't know how much more praise she could stand.

"Have you had breakfast?" Chen asked, changing topic as he noticed her discomfort.

"Yes, but more coffee would be wonderful, please."

"Please come inside," Chen offered, gently guiding her to follow.

Pryderi shot Cerys a look which suggested 'he's making himself comfortable'.

Cerys' answering look was one of smug happiness. She was more than happy that Chen was here and was showing no intentions of going back to China.

Kiera slumped into a big comfy armchair as Chen made them all coffee.

She brought Cerys and Chen up-to-date with everything that had transpired with her father.

"So, what should I do now?" Kiera asked the small group once she'd finished her tale.

Cerys was about to answer when her mirror signal went off. She went scurrying to her bathroom to answer it.

"Kiera," she called back to the lounge.

"Kiera, come here dear."

Frydah's image was in the mirror.

"She came out of nowhere. We were all so shocked, and we didn't know what to do," the fae was babbling.

"Who dear?" Cerys enquired.

"Althea of course. She's not very happy. She was demanding we contact you straight away last night, but we explained about what was happening in the clans and she agreed to delay. But she's now more insistent than ever that Kiera must come here."

"Althea, the sorceress. The one who trapped my father?"

"Yes, who else? Stupid. Now get here quickly."

Kiera rolled her eyes, "No rest for the wicked," she sighed.

Cerys bristled and made Kiera look straight at her.

"No rest for the righteous. I shan't let anyone call you wicked, not even yourself."

Kiera rolled her eyes again and let out an exasperated sigh.

"When will this all end?"

"The sooner you go the sooner it'll end," Cerys attempted to sound helpful.

"Fine. I'm going, I'm going."

She went back to the lounge where the boys were getting to know each other better. Pryderi thought he could like the strange Chinese witch, and could see how he was a good match for Cerys. He'd not known about their history, but it explained a lot.

He leaped to Kiera's side as soon as he saw her frazzled look.

"What is it?"

"I have to return to my father. I mean, I was anyway, but I have to go now. The sorceress, Althea is there and is demanding my presence."

"I will not let you go alone."

"I wouldn't expect you to," she said, stroking his cheek.

"Right. Are you two staying here?" she asked, turning to Cerys and Chen.

"And miss all the fun?" Chen replied gleefully.

"Very well. I think I can take all four of us at once."

"What? You're going to whisk us there? No portal?" Cerys asked, wary of such transportation methods.

"It's fine. I'm getting used to it."

"Hmmmm…." came the unconvinced response.

Kiera made them all hold hands and in the blink of an eye they were at the barrier she'd created.

Chapter 33 – Sorceress

"Oh poopey," Kiera exclaimed, realising Pryderi would still not be able to get through her barrier.

"OK, you three. Release any ill feelings towards my father you may be harbouring."

"But he kidnapped my mate," Pryderi growled.

"And you found me."

"You found me, but fine. He was going to kill you."

"But he didn't. I'm fine."

"He killed elinefae and started war."

"Are we going to go through the whole list? Yes, he's done some very very bad things, and we're going to make him answer for them. But you must leave that up to me. You must not go through with the intention of harming him yourself."

"Fine," her mate gruffed.

"Let it go," she compelled him.

His breath came out long and slow as his immediate anger towards his mate's father was released.

"Besides, I wouldn't be here without him."

Pryderi smiled as he realised she was correct. Yes, he had something to thank the sorcerer for. He had his soul match because of him.

"Now, if we're all ready?" she checked before leading them through the barrier.

"Ahh Miss, good to see you," the butler welcomed her as they all walked through the front door.

She put a hand on the servant's arm as she checked, "You do understand why I must do this, don't you?"

"Oh yes, Miss. I'm only too happy to help. But if I may, I believe you may need to alter your spell just a smidge."

Kiera was just about to ask for clarification when a tall, elegant lady in flowing purple robes glided into the entrance hall.

"You must be Kiera," she acknowledged condescendingly.

"Yes, hello. Althea?"

The female standing in front of her gave a slight nod.

"Umm, I brought my mate, Pryderi. And this is my good friend Cerys. And Chen," Kiera added, pointing behind her.

Althea raised one discerning eyebrow slightly, casting a brief look in their direction.

"I see," she said, sounding unimpressed.

"Err, shall we go into the parlour? I'm sure we can get some tea. You must have a lot of questions."

"As you wish," Althea granted.

The butler had taken a step to lead the way, but faltered as he found himself in the suggested parlour. Althea had taken them all there without batting an eyelid.

"Would you like some tea, m'lady?" the unnerved butler asked.

Althea merely rolled her eyes and wafted her hand over the nearest coffee table, where an array of tea and coffee pots appeared.

"Very good. If you'll excuse me, please," the butler bowed, backing out of the room as fast as he could.

His Master was offhanded and abrupt, but never made him feel so utterly useless. He scurried off to stand guard outside his Master's rooms, not that he'd be much use if that woman decided to barge in, of course. But he felt better being at his post and out of her presence.

Kiera sat down in a chair, and used her own magick to light the fire in the fireplace. She refused to be cowed down by this woman.

Kiera was bristling. She was completely fed up with people trying to intimidate her. She'd been wrong-footed for what felt like months, but was merely weeks in reality.

Well, she was growing into her power now, and had made huge steps in the past twenty-four hours. She'd be damned if she was made to feel inferior now.

Althea calmly poured herself some tea, leaving the others to help themselves. Pryderi poured some coffee into a cup and handed it to Kiera.

Althea looked down her nose at the young sorceress, "So, you saw fit to dispose of my curse, did you?"

"Yes, as a matter of fact I did," Kiera replied through gritted teeth, trying to force a smile.

She really wanted to slap that arrogant look off the woman's face.

"It required an upgrade," she added.

"Did it now?" Althea sneered, "And just how did you break the unbreakable?"

"I didn't break it. I fulfilled it. I apologised on his behalf."

"*You* apologised?"

"Yes. I am his daughter."

"Well, well," Althea murmured, masking her shock.

"You see, he has been enslaving others in this place. He kidnapped me. Actually he created me to break his curse. He was going to kill me, but I stopped him," Kiera babbled.

"Clearly."

"Well, your curse meant he was still able to leave the confines of this gilded cage. Even in those short spells he was able to wreak havoc."

"That was an unfortunate loophole."

"Exactly, so I had to adapt it. It wasn't direct enough. Threaris may be a sorcerer but he is still male. After all this time he still couldn't break your curse."

"Well it was perfectly simple."

"Not to him. He has killed many in his grief, needing others to feel the pain he did. He started to numb himself to the horrors of killing."

"Which is why I stepped in."

"Yes, but he couldn't apologise. You told him to go on bended knee and seek forgiveness, but like he said, the dead cannot forgive."

"No, I don't suppose they do."

"So he got stuck. And the more he felt trapped the more frustrated he got. And the more frustrated…"

"Yes, yes. No need to spell it out, girl. I can follow the train of thought, thank you."

Kiera glared at the interruption. She jumped slightly as she felt a touch on her shoulder. It was her mate.

'*Calm*,' he thought to her.

"I freed his servants, and would only allow those who meant no harm to come back through," she carried on more gently.

"Hence his small entourage," Althea mused.

"Well, you can't blame them. But you got through, so I'm guessing you're not here to harm him."

"No. I was brought back by the curse itself. I was called back when it was fulfilled. My intention had been to ensure he showed true penitence before truly releasing him."

"I'm afraid he's not there yet. But I have a plan. I'm working on it."

"You would help him? After all he has done?"

"He's my father," Kiera replied, tears rising to her eyes.

"Very well, I relinquish the power over him to you. But I shall return. Once you think you have cured him, as you so naively think possible I shall return to ensure he is. We can't have a psychotic sorcerer on the loose now, can we?"

With that Althea vanished away.

The remaining three were left trying to catch their breath.

"Well, my father was right about one thing. She is a bitch," Kiera snipped snidely.

"What a horrible woman. I never thought I'd see the like. She waltzes in, acts like you've done something wrong, with that look on her face that suggests she's trodden in dog's mess. I bet she thinks her own shit don't stink," Cerys burst out.

The witch was so angry with the sorceress for her overbearing interference. She'd been powerless to come to Kiera's aid. She hadn't a fraction of power that woman had, and would be toast if she so much as looked at that sorceress scornfully. So she'd had to bite her tongue. But now the sorceress had gone she blurted out all her frustrations.

"Thank you," Kiera said, kissing Pryderi's cheek. "I think I was about to hit that bitch."

Ever practical, Chen asked, "So what do we do now?"

"Well, I'm going to finish my coffee," Kiera announced, sitting back, taking a sip of the hot black liquid.

"Is she truly gone?" a tinkling voice piped up.

"Frydah, there you are."

"Sorry, I was hiding. That sorceress is the rudest person I ever came across. And that's saying something. Someone should teach her some manners."

"Perhaps they will. Is Zondra here?"

"No, even with Miss High and Mighty insisting we hold no intention of harm, Zondra could not cross the barrier."

"Really?"

Frydah giggled, "No. The nereid's wrath is even stronger than Miss Snooty Pants' compulsion."

"Wow, remind me not to get on the wrong side of her."

"Kiera, before you release your father you will need to speak with Zondra."

"Let's cross that bridge when we come to it."

They all needed the refreshment, so finished their hot drinks, taking advantage of the opportunity to rest for a few minutes.

Kiera stood as she stated, "I should go and check on him."

"I will come too."

"No, my love. I need to do this alone. He cannot harm anyone. I am safe. Please remain here with the others."

Pryderi didn't like it, but knew there was no arguing with his mate on this.

The smell of urine hit Kiera's nose as soon as she walked into Threaris' room.

"Oh, I'm sorry. I see what you mean," she told the butler.

Threaris had been unable to move from the spot she commanded him to sit in. He was stuck staring at the painting of Azi.

He'd not been able to sleep or even get up to go to the bathroom.

"You may get up to go to the toilet, eat meals and retire for up to eight hours of sleep per day," Kiera added as she swirled her arms. "But there will be no other interruptions to your lesson."

Threaris immediately tried to stand, but fell. His legs were weak and his energy was drained. His butler went to his aid.

Kiera looked on at the pitiful sight, dumbfounded. She'd not meant for this to happen. She looked at her father's red puffy eyes. He truly was a sorry state.

"Please, help him clean up," she asked the butler.

He nodded and quietly helped his Master into the bathroom.

Kiera looked around the room and found a smallish mirror. She placed it above the fireplace, next to Azi's picture.

"I will help him," she promised the lady in the painting.

She could've sworn the image smiled at her, but she shook her head to clear the thought away.

Kiera also exchanged the soiled chair for a clean, dry one.

It didn't take long for the butler to bring Threaris back. He was freshly showered, and dressed in his usual neat attire.

Threaris seemed oblivious to what was transpiring. As soon as he was back at his chair he continued his picture gazing.

"Father, look at me," she commanded, kneeling down to his eye level.

She took his head in both her hands.

"You will learn your lesson from this. You will return to your old self. You just need to realise what you've done. You need to feel again."

There was a mild flicker of recognition in his eyes before he turned his gaze back to the picture.

Kiera chanted and waved her hands in front of the mirror next to the picture.

"Upon this mirror you may also gaze,

To witness the horrors of former days.

When once more all the past pain you can feel,

Then at last you can start to truly heal."

She turned to the faithful butler to tell him, "This will not be easy. He will be tormented by what he sees."

"I understand, Miss."

"He will need your help to get him through. I will visit as often as I can to help. But is there anyone you know who can come in to help you?"

"I'll be fine, Miss. Don't you worry about old Jeffers."

"I am so sorry. I didn't even know your name."

"Jeffers is what I answer to. It is not important, Miss. Truly, do not feel bad for it."

"Are you able to use any magick? Can you communicate with the outside world?"

"Thanks to you I can again now, Miss."

"Brilliant. If you need anything you are to contact Cerys. She will be able to reach me. Promise me."

"I promise, Miss."

"One more thing, Jeffers."

"Yes, anything, Miss."

"Please call me Kiera."

Jeffers blustered and flustered a little, feeling awkward, but he agreed.

Chapter 34 – Reflection

Jeffers walked Kiera out of Threaris' room. Pryderi was immediately by her side.

'He's OK,' she thought to him, leaning her head on his shoulder.

"Miss, would you like to retire to your rooms to gather your thoughts?" Jeffers offered.

"Oh yes please. That would be lovely."

Jeffers started leading the way, and informed her as they walked, "You know those rooms were hers, of course?"

"Who's?"

"Why, Mistress Azalea's. Master really did try very hard to bring her here. He would have moved heaven and Earth for that lady. Such a pity."

The knowledge gave Kiera some hope. There were other rooms in her father's home. She'd walked past many many doors. But he'd chosen to put her in the ones intended for the love of his life. He must have always harboured a little fondness for her, his daughter.

Kiera worried her lip as she tumbled the idea around in her mind as she walked. She had hoped her father wasn't truly evil. Indeed, his loyal servants had told her so. And he had confessed himself he was not always that way.

She had hoped, and she had set plans into motion to aid his recovery. But she'd not honestly dared to believe. Althea had called her plans naïve. But perhaps she really could help bring him to salvation.

Opening the door to her suite, Jeffers let her lead the way inside.

"I'll be right back with some lunch for you all," the kindly butler offered.

She'd not seen him much before, but she was sure he'd softened. Maybe because he too now had hope.

Kiera, Pryderi, Cerys and Chen took comfortable seats in the sitting area, and Frydah hovered. Kiera magickally lit the fire, more for its cheery glow than warmth. She smiled as she mused it was the same location as she'd made the chain for her father. Was it really so short a time ago? The past twenty-four hours felt like years.

"Penny for them," Cerys offered, enquiring what Kiera was thinking.

"Oh, nothing much. Just how much has happened, and how much there is left still to do."

"Yes, it must all feel very daunting. But you can do it," the witch said, leaning forward to pat Kiera's hand encouragingly.

Kiera rubbed her face with her hands. "I wish I could just be sure of a successful outcome."

"It seems you have been successful already. You have no reason to doubt you will be in times to come too," Chen soothed.

"I believe in you," Pryderi told her, leaning in close to brush cheeks.

Their lips briefly met as Kiera thanked him for his faith.

Frydah had kept flitting around, but now settled on the table.

"You are very powerful. And you are good. Just like I said," the faery smiled.

"Thank you too."

"I like your memory replay mirror," Frydah added. "Cruel to be kind."

"Yes. It pains me to do it. But seeing exactly what he's done seems to be the best way for him to face it."

"And that pain is what makes you good. You take no pleasure in his torment. And torment it is, make no mistake."

"A torment of his own making," Cerys added.

"I wish there was another way," Kiera sighed, looking utterly defeated.

Her mate knelt on the floor at her feet. He cupped her chin in his hand.

"Not your fault," he told her, gazing directly into her eyes.

Her tears began to fall at his words.

He picked her up, and sat back down with her in his lap.

"Shh, Kiera. You are doing right. He will be well," he whispered into her hair, hugging her close.

Jeffers came back in with a tray of food offerings, which he laid on the small table near them.

"Everything alright, Miss?" he asked, concern etched on his face.

Kiera wiped her tears away. "I'll be fine. Sorry."

"No apology needed. You are brave to even be here. I am not sure I would be after the way you were treated. But I say too much. You ignore old Jeffers. I'll leave you be."

Kiera managed a smile at the butler. Really, how had she not seen this side of him before?

Her mouth watered as she smelled the delicious food. Now the two servants were able to come and go they'd managed to catch some wild rabbits.

Kiera had no idea how they managed to cook the stew so quickly, but she suspected a little magick had been involved.

There were even nuts and fruits cut into small pieces for Frydah.

They all tucked into the food eagerly and in silence. Kiera even had a little red wine to wash down her stew. The combination of delights revived her.

Pryderi noticed the change in her mood immediately, and looked up over the rim of his wine glass with gleaming eyes. Catching her attention he gave a subtle wink, making her smile broadly and sending butterflies fluttering wildly inside her.

He reached over the table and gently took her hand. "Time to meet family?"

Worry furrowed her brow instantly.

"Y...y...yes, I suppose so," she stammered and hissed.

Frydah flew over to pat her friend's cheek.

"You'll be fine. Everyone loves you."

"But I'm not pure elinefae," she mumbled, biting her lip.

"Did Dougal and Loth chase after you with torches? Did Ailene not say half sorceress was different from halfling?"

"Impure is still impure. They really may not like me."

"Sorceress is different. Better," Pryderi informed her. "Look at what you did. We were wrong to worry."

"And so what even if they don't like you?" Cerys asked.

The others glared at her.

"No. Hear me out. Even if they don't, then what is it to you? They can't kill you. I think you've proven that."

"But they're Pryderi's family."

"Oh, and in the human world people always get along with their in-laws, I suppose? You're being twp. Rhion has had time to get used to the idea."

"What? He knows already?" Kiera asked, startled.

"Oh, didn't I tell you, dear?"

"Err, no. How did he take it?"

"Well, you'd just been abducted, so there was the added threat of an insane sorcerer on the loose, so we can't really judge by that."

"That well?" she asked glumly.

"He only punched me once. I think it went well," Pryderi supplied, thinking this was helpful information.

Kiera hid her face in her hands with a groan.

Pryderi rubbed one of her hands, making her take it away from her face. She gripped onto one of his big sturdy paws of hands.

"I will be with you. He is a good Leader. He will be alright now."

"You can promise this?"

Pryderi had to shake his head, but added, "But I believe it will be."

"Well, there's only one way to find out, I suppose."

"You ready?"

Kiera nodded sharply.

"Um, what should I wear?"

"I like your green robes," Cerys offered.

"But you want to appeal to elinefae," Frydah contradicted. "You need to let them know you're one of them."

The witch and faery started to argue their point, making Kiera's head swim.

"Be you," Pryderi told her.

"Who am I?" she genuinely asked.

He kissed her forehead as he replied, "The strongest female I have ever met."

Her heart fluttered at his words.

She closed her eyes, and felt what she truly was. She was elinefae. She was a sorceress. She was Kiera.

When she opened her eyes she looked into the mirror. She saw brown leather trousers, similar to Pryderi's, but more figure hugging.

The female elinefae she'd seen at Ailene's camp mostly wore some sort of short leather skirts, but that wasn't her style.

Her brown leather boots matched her trousers, and were knee high.

Her midriff showed below her short sleeved green crop top. A golden tree of life was embroidered in the middle. Her cleavage spilled over the top.

'A little showy,' she mused, but decided her new feline figure should not be hidden. Others displayed theirs proudly. Her own mate openly showed his chest under his open vest top most of the time.

Her dark green velvet cape draped across her shoulders and cascaded behind her.

"Wait right there," Frydah instructed her, and disappeared from view.

The others were admiring her outfit, especially Pryderi, who was clearly aroused. He was trying hard to control his ardour, knowing he wasn't able to do anything about it just yet.

Frydah finally re-emerged, holding a circlet made of twigs and ivy. There was something clear and sparkling at its centre.

"A dew drop," Frydah informed the gaping girl.

"It's beautiful," Kiera breathed.

"A present from the fae so you never forget us," Frydah grinned, flying up to kiss Kiera's cheek.

"I don't know what to say. Thank you."

Frydah wiggled her fingers, and Kiera's lustrous brown hair was gathered into a loose half ponytail, with the circlet carefully placed perfectly in situ.

A little makeup had been applied as well, highlighting her high cheekbones and sparkling green eyes.

"The strongest female I have ever met," Pryderi repeated breathily, kissing her cheek tenderly.

Cerys thought she was being subtle as she wiped the tears from her eyes, but Chen noticed.

"You care," he teased.

"Well of course," she bristled.

Her man caught her in his arms and hugged her tightly, planting a kiss on her neck. Cerys, although happy with Chen's attentions, wriggled free.

"Very well, very well. Be off with you now. You'll not be readier than you are," she gruffed at the elinefae pair.

Kiera reached out and took both Cerys' hands in her own.

"Thank you," she smiled as she kissed both of the witch's cheeks.

"Pah," Cerys waved her off. "Go on now."

But as Kiera transported Pryderi away Cerys wiped more tears away and found a handkerchief to blow her nose.

"She is beautiful, isn't she?" Frydah gushed.

"She's everything we hoped for and more," Cerys sniffled.

Chen pulled a mobile phone from his pocket.

"It's OK, I caught the magick moment on camera," he smiled.

"Oh you sly fox. What are you doing with a gizmo like that?"

"I'm a modern witch. Tell me you don't have one," he winked, knowing full well she did.

"We'll be able to show Lily when we see her later," he added.

"Oh crumbs. Lily, I almost forgot. Oh, the poor dear."

Chen and Cerys made their farewells to Frydah, who insisted on transporting them to their sister, rather than trying to find a portal where they were.

"I'll just sit here and babysit a sorcerer all alone then," Frydah said to thin air once she was by herself.

Chapter 35 – Meeting

Kiera transported herself and her mate to the clearing where she used to run to. It felt like a lifetime ago since she'd gone jogging to this very spot.

"Hmmm, a tree indeed," she chuckled, looking at Pryderi.

He shook his head at her foolishness and took her hand.

"Come. We walk. I will show you my home."

He was as excited as a puppy as he strode along the paths so familiar to himself.

Kiera admired the flora and fauna he showed her, and there were some stunning views despite the fact it was an overcast day.

Her soul felt soothed as they strolled along together. She almost forgot about her nerves over meeting the in-laws. Almost.

Pryderi leaped in front of his mate as they heard a twig crack in the bushes to the left of them. His fangs were showing as he snarled his warning.

Kiera was doing likewise, taking her cue from Pryderi. This was his territory, he was the best judge of any potential threats.

As they circled around to distance themselves from the bush they slightly crouched, poised to pounce on whatever leapt out at them, they heard a spluttering.

Arwyn had been unable to contain his laughter anymore, "*You should see your faces*," he guffawed.

Not understanding the deranged maniac in front of her, Kiera was still snarling. Pryderi calmed her with just one look. She cocked her head to the side quizzically in response.

"This is my friend, Arwyn," he explained, and slightly bowed.

Giving her his most formal bow Arwyn greeted her.

"So this is the female who has captured Pryderi's soul," he said, kissing the back of her hand.

Pryderi snarled a warning at the contact, which just made Arwyn laugh more.

"Yes, you are truly mated. I apologise," he put his hands up in surrender taking a step back.

"Why are you sneaking around here?" Pryderi asked, trying to calm himself.

"I was curious. I've been roaming around for ages, hoping you two would show up."

"Curiosity killed the cat. Did no one ever tell you?" Kiera quipped.

"Ooh, sassy. I like her," he admired, turning to Pryderi with a cheeky wink.

"And part sorceress," his friend cautioned.

"Of course," Arwyn acknowledged with a head bob.

"Shall we make our way?" he added nervously, starting to walk on.

'Your friend?' Kiera asked silently, emphasising the word friend.

'Yes. He thinks he's funny. He usually is. I think you just make him nervous.'

'Me?'

'It is not every day a sorceress meets our kind.'

Kiera smiled wryly, allowing herself to enjoy the feeling of power over this obviously strong elinefae. He was slightly taller and broader than her mate, yet little old her could make him nervous.

She reprimanded herself immediately. She wouldn't allow herself to get like her father. Power must be balanced with care. She would not disrespect others. And she had to make herself humble for these people. She was the stranger here.

Kiera felt Pryderi squeeze her hand reassuringly as they walked through the forest. Her heart was beating faster the closer they got. She was desperate to make a good impression. She was only just beginning to appreciate how much she wanted to belong here.

As they'd wandered along she had found an inner peace warming her insides. She had the sensation of being home.

But the clan may not accept her. They may still reject her as a halfling. Just because others had accepted her didn't mean Rhion would.

Pryderi pulled on her hand, bringing her to a stop. He stepped in close and sucked on her lower lip. She'd been biting it again, and this was his way of telling her he'd noticed. He was doing his best to tell her not to worry.

Mistaking it as a signal of pure lust, Arwyn rolled his eyes and urged them, "Come along. Rhion awaits."

Pryderi looked back over his shoulder at his friend and grinned his apology. He was happy to let Arwyn think he was being randy. He did not want others to detect his mate's uneasiness. Taking his place back at her side and her hand in his, he urged her to continue to following Arwyn.

Kiera's knees felt wobbly as they entered the encampment. It was still daylight so most inhabitants were still in bed. But the ones who were awake had gathered. Arwyn had apparently announced their arrival through the thought channels.

There was quite a hubbub, and Kiera was starting to get fed up with being treated like a spectacle.

The elinefae all saw her as a curiosity, and seemed to forget she was a person. But she also sensed fear from these elinefae.

Happily Rhion came to her rescue. The crowd parted to allow him entrance.

He looked so gruff that Kiera wasn't terribly sure she was that happy he'd come to her aid after all. She wondered if she'd be better off with the curious crowd.

Pryderi kneeled to his Leader, so Kiera followed suit.

"*You are the one who stole my Watcher?*" Rhion asked her.

"*Sir, with regret, my mate does not yet speak Eline,*" Pryderi informed the mighty Leader, with his head bowed.

The Leader's whiskers twitched as he grumbled. His red mane of hair was matched by a full face red beard which moved as he spoke.

Kiera was trying not to stare, but was failing miserably.

"You stole my Watcher," he accused, this time in English.

"I apologise. I did not mean to. I was just thinking of him and he sort of appeared in my room."

"Just like that?"

"Just like that. I was still getting accustomed to my powers. I still am really," she began to babble.

"I am aware of your heritage. I am also aware you were not."

"That is correct, Sir."

"Very well. You'd best come inside," he said with authority

His small, beady green eyes were peering at her sceptically.

The crowd dispersed, busying themselves with their duties as the couple were taken into Rhion's meeting place.

Kiera took in her sparse surroundings. This was clearly where the Leader held smaller meetings. It was nowhere near as grand as the large meeting place she'd been in with Ailene.

She took a seat on a simply carved wooden stool, noting it was beautiful in its simplicity.

"Now Kiera," Rhion started.

As he pronounced her name he made a guttural hiss at the back of his throat instead of a hard 'k'. It made her name sound more like 'Hera'.

"I must speak true," he continued, "I thought you an abomination when I was told of you."

Kiera balked at these harsh words.

"There are tales of elinefae mixing with others long ago, and it led to disease. One of our most sacred laws has been to protect the race by birth."

Kiera was grinding her teeth as she heard what this person had to say. Her own father detested her lineage, and now her mate's clan was repeating that antipathy. Would she ever belong anywhere? Would she always remain a halfling with no home?

"Your own parents were executed I understand, because of this law."

Tears were pricking Kiera's eyes. How many times would she have to hear of this travesty?

He held up his hand again to still the squirming sorceress. He was getting restless himself at her increased ire.

"So it comes as no surprise to you. Our laws were made with good reason."

Kiera gulped. This was not going well.

"Sorcerers are stronger than humans. They may not harbour disease but they still bring great danger. Your father, the sorcerer Threaris, has himself waged war on our kind."

"Yes Sir, but he is not me," she stammered.

"But you are of him."

"I have not known him. I don't share his views. I am trying to help him," she tried to explain.

"But his blood still flows in your veins. Your magick is mighty. I feel it. I admit I fear it. Power such as yours is not to be trusted."

"Please. You can trust me. Have I not proved this?"

"You speak of your dealings with Ailene? Would there have been a battle at all without you? Consider that before you think of it as success," he hissed.

Kiera's mouth hung open as she saw things from his perspective. It was her birth, her family on all sides, her father's meddling that had led to that dreadful fight. She could not disagree with the Leader.

Her eyes were cast downwards as her shoulders slumped with the heavy burden now placed upon them.

"I see you acknowledge this. I cannot allow such a viper to hide in my nest."

Pryderi knelt before Rhion.

"She is my soul match. She is my mate. She is brave. Does this mean nothing?" he pleaded on his mate's behalf.

"It means sorcerers are still causing pain amongst us. It strengthens my resolve. Pryderi, I cannot allow her kind to be here. It endangers us all. My duty is to protect clan, and this I will do until my last breath."

"She can help protect us."

"Enough. I will not be argued with. She has said herself she is still learning to control her powers. She is as likely to destroy us as she is to protect us. I may not have the ability to have her executed. Elinefae would not physically be able. But I can deny her access to my own clan."

Pryderi was staring at his Leader, unable to believe what he was hearing.

"You have a choice to make, Pryderi. Your mate or clan."

Pryderi was stunned. He couldn't seem to inhale. The wind had been knocked out of him.

Clan or his mate? Banishment and love, or home and heartbreak? Either way his soul would be torn in two. Either way he would never be whole. He was doomed.

His sworn oath was to protect clan. It was a binding pledge he'd made as Watcher. To turn his back on that was unthinkable. But to live without Kiera was unimaginable.

There was a loud scraping noise as Kiera physically reeled, taking the stool backwards with her. She saw the confusion on Pryderi's face. She also saw the very moment his choice was made.

He was not choosing her.

To be continued...

Glossary of Names

Name	Pronunciation
Ailene	a-*lean*
Althea	*ael-thEE-uh*
Arwyn	*aar-wihn*
Azalea	*uh-z-ai-lee-uh*
Cailean	*kay-lun*
Cerys	*keh-rihs*
Colle	*kohl*
Donnagan	*don-uhg-un*
Dougal	*do-gawl*
Eileithyia	*eel-eeth-EE-aa*
Eirlys	*ayr-lihs*
Elan	*ee-lan*
Elinefae	*ee-LINE-fay*
Frydah	*free-dah*
Kiera	*key-air-uh*
Pryderi	*pruh-DAIR-ee*
Rhion	*ree-on*
Roarke	*rawrk*
Shakira	*shu-KEER-uh*
Shui	*shw-aay*
Sinead	*shin-ade*
Terrah	*tehr-rahr*
Threaris	*three-AH-is*
Una	*oo-nah*
Zondra	*zon-drah*

About the Author

TL Clark is a British author who stumbles through life as if it were a gauntlet of catastrophes.

Rather than playing the victim she uses these unfortunate events to fuel her passion for writing, for reaching out to help others.

Her dream is to buy a farmhouse, so she can run a retreat for those who are feeling frazzled by the stresses of the modern world.

She writes about different kinds of love in the hope that she'll uncover its mysteries.

Her loving husband (and very spoiled cat) have proven to her that true love really does exist. Writing has shown her that coffee may well be the source of life.

If you would like to follow TL or just drop in for a chat online, @tlclarkauthor will find her across most social media:

Instagram, Facebook, Goodreads, Twitter…

She also has a **blog** where she shares random thoughts and book reviews. She's very kind and supportive, so often reviews other indie authors.

You can also sign up for her newsletter on her blog, to ensure you don't miss any exciting news (about new releases or special offers).

www.tlclarkauthor.blogspot.co.uk

Other books by TL Clark:

<u>Young's Love</u> – Striving for independence and finding gelato in Tuscany.

A gentle journey that explores Samantha's cry for freedom. She has an unhappy, controlled marriage which just keeps getting worse.

At breaking point, she goes on a couples' holiday to Tuscany. As she finds independence can she also find love? Can she become the woman she always wanted to be?

<u>Trues Love</u> – Suspense and suspended reality in Ibiza.

Amanda Trueman loves her single, wild and carefree lifestyle. Read about her erotic adventures in this rollercoaster of a book.

She heads off with her best friend to the sunny skies of Ibiza for a holiday which promises to supply even more fun memories.

A blonde bombshell certainly fits the bill, but he soon has her heart exposed as well as her flesh.

Feeling vulnerable, will Amanda sink or swim in the world of true love? Danger lurks. Is their relationship doomed to end in disaster?

<u>Dark Love</u> – A romance novel with BDSM in it too.

This book follows Jonathan, a male Submissive. His attention is grabbed by another woman, but can he bear to turn his back on the life he's always known and loved? Is it even possible?

This book investigates the love that exists in a BDSM relationship and beyond.

<u>Broken & Damaged Love</u> – a book with an important message.

This one comes with a trigger warning, as it features a sexually abused girl.

It was written to give hope to CSA survivors. They too can go on to have healthy, happy relationships.

It also aims to help others watch out for signs, so they can help stop abuse.

Profits are regularly donated to charity from the sale of this book.

<u>Rekindled Love</u> – Hatches, matches and dispatches.

We join Sophie just in time for her first 'experience', but she gets torn away from her first love.

We go on to follow her life, through marriage, birth and death. Hers is not an easy life, but hold her hand through the bumpy bits to get to the good times.

There's a rollercoaster of emotions waiting for you.

That's all for now.

Thank you for reading. Don't forget to post a quick review.

Love and light,

TL Clark

Lightning Source UK Ltd.
Milton Keynes UK
UKOW04f2322171017
311154UK00001B/125/P

9 780995 611733